SILVER GHOSTS

WILL SHROPSHIRE

Silver Ghosts

ISBN: 978-1-914615-22-1

Published 2022 by Tricorn Books

www.tricornbooks.co.uk

Aspex
42 The Vulcan Building
Gunwharf Quays
Portsmouth
PO1 3BF

Printed & bound in UK

Cairnton Fishings

River Dee

COLONELS
PLANK
WHITLOCK
UPPER FERROCH
MID FERROCH
LOWER FERROCH
ISLAND
GREY MARE

HOLLY BUSH

COTTAGE
COTTAGE RUN
POTTERS

SPOUT
GLISTERS
LONG POOL
LONG JETTY

SANDY BAY
CANABY
RUSSELL

GARDEN RUN
OLD GARDEN

MALT STEEP
ROCK HEADS

UPPER SALT VAT
MID SALT VAT
LOWER SALT VAT

INVERCANNIE

MILL

N

BALMORAL

With thanks to fishingmaps.co.uk

The River Dee

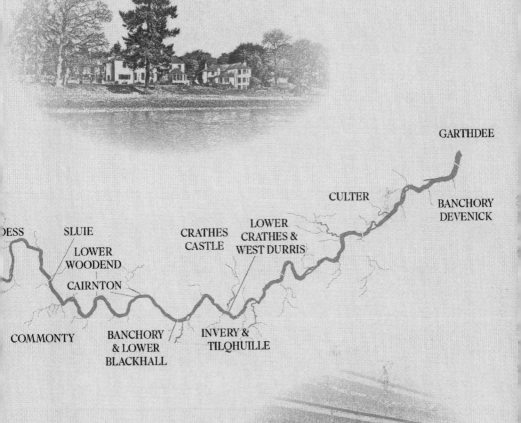

GARTHDEE

CULTER

BANCHORY
DEVENICK

DESS

SLUIE

LOWER
WOODEND

CAIRNTON

CRATHES
CASTLE

LOWER
CRATHES &
WEST DURRIS

COMMONTY

BANCHORY
& LOWER
BLACKHALL

INVERY &
TILQHUILLE

This marks the
height the water
reached following
Storm Frank
30th December 2015.

FOREWORD

I never really thought I would ever write a book, but I'm sure most people who have run across a desert, reached base-camp or swum the Channel didn't plan that either, until one day they felt a true purpose in doing so.

For my mini challenge the driver came in 2019, when I was learning to fish on a Scottish river and listened closely to the discussion of my fellow anglers over lunch. I learned that the cleanliness and ecological diversity of our rivers is in decline and at the same time the number of salmon returning to our rivers has fallen dramatically. If we can't appreciate our environment, and more importantly the creatures we share it with, then this world is going to be a worse place for future generations.

Spending time on a river in the pursuit of the king of fish opened my eyes to the natural beauty of such places.

Standing in that cold river, trying to cast that little bit better distracted only by wildlife has brought me true mental wellness. It is something I want my children (and grandchildren) to be able to experience.

The Atlantic salmon is an incredible creature; the journey it makes to feed and the challenges it faces to reproduce are astonishing. It has been doing so for millions of years across the entire North Atlantic, until the recent past, when its fate has been dramatically changed by the actions of man.

The threatened demise of the salmon is an early warning of things to come, and investment in the science behind the change is crucial. But a wider awareness of the issue is essential too, and I hope in some small way, through a teenager reading this book, that might be achieved.

This book would not have been possible without the help and support of many people, especially my darling wife Josie – my finest ever catch. I am truly grateful to my loving sister Kate, whose encouragement was critical when things were a bit choppy, and for introducing Sarah Law, who gave me the confidence to finish it.

Thank you to Chris Newton, my fly-fishing editor whose guidance turned a messy word document into a nice story.

I have great admiration for the River Dee Trust, who are guardians and protectors of the special river for future generations. Thank you Lawrence and Debbie, and special thanks to Mel for your light-hearted, constructive comments on draft 1!

Thank you also to all the ghillies who for many months of the year do all they can to make each day special for us, and none more so than my good friend Brian.

But my biggest thanks goes to those friends with whom I have spent time learning how to enjoy the beauty of fly fishing for salmon. Some, like Kempy, Ben, Guy and Roly, arrived at the river with me, but many of them became friends afterwards.

PROLOGUE

Ian Anderson watched his eighteen-year-old son as he effortlessly swung the rod, directing the energy forward like a wizard with a wand seeking to conjure some magical response.

Donald, Ian's father, stood a hundred metres upstream, in the middle of the river, silhouetted by the evening sun. His goal was the same, but his movement was smoother and slower.

It's not always deepest in the middle; sometimes you are standing on the edge without even knowing it.

Ian looked down at Callum, who was sitting on a blanket with his toys, legs still dripping wet from releasing a fish, eyes fixed adoringly on his brother.

"It's nearly your turn, lad. Your journey's just begun," he murmured.

This was one of those moments, borrowed from history, that Ian often thought about when he watched the sunset over the North Sea.

This was when nature was at her kindest.

CHAPTER 1

It had taken nearly a hundred hours, but Callum had finally levelled up to Commander. For most it took a lot longer, though there were exceptions, and he couldn't help but smile, he had this Call of Duty game cracked. He threw back the clammy duvet and walked into the cool bathroom for the first time that day; brushing his teeth, he noted a shave was overdue. He ran his wet hands through his curly biscuit hair, lifting the locks away from his slightly bloodshot green eyes.

Breezing into the living room, eyes down, dressing gown flapping, he nearly knocked his mother over.

"Hey Callum, watch what you're doing!" she protested. "Don't walk and text! You can hardly master walking and breathing at the same time, let alone texting."

"Huh, texting?" smirked Callum. "Nobody texts nowadays Mum, apart from you and Granda." He continued towards the breakfast table, punching emojis and posing for snaps as he went, grinning at the digital respect coming his way. Perhaps breakfast wasn't the best description, given that it was past noon, but that had been the pattern recently.

"What time were you back last night?" asked his mum sharply as she bustled past him, placing the empty coffee cup in the kitchen sink. She turned to face him, pulling a brush through her greying hair.

"Just before midnight," he lied. "We were gaming at Jake's and

I didn't realise the time."

"Hmm," she muttered. "It was more like two when I heard you crashing up the stairs."

But she had no time to argue now and Callum watched as she took the insulated bag off the side which contained the lunch he knew she would drop at her father-in-law's on her way to the hotel. This was something she had done each Saturday since Morag, her mother-in-law, had died. When she was in a rush it was simply left outside his front door, whether it was appreciated or not.

"There's three things for you on the board, please do them Cal, I don't ask much. See you at six and we can have a catch up over supper." She kissed him on the head, and he heard the front door close as she scurried onto Auchinyell Road.

Of course it had been well after midnight, but he seemed to have got away with it again. The Aberdeen nights were long in July yet they had drunk and smoked until it was pitch black, then cycled to Jake's dad's place and the retreat that was the garage where the sound from his PS4 drowned the rap music. More lager was accompanied by THC-laced juice for their vapes and the four of them had chuckled away until Rory was snoring on a beanbag. Soon after, Callum had wobbled outside, steered his bike home and made it to bed.

This kind of evening had become routine over summer, in fact for much of this year. His injury last October had definitely contributed. Until then he had been training three times a week and playing twice, which left little time for messing about. But that had gradually changed, especially once his exams had been cancelled. He didn't have the same energy for rugby now, perhaps because he was frustrated that his season had ended so early, or possibly the smoking and booze had done it. Since finishing his Nationals, life had been one long cruise, and his attitude was creating some tension at home.

He looked at the scribble board on the wall: 'Clean room + bring down laundry. Clear away breakfast and wash dishes. Walk Fergie'. He poured a second bowl of cereal, munching away whilst still tapping on his screen. Placing the empty bowl next to his mum's cup, he took a long, thirsty drink directly from the tap, then headed upstairs to shower. He started the music from his phone as usual, taking the speaker into the bathroom so he could hear it in the shower. The shave would have to wait a bit longer. He quickly dressed and headed back down, his bare feet hammering the stairs in time to the beat.

Pulling his hoodie on, Callum slipped into his trainers and headed to the front door, where he took the dog lead off its peg. At the sound of the jangling chain, a brown cocker spaniel appeared, tail wagging furiously, and they both left the house and headed towards the park. Fergie was a fit ten-year-old, probably from all the running he had done with Callum these past years, though that too had slipped since the end of last year. The previous Fergie had lived to be fourteen, and though Callum was too young to remember, he knew he had always been his brother's dog.

But there was no jogging today. It was bright and sunny, just as it had been all week, as they set off on another visit to the park. Callum plodded slowly along Garthdee Drive, lifting his feet as if it was all a big effort, which may have been down to the hangover. He took a deep breath through his nose and blinked rapidly as if preparing for something. They entered the play area and Fergie scurried off as soon as the lead was removed, heading straight for a small gathering close to the trees.

"Fergie!" croaked Tomas from his seat on the grass, firmly embracing him as he arrived and rolling straight into a play-fight, which they both clearly enjoyed. "Och, you're the best manager we ever had." This was precisely the same thing he had said to the dog every day for months now, usually in the very same location.

"Well done," said Rory, who was already rolling one up. "Do we have to call you Commander now?" he smirked. Callum dropped the lead on the grass and slumped down next to it, then cupped the back of his head with his hands and rolled back, facing into the sun.

"Sir will do, dickhead,' he said. A brief pause, then he added "What the fuck happened last night? I can't remember much, don't even recall leaving your place, but I woke up in the right bed. Miracle I didn't stack the bike on the way back."

"We was all pretty pickled, again!" replied Rory and giggled before lying back and lighting the cigarette.

They fell quiet, other than the sound of Fergie tussling with Tomas. They always occupied this slightly concealed section of the park; it was a long south-facing bank just beyond the football pitches. It gave shelter from any breeze but was open to the sun. The park had become a favourite, not only for young children but also for teenagers during this difficult summer, a social oasis you might say. Whenever it was dry, groups assembled, usually consuming something intoxicating, and so the days passed. There had been very little else to do this summer, and most people had just stayed home. They were halfway through the school holidays and there was no reason to believe the second half would be any different.

The quiet was broken by the sound of music approaching from behind, but Callum didn't need to turn to know who it was. From the type of music and the volume he knew it was Jake, who lowered his rucksack and portable speaker, then sat amongst them. A monosyllabic attempt at conversation was struck up, with the previous evening's activities the main topic. After Callum had left it sounded like Jake and Tomas had stayed up playing for a few hours before crashing out themselves. It had been a slow start to the day, that was sure.

His attention had been grabbed when Jake informed them that he had asked Chloe, Megan and Sophie to join them that afternoon for a chill. There was no denying all three were attractive in their own way, but they were also mature, cocky and assertive. Callum felt a little insecure in their company, being less confident than the other three, and he was always a bit anxious about seeing them. They were certainly lively, which could always mean a chance to get off with one of them. They were no strangers to alcohol but it was because of what they smoked that they had become known as the Spice Girls. Callum could see Jake was watching him and he shifted nervously.

Jake reached into his bag and pulled out a four-pack of cider, handing one to each of them. It was the cheap, strong, fruit-flavoured stuff you can get from the supermarket by the river and luckily for them, Jake's fake ID always stood up there. They supped away and before long Rory was handing round a spliff. Callum's intention to clean his room and do the washing-up was soon replaced by fuzzy giggles and banter. Fergie had loved the attention, but now he lay with his head on Callum's lap, one ear pricked. He raised his head to investigate a sound that he was the first to hear. The girls were inside the park and closing in.

Callum sat up, leaning back onto his extended arms, which made him feel his chest looked bigger. He casually ran his fingers through his wavy hair, which had now dried, making sure it didn't look like it was anything other than habit.

"Hey Jake," said one of the girls, Chloe, who was tall and dark-haired with a suggestive smile. As she spoke, Callum caught sight of her tongue piercing. She was the one he liked, but her confidence made him nervous.

"Hey trouble," Jake replied, and patted the grass next to him. Chloe sat and wrapped her bare arms around her knees. Then, cocking her head to face into the sun, she lifted Jake's can to her lips. Megan and Sophie had spotted Fergie and sat either side of Callum petting the spaniel. They were intimately close to Callum's leg, adding to his feeling of tension. They were sharing what was left of a bottle of vodka and their actions suggested it had been full not long ago.

Their attention drifted between Fergie and the boys. Jake cranked the music and Rory skinned up again; the sun edged towards the trees and they drifted a little closer to each other. It was a laugh, pushing boundaries they would not have approached a year ago.

When the vodka was finished, Megan, whose face was now nearly as red as her hair, suggested they play spin-the-bottle, an old favourite.

"Whoever it points to has to kiss someone else from the circle but differently to all previous kisses," she announced. She knelt over the bottle, her large, freckled breasts almost tumbling out of her sleeveless shirt. She glanced towards Callum, causing him to look away, slighty flustered, then gave it a spin. It landed on Jake, who without a moment's hesitation grabbed Chloe with both hands and thrust his tongue into her mouth, meeting no resistance. They rolled around as they kissed, adding to Callum's embarrassment, which he tried to hide with a grin.

Thankfully they eventually stopped and Jake leaned over to give the bottle another spin. This time it fell on Rory, who was much slower in his actions than Jake, possibly because he was less sure about what he wanted to do, but probably due to the weed. He reached down and took Megan's foot, removing her wedge shoe, then placed her big toe against his mouth and groaned as he kissed her.

"Yuck!" she squealed, withdrawing her foot. Rory spun the bottle and it fell on Sophie. She raised her eyebrows and slowly reached into the pocket of the bag she was carrying, clutching something in her palm. Then she crawled on all fours towards Callum and pushed his shoulders. Maintaining the nervous grin, he lowered himself until he lay flat and Fergie moved to the side. She straddled him and he watched her pull a vape to her mouth, drawing as much as she could. She leaned forward, pressed her mouth onto his, and exhaled, leaving him to breathe it in. He struggled not to cough, just managing to inhale the alien flavour before slowly releasing the smoke back into her grinning face.

"Cool!" she hissed and returned to the space next to him. He sat up, pretending nothing had happened, and reached over to spin the bottle. As it spun, his head began to rotate with it and he sank backwards onto his elbows. A wave of nausea hit him as his ears began to ring. He allowed his heavy eyes to close and sank further back.

CHAPTER 2

Rather than head straight home, Mary Anderson decided she would return to Donald's again. It would give her a chance to collect his empty lunch containers, but the main reason was that she needed to talk to him about Callum.

Working at the hotel was a key part of her life. It provided welcome income, but it meant more than that. She enjoyed the social interaction with the guests nearly as much as with the other staff. They were a good team and she had been hoping to get a job for Callum during the holidays, but none had been available. He needed something to keep him busy, to get him off that damn video game and engaging with a different group of people. Things had been going the wrong way over the past few months, she was well aware of that, but she didn't know how to change them. They had always been very close, as you would expect given the circumstances, but recently the bond between them had been stretched, which both frightened her and made her angry. It had bubbled over into fiery arguments; they had never fought before this summer. She would try yet again, when they sat to eat their supper that evening, to see if she could push him to get back into exercise and mountain biking; anything would be better than this. But whenever she tried to picture what sixteen-year-olds in Aberdeen should be doing to occupy themselves in the summer holidays, she always arrived at the same place.

"Just me Granda," she called as she let herself in through the front door. Knowing precisely where he would be, she slipped off her shoes and joined him in the front room.

"Aye aye Mary, how was work?" He removed his glasses, placing the newspaper on the side table, and smiled at her, bringing his wrinkled face to life.

"Nae bad. I'm a bit preoccupied with Callum to be honest, so I probably wasn't at my sharpest, but it's all OK thanks."

"Aye, ye mentioned that in your text. And thanks for the dinner dear, highlight of my week! Can I get you a cuppie?" he asked, preparing to rise from the chair.

"No, thanks, I won't stop long. I just wanted a quick chat."

"Aye. I've not really seen Callum these past few months myself, but is it getting worse? I could sense how worried you were last time we spoke."

Mary had shared with Granda how Callum's knee injury, along with the restrictions, had really narrowed his world. But she now told him of the monotonous routine that had developed involving video games, late nights, smoking and drink, such that the boy was seldom up before noon. There were only a few weeks before school restarted, and Mary was convinced his mind needed to be in a better place.

"Ah, I think we both feel he should be doing what Finlay was doing at his age and in fact what most generations of Andersons also did, including myself during summer holidays. I must take responsibility for it not being the case."

"It's nobody's fault, but he needs our help through this tricky patch. A stick and carrot approach is what I was thinking."

They discussed how they were going to steer Callum into trying something new; they just hoped it would stir an interest in him.

As Mary walked along the road, she had more energy in her step.

The sun was still shining and the sky was the darkest shade of blue. It was the end of another week's work and she had agreed a plan with Granda.

Swinging the empty lunch-bag in time to her steps, she turned into Auchenyell Gardens and rehearsed what she was going to say to Callum. The message was clear, and she just hoped he would agree. She reached for the keys from her handbag and looked towards the house.

What she saw stopped her in her tracks. She froze twenty metres from the front door, uncertainty and fear engulfing her.

CHAPTER 3

Callum stirred and slowly emerged from the fog in his head. He was lying on his side, head on his rucksack in the shade of the trees at the east end of the park. Gradually he raised his upper body until he sat looking towards the playground, elbows on knees, rubbing his eyes. He sensed he had slept for quite a while, as there were very few people in sight; most had headed home, including his so-called friends.

His tongue sought moisture from the bridge of his dry mouth, and found a sharp, bitter and unpleasant taste. Letting out a deep breath he reached to his jeans, looking for his phone; thankfully it was still there. It was almost out of power, but he could see a missed call from his mum and numerous unopened snaps. He clicked to open them, but as he did so the screen went black.

He tried to piece the afternoon together. He could remember the sesh with the boys and the giggling when the girls arrived, but he had blacked out after inhaling from Stacy. What the hell had been in that vape?

Slowly he got up and reached for his rucksack, and just then he noticed the lead next to it. His stomach lurched. "Fergie, shit!" he muttered. He spun round to look towards the trees.

Moving erratically, he peered over the park, but could see nothing other than the small group across from him. He slung the warm rucksack over his shoulder and began to circle the perimeter, calling as he went. His mind began to race, it was well known that the huge demand for dogs through lockdown had led to a sharp increase in theft. A growing fear rose into his neck and dulled his shouts to a croak. Maybe the dog was asleep in the bushes out of the sun?

Callum's quest became more urgent as he paced around, repeatedly shouting, "Fergie! Fergie!" He was pleading now as he continued around the outside of the park. He looked with misty eyes through the fence towards the main road beyond. As he approached the four remaining teenagers, they stood in unison and turned away from him, looking towards the exit of the park, where a police car had stopped, blue lights flashing. Not knowing what had happened, one of the girls swivelled and said with a grin, "Hey Callum, nice sleep?"

This hugely irritated him, but using all the control he could manage replied, "Um hi Alice, yeah good. What's happened over there?" The fear was now overwhelming him.

"Dunno, something's happened on the road there and the police arrived but we didn't see anything."

"Oh OK, I'll go take a look. Hey, you haven't seen Fergie, my dog, have you?"

Alice looked him in the eye and they both had the same unspoken thought. She shook her head and he felt even worse. This was his fault, and he was struggling to avoid tears. He walked swiftly past them, directly to the exit, and said a silent prayer, promising to be a better person if only his dog was safe.

Approaching the exit gate, he slowed, trying to determine what had happened. He could see the two officers were standing in front of the car looking at the floor; one of them crouched down and extended her hands. Callum nervously walked through the gate, fearing the worst. But then, to his relief, he saw the officer's gloved hands take the hands of a teenage girl who was slumped on the kerb. She helped the girl to her feet, asking questions about how she was.

Callum sighed with relief, but then guilt hit him as he saw the lost look in her eyes. He turned away and headed back along the pavement in the direction of his home. He needed to charge his phone so he could check whether any of the gang had Fergie or knew what had happened to him. He would have to tell his mum; there was no choice if he returned without the dog. Her anger did not worry him. He was overcome with worry about Fergie and how to locate him.

Questions and scenarios ran through his head. If the others had taken him, surely they would have taken the lead? If he had to report him missing to the police, they were going to want the details of how he had disappeared, and Callum did not want to go through that explanation. What if they just couldn't find him, if he had been taken and sold to another family far away? He tried to control himself with slow, heavy breathing, but the fear was overwhelming.

He trudged along until he reached his front door. It felt strange walking without peering at his phone as he went, like he was being watched. He moved faster, plunging his hand into his front pocket. He reached the front door, opened it a fraction and then paused. He closed his eyes and composed himself before pushing it further.

As he stepped in, his mum came through into the hall hurrying towards him.

"God Callum, what happened? I've been worried sick. I was just about to try calling your friends."

"Mum, I'm so, so sorry, we had a few drinks, then it all got out of hand and I fell asleep. Mum, I've lost Fergie."

With this he began to sob. She stepped forward and he embraced her, his head resting against hers. She held him tight, then stepped back. Callum could see there were tears in her eyes too.

"He's here, son. He was at the door when I returned. That's what frightened me, I knew you wouldn't normally let him out of your sight and my mind started racing about what might have... happened to you." Her voice trailed away with these last words.

"Fergie's *here?*" exclaimed Callum. At that moment, as if responding to his name, the dog scurried round the corner and into the hall, where Callum scooped him up. "I'm so sorry," he whispered, pressing his ear against the dog's muzzle.

After taking a moment to regain her composure, Mary spoke. "Callum, this can't continue, it's sending me to despair. You used to be so active and engaging, now you spend all your time drinking, smoking or on that damn video game. You can't even bring your laundry downstairs or clean away your dishes. I'm near to a breakdown and I have nobody to help me. If your father was here he would never stand for it. Now go and take a shower, clean that mud off your face and come back down so we can speak more. I am too angry to talk, and it will only make me cry again."

"Aye, I'm real sorry ma," he said, now noticing her tired, red-rimmed eyes. He slowly nodded his head and made his way upstairs.

Half an hour later, looking slightly more human, Callum entered the sitting room and sheepishly sat down opposite his mum. She looked more composed and held a mug of tea.

"You need something to occupy your time before school starts again," she began. "You don't seem to be too bothered by rugby training and you haven't found a job. There's no farm-owning family I can send you to or any such obvious solution. Cal, I have registered you for something this coming Friday and Saturday that I want you to attend without any argument. Today was as bad as it can ever get, do you understand? At least as long as you live under this roof. I truly do not want to be any more alone than I already am."

Callum looked towards her, relieved that Fergie was safe and apologetic for what he had done. The afternoon had shaken him.

"OK Mum, I'm sorry, I really am," he said. "Yes of course I'll do it. What is it?"

"I have registered you for an introductory salmon fishing course taking place at Banchory. Outdoors, without screens, away from that bunch of friends it will be a chance to learn something new in a nice healthy location."

Callum stared at her ageing face in disbelief.

Shortly afterwards, still feeling dazed but with his phone recharged, he checked his messages and replied to the latest from Jake asking where he was. 'Home, feel pretty shitty. Lost Fergie. Found him now. Mum's vexed and forcing me on a course this wknd at Banchory.'

'Banchory, what course? Golf?'

'Nah, fly-fishing. Grounded til done it. cu sat eve.'

'Fly fishing? FFS.'

CHAPTER 4

The following Friday morning, Callum cycled to Cult's hotel, parked his bike round the back and just about made the 08.10 bus. It had been a huge effort, overseen by his mum, but he had made it as agreed. He ate the sausage and egg sandwich she had packed for him and drank the orange juice carton dry whilst messaging his friends. Arriving at Banchory 40 minutes later, he cut through to the Banchory Lodge Hotel and ambled across the car park towards the group on the lawn that ran down to the river.

It was a pleasant day and the sun shone between the tall lime trees that surrounded the car park. There were two trestle tables with eleven youngsters gathered around the two adults; eight boys and, perhaps surprisingly, three girls. The adults were wearing the typical fishing clothing, olive and khaki colours with peaked caps. He figured they were both in their forties. The crowd were paying attention, and they turned towards him as he shuffled across the gravel onto the grass, putting his vape in the front pocket of his ripped jeans.

"Hey, welcome," said the taller adult. "What's your name?"

"Callum," he replied, without eye contact. "Callum Anderson."

"It's good to have you with us, we just got started. My name's Ross and this is Scott. Here you go." The man tossed a branded baseball cap across as he continued to talk to the group, who had all turned to view the newcomer. Callum returned their attention with a slight raise of his head, which the eldest of them acknowledged.

The instructor continued in his strong, accented voice. "Thank you again for joining us for the next two days. We hope you will gain the knowledge and skills that will provide the right platform for your fly fishing careers and have a lot of fun on the way. Scott and I will be splitting you into two groups based upon your ages, but we'll be covering the same topics. This morning we'll talk about the salmon and what a unique, wonderful fish it is. You will learn exactly what is so wonderful about it, where it can be found and the many threats the species currently faces. We'll do some casting practice, so that after lunch we can get you fishing with a visit to Raemoir fishery. It should be a cracking day. Please ask any questions you have and enjoy yourselves. Now, all those born in 2007 and earlier come with me, the rest of you go with Scott."

The group slowly split and followed the instructors.

"Hey Callum," said Ross firmly as he turned. "Pop your phone in your pocket and come with me, lad."

Begrudgingly, Callum followed the group to a space on the lawn where there were some floor cushions and some neatly stacked items. He recognised two of his group from school; both were a year younger than him, which added to his embarrassment. He didn't recognise the other three; perhaps they were in the area on holiday and like him had been pushed into the course by their tired parents. They looked engaged in the new experience and were laughing at something. *They'd better not be laughing at me*, thought Callum as he grabbed a cushion and tried to sit as far from anyone as he could.

"There she is everyone, this beautiful river in front of you is the majestic River Dee," said Ross. "It rises to the west in the Cairngorm mountains and flows for over 80 miles to the sea at Aberdeen. There are hundreds of rivers in Scotland, many of them quite small, that have salmon in them, though this number is sadly decreasing rapidly. The Dee is one of the famous Big Four Scottish salmon rivers, the others being the Spey, the Tay and the Tweed. For millions of years fresh water has run down this river and salmon have run up it, following the same incredible migratory pattern. Eggs are laid high up the river, hatch and gradually mature in the cool, clean fresh water until after about two or three years these young salmon make their way out to sea and head to waters off Greenland, where they feed and rapidly grow before returning right back to the very reaches of the same upper river with one purpose, to spawn. If they return after just one year at sea they are known as grilse, those that stay at sea longer grow to be the biggest."

Ross paused and reached down to the floor, lifting up a fibre-glass model of a very large salmon. "Within four years, those precious new eggs can become beautiful strong fish which battle the elements, leap the rapids and evade all sorts of predators so they too can perform their goal of producing a new generation of fish. They have an incredible ability to sense when they are in the estuary of their birth river, and assuming the river level isn't too low, they will head upstream, changing from salt water to fresh. This is known as being anadromous. It's during this window in their journey, when they are between the sea and their spawning grounds, that many passionate anglers try to catch them." He wiggled the salmon light-heartedly in a swimming motion before placing it back on the floor. Then he turned over the first page of the flipchart, which had a hand-drawn map on it.

"Atlantic salmon are now primarily found in north-east America, Iceland, UK, Scandinavia and Russia, although a hundred years ago they were present in large numbers across Europe. At the beginning of the last century, over a hundred thousand fish were caught in a single year in Germany and Holland alone. Sadly, for a variety of reasons, the number of wild salmon in the North

Atlantic has dropped significantly in recent years and whilst we work hard to address that decline, it does mean catching one is even more special than perhaps it used to be. They are remarkable fish and broadly recognised as the most prized fish to catch. The king of fish."

Ross waited, partly for effect, but also to give people a chance for questions. Callum looked at the map. The salmon's distribution had shrunk to just the most northern countries, and Scotland was right in the middle of them.

One of the boys from the year below Callum raised his hand and asked about the size of the salmon in the river. *Keeno*, thought Callum with a sneer, but he was surprised to hear that some were over 20lbs in weight and a few even over 30lbs. That was heavier than Fergie. Another asked what the salmon ate in the river – did they take ducklings and frogs? This caught everyone's attention, as the mental image of a fish taking a duck off the surface like a scene from a nature programme was vivid and pretty gruesome.

"No, Angus, they don't. In fact, one of the peculiarities of the salmon is that when they return to fresh water they stop feeding. Sometimes this can be for many months and in extreme cases for a year, yet they manage to survive on the energy reserves they have stored from time at sea and pursue their destiny to reproduce. There are a few theories about why this happens. Can you think of any reason?"

After a brief silence, Angus offered, "Maybe it's to do with the effect of changing from salt to fresh water?"

"Good answer," said Ross. "There is certainly a school of thought that the shock of the transition from salty to fresh water is what changes their behaviour. Another idea is that when in fresh water, the stomach of the fish contracts to make room for eggs and sperm. I can see some logic in that." One of the group of three boys was rubbing his own stomach and giggling. Ross continued, "This could explain why salmon will still seize food items, including an angler's fly, through habit, although their hunger is suppressed. Insects and small fish are sometimes found in the stomachs of salmon that have recently entered the river, but not in large amounts. The other suggestion, one that I like and which you might think is more in line with Charles Darwin's theory, is that over long periods of time salmon have evolved to stop feeding in fresh water as the majority of available food in these cold rivers is young, developing salmon. If adult salmon were to feed as they swim upriver towards their spawning grounds, surely they would cannibalise their own offspring and threaten the very existence of their species. Interesting thought, isn't it?"

Ross then turned the page on his flipchart showing the life stages of the salmon. "There is so much we don't yet know, but science is slowly uncovering it for us. Right, I think that's enough talking on my part for a while, let's start on something practical."

He beckoned the group to follow him and walked down to the water. Callum followed and they bunched closer. Laid on the grass in front of them were four sets of fly-fishing tackle, each consisting of a tube which clearly contained a rod, a reel and a small pouch. He had expected there to be more kit, as it appeared quite simple.

"I'm going to show you how to set up a fly rod, and to start with we are preparing for trout fishing," said Ross. "Trout rods are shorter and lighter than salmon rods and can be cast using one hand. Please watch carefully, because then you are going to try for yourselves. I assemble the rod by pushing the sections firmly together so they are gradually getting thinner and make sure that the rings, or eyes, are all aligned so the fly-line can run through them. I then attach the reel to the rod. Some people like to reel in with their left hand and some with their right. Each reel has a metal foot at the top that fits into the seat on the rod. It is then locked in place by screwing the fastener. Ask an instructor to check this once you have done it and then thread the line through each of the eyes. This line I am threading, the fly-line, is quite thick, and that's what gives enough weight to allow us to cast it some distance."

Ross demonstrated this, and Callum thought it seemed pretty straightforward and logical. Ross then laid the rod back down on the grass, fully assembled. The line ran through the eyes and back down towards the reel. He then turned over to the next page on the flipchart, where the steps were already drawn.

"Right, get into pairs and assemble your trout rods," was the instruction. Callum found himself pairing with one of the three other boys. He was wearing a Chelsea shirt and a pair of shiny shorts as if he had just finished playing football. Callum found this amusing. *What were you thinking kid, get a grip*, he thought. With a grunt they connected the rod together. It took a moment and a few glances at the one finished by Ross to work out how the reel attached, but it was soon in place and whilst Callum held the rod the line was threaded through the eyes, to the approving look of their supervisor. Once all three rods had been assembled, Ross asked them to swap roles, dismantle the rods and repeat the process.

Each of the three pairs now had a rod with a reel that was threaded with a fly-line. What remained was to attach a length of see-through nylon and tie a fly onto the very end. In each pouch was a small plastic envelope that contained a coiled, three-metre length of fishing line which, when carefully unpacked, was linked to the thicker fly-line by connecting the loops. Ross demonstrated this twice and each group followed suit, pulling both lines so the link was tight. Without a word, they all rushed to get theirs finished first. They gave a brief smile when they did so.

"OK, well done all of you," said Ross. "We would normally now tie a fly on the end, but we'll hold off doing that whilst we do some casting practice – we don't want any accidents with the hook until you've got the hang of it. OK, good work, let's take a fifteen-minute break now, chance to go to the loo and there is juice available up at the tent."

The group quickly dispersed. Callum wandered along the river-bank and took a seat on the bench, pulling his vape and phone from his pocket.

He was finding it tiresome and sat with a pained expression. Perhaps it was the activity or perhaps it was the company he was in, but either way he couldn't wait for it to be over. He messaged as much to Jake, Tomas and Rory; he was planning to meet them tomorrow and let his hair down amongst a decent crew rather than these losers. Why had his mum pushed him to do this, couldn't she have chosen something else? Had he really done something bad enough to deserve this?

Pressing the button on his vape, he took a hit, then headed to the tent, where he grabbed a drink. He could see both groups already under way again and he sauntered over to join Ross, who acknowledged his arrival without warmth. The kid he was with before was waiting for him to rejoin, but he did not rush. Ross had the trout rod in his hand and had moved to the front of the group with his back to the river.

"OK, so you've assembled your rod. Let's imagine you've tied on your chosen fly and now you want to start casting it towards where you think the fish might be. As I mentioned before, when fly fishing we use the weight of the line as the means to propel the fly forward."

Ross lifted the rod and with a short flick backwards and then forwards, the line flew onto the grass in front of him. He then pulled a few yards of line off the reel and repeated the process, and each time the line went further. He laid the rod on the floor and walked along the line, placing an orange cone on the grass at the point where the end lay, some fifteen metres away.

For the remainder of the morning the group practised casting, trying to get the line to reach the orange cone. It was pleasantly warm, and Callum participated as little as he could get away with, until it was his turn to cast towards the orange cone. Then he made sure the younger kids could see how much better at this he was. The rest of the group were clearly enjoying the instruction, and loud laughter came regularly from the younger team. When not practising the cast, Callum stood at the back peering down at his part-hidden phone, but he looked up at every outburst of laughter or chatter just to be sure he wasn't missing out.

He ambled towards the two girls. They hadn't finished the assembly and Callum was just about to show them how it was done when Scott called them back to the tent, where there was a picnic lunch laid out.

"Grab some food and find a space on the grass or on those tables over there," said Ross. "Once you've eaten, feel free to practise some more. We'll be leaving at one o'clock sharp, so please make sure you are here and ready to go for then."

Callum waited his turn to fill his plate and piled it high. Being awake so early had made him hungry and he made for the table that was furthest away, where he sat alone until almost one o'clock.

The two minibuses pulled onto the grey tarmac close to the main hut, with both drivers opening side doors for the groups to exit. Callum had sat on the back seat and was last off. He slipped his phone away just before stepping down and following the group to the outside tables. A series of small lochs sat naturally in the landscape, surrounded by woodland, their gleaming surfaces reflecting the deep blue of the sky. A smiling, long-haired woman in her early twenties approached them and extended her hand to Ross. Her green Raemoir Fishery T-shirt confirmed that she worked there. As they chatted, Scott placed six rods he had brought in the minibus alongside the ones that already stood in the rack before joining them, shaking hands and turning towards the group.

"Afternoon everyone and welcome to Raemoir. We are very grateful to Sally for hosting us today at this wonderful fishery. She's going to provide a few instructions, then with the help of her three volunteers, who regularly fish here, we'll see if any of us can catch something."

"Hi there guys, and thanks to Ross and Scott for bringing you to join us today," said Sally. "We are all really pleased to have you and hope your first experience of fly fishing will be memorable and successful. Raemoir is purpose-built for trout fishing. Twelve years ago the lochs you can see were dug and planted with a wide array of plant species to create a very natural home for our trout. You will all be fishing at the same time with the team of us on hand to help, and given the lovely weather you are going to be using dry flies, which sit on top of the water's surface, until a trout grabs them, that is. We have exclusive use of the loch in front of you, and it's divided into six sections, so each section will hold two of you. All fishing is from the bank or the short wooden pontoons, so no getting wet. We will each take two of you and show you how to tie the fly onto the leader – that's the clear fine line at the end – then you can get going."

The group was split between the instructors. They each collected a rod and were shown how to tie a 'clinch knot', though for the younger kids the knots were tied for them. Callum quickly mastered the knot – as the eldest, he felt he needed to – then headed with suppressed enthusiasm for the section he had been allocated. He looked across the water, where fish were continually breaking the glassy surface of the loch in pursuit of insect food.

Once everyone was in place, they began attempts at casting.

The instructors needed to provide more help to some, though most were able to get the fly out onto the water to varying distances.

After a few curses, Callum had the line going out quite nicely and was watching the floating fly carefully. He wanted to catch one, wanted to show it was easy for him. He was waiting for a fish to take the fly when he heard a commotion coming from the far bank. He looked over to see that one of the girls from the other group was towing a splashing trout towards the net, which was held by Scott.

Callum shuffled his feet a little, drew his line in and cast again. The fly-line extended nicely over the water before the fly dropped gently onto the surface, just as the instructors had done it. He mumbled approval to himself and was stunned to see a swirl around his fly as it disappeared. It took a moment to appreciate what had happened, but then he lifted the rod and tightened the line as they had been shown that morning.

"Hey hey, Ross!" he yelled in excitement, forgetting to be cool for a moment. The trout was pulling against him and he wasn't sure what to do.

Ross was soon at his side. The fighting fish was splashing defiantly.

"If he tugs hard, let the line pull off the reel or there's a chance it'll either snap or the hook will come out," he said. Callum managed a nod in reply as the fish zigzagged at the end of the line.

"You're doing great, Callum. When the line gets loose like that, reel it in so you keep the tension on the fish," said Ross.

Callum concentrated, following the instructions. "Good, now slowly draw it towards me and I'll net it."

The fish kicked and twisted but remained on the hook until it was safely in the net, which Ross now placed on the bank. Callum remained transfixed by the shiny fish and its pink hues, worried it might jump back in if he took his eyes off it. Ross withdrew a short truncheon from his pocket and held the back of the fish steady before cracking it firmly on the top of the head.

"This is called a priest," he explained, holding up the little club. "We use one of these to swiftly dispatch any fish we are not returning. In this lake, all fish are to be dispatched, as beginners handling them and returning them creates potential problems and disease. The fish are all reared on site, so there's no issue with harming native wild populations."

Callum was only half-listening, fascinated by what Ross was doing and shocked when he handed the fish to him.

"You're welcome to take this one home with you this evening to cook, Callum, it'll be delicious. Well done, your first fly-caught fish is a 3lb rainbow trout!"

Callum smiled at Ross, not sure about the slimy texture of the fish but wanted to appear capable and unbothered.

They continued for more than an hour and although a few more fish were caught by the others, Callum had to be content with just the one. His attention span was dwindling. He ambled back to the hut carrying the trout, which one of the staff took and placed in a bag with some ice before returning it to him. He took a seat in the sunshine looking over the lake and opened a drink can. Although he was still annoyed that he had been pushed to attend this session, he felt that perhaps this fishing lark wasn't all bad.

He went through his messages. His mates had done precisely nothing all day, so he hadn't missed out.

Before long, the rest of the group had returned to the hut where the rods were stowed, and they were all buzzing from the day as they boarded the minibuses. Callum sat alone. Once they reached the Banchory Lodge Hotel he gave a nod to Ross before heading back to the bus stop. He took the bus back to Cult's and cycled to Garthdee.

When he reached home, Fergie and his mum met them at the door as he wheeled his bike into the hall.

"Well, how was it?" Mary asked.

Callum smiled, handed his mum the bag containing the fish and continued into the kitchen. "It was all right," he said.

"You caught one?" she pressed her hand to her chest and followed him.

"It's just a trout, Mum," he said. He knelt down to fuss Fergie.

"Yeah but come on, that's great. I'm going to cook that beauty tomorrow night, Cal. I have a special family recipe for it." This gave Callum a strange feeling of pride.

They chatted more as they ate tea, but Callum didn't offer to say anything else about the day. He helped clear up, then sharply marched upstairs and pressed the power button.

Eleanor Scougall

CHAPTER 5

Callum had not been allowed to meet the lads in the park, so he had spent the evening in his room with his vape and video game controller. Tiredness from a busy day and fresh air ensured he was asleep by eleven. He knew that if he could put up with one more day on the fishing course, he would get his freedom back.

Saturday was again bright and warm. He had followed the previous day's routine, just about making the 201 and guzzling his packed breakfast as they motored along North Deeside Road. He found himself occasionally lifting his gaze from his screen and peering through the left window at the river until they came to a stop in Banchory.

As Callum traversed the hotel car park again and glanced across at the gathered group, something caught his eye. It was the unexpected sight of a girl; one he had certainly not seen the previous day. She was quite tall, with long, heavy, dark locks and a smiling face. She was beautiful. He lifted his shoulders, and his slump was transformed into a steady gait as he walked towards the meeting point. He tried not to stare and pretended to focus on the river, but he could not resist looking at the girl. She was chatting with another new face who looked of a similar age to Scott and Ross, but she was much younger than them, most likely sixteen or seventeen, he thought. Her head tipped backwards as she laughed and Callum could see her big, attractive eyes and her fresh, pretty face.

Others in the group began to acknowledge Callum's arrival, but he remained at the rear of the group, his lack of interest in the occasion apparent. His shoulders were hunched forward, his earphones remained in place and beneath the peak of his NY cap – not the fishing cap. His eyes were lowered.

"Good morning," said Ross enthusiastically as he and Scott arrived. "Glad to see we didn't scare any of you away yesterday. Welcome to Day Two. Today we're going to take what we learned yesterday to the next level. This morning you will learn the basics of casting with a two-handed rod, and this afternoon we'll bring it all together on the river itself and see if we can hook one of those precious bars of silver. I'm delighted to introduce Honor Garba and Fergus Grey, our AAPGAI-qualified instructors, who are kindly joining us today." Following a brief round of appreciative applause, Ross concluded, "Same groups as yesterday, let's make today special!"

Callum had removed his earphones and now followed Ross towards their space on the grass, conscious of his disappointment as he watched Honor head towards the younger group. She had a natural grace in her movement, and her plain waders and boots somehow seemed to amplify her femininity. She was passing her thick hair, now in a ponytail, through the back of her baseball cap, and he quickly turned away as she glanced in his direction.

As yesterday, on the ground were a fishing rod case, a reel, a spool of line and a closed box bearing a bright painting of a salmon fly. With the six teenagers and Fergus around him, Ross assembled the rod, attached the reel and threaded the fly-line through the eyes of the rod, just as they had done the previous afternoon, although this time the rod had more sections and was longer. Ross then explained that whilst the fly-line gave the weight to cast some distance, he needed to attach a short length of clear line, the leader, before tying the fly so that it would be invisible to a fish. This was just what they had done the previous day.

"The last remaining piece of the kit is the fly itself, the little bit of magic we hope will drive the salmon to snap at it," he went on. "As I mentioned yesterday, a mystery of nature, and one more thing that makes salmon fishing unique. The salmon does not feed in fresh water, yet it is possible to trigger the fish to take our flies. Is it habit, is it frustration or irritation, who knows?"

The group listened intently, even Callum. Being so close to the river created extra excitement.

"This morning we are going to use a piece of wool instead of a fly, so we don't have any accidents whilst we teach the basics. We have set out a grid to practise a bit further upstream, opposite that hut you can see on the far bank. There's a nice shingle beach here and the water is shallow, so you can learn in your casual shoes. This afternoon we'll put on waders, add flies and see if we can get them to swing across the current."

Fergus tapped Callum on the shoulder, indicating for him to follow along with the two others from Callum's school. He walked for a minute along the grassy bank with fishing rod in hand, then down onto the stones where he stopped the three boys. They all turned to face the river, which was just a few feet in front of them.

"Casting a salmon fly is all about timing and technique, there's very little force involved," said Fergus. "By using the flex of the rod and the weight of the fly-line it's possible to send the line thirty metres, even forty. It's not like golf, which can be daunting for beginners – everyone can cast the fly in the intended general direction, even if only a short way. Through practice, you can improve distance, accuracy and delicacy. It's something you can do at all ages, nine to ninety – the timing and technique are what count, it's not about muscle. Some of the greatest fly-fishers are female. You'll soon see how easy Honor makes it look."

The mention of her name focused Callum's attention. Fergus turned to face the river with the three boys behind him to his left and slowly talked through the technique for a short cast.

"Yesterday you were using a nine-foot rod that you held in one hand and were able to present the fly onto the water through a back-and-forth motion, flicking the line behind you, then pushing it onto the water in front. This is known as an overhead cast, and it's not too difficult to master the basics. For salmon fishing, where the rivers are typically wider and the fish larger, we normally use a bigger rod that requires two hands to operate, like this one. This rod is more than thirteen feet long and as you can see would be too much to hold in one hand, so we use two. It's certainly possible to use the overhead cast with a double-handed rod but this morning we are going to teach you a basic form of Spey casting known as the roll cast. It is called Spey casting because it originated on the River Spey. Now why might we want to use this type of cast?"

"So that we can cast when it isn't possible to flick the line behind us?" came a reply from one of the lads.

"That's right Marcus," confirmed Fergus. "Long stretches of this river are lined with trees. It makes it very attractive, but if we did an overhead cast our lines would end up caught in the branches. Nor would we want to hook someone out walking along the riverbank, so we use a roll cast like this."

Fergus pulled some line from his reel, then slowly dragged the rod backwards over his right shoulder and he paused with the rod at forty-five degrees, which created a loop of line from the rod tip to the water in the shape of a letter D. He then accelerated the rod forward, crisply stopping it when the rod was forty-five degrees in front of him. A loop of line followed the rod forward like a wave, accompanied by a crisp whooshing sound. When the line had fully extended, the piece of wool fell to the water.

Fergus demonstrated this a few more times before calling Marcus up to try. Soon it was Callum's turn, and he shuffled up to the instructor and took over the rod. This couldn't be too difficult, he thought, having mastered the overhead cast yesterday. He drew the rod tip back over his shoulder, which left the line hanging in a loop below it and thrust the rod forward. The line went in the right general direction, but it didn't extend as far as when Marcus had tried, and the last few feet collapsed into the shallows.

"Sweep the line backwards and gradually raise your tip to create a large D-loop," said Fergus. "Then when you accelerate forward, stop it crisply when it's pointing to the tops of those trees. Imagine you have an axe and it's hitting a tree trunk." Callum composed himself and followed the instructions with a smooth rhythm, and the line shot straight out.

"Excellent, Callum. Now pull two more lengths of line off the reel and see if you can do the same again."

Callum tried again, and the line shot out again just as Fergus' had. He wound in the line and placed the rod back on the ground. As he walked back to his floor cushion he caught the eye of Ross, who raised a thumb. The recognition gave him quite a buzz. He felt slightly conceited but was pleased he had looked good in front of the group.

He glanced over to the younger group, where Honor was demonstrating. The morning chill had receded, so she had removed her fleece, revealing slender bare arms beneath the contrasting white T-shirt. As she drew the rod back to cast, he could clearly see the feminine curve of her chest before she gracefully completed the action. Her movements were seemingly in time with a silent orchestra. He was captivated.

He mimicked the casting motion himself with an imaginary rod, trying to copy her smooth motion. He stopped abruptly as he realised what he was doing.

For the following hour the group practised casting a longer line. There was a large boulder pointing above the surface about fifteen metres out that they were all trying to reach. Callum's naturally competitive spirit came through as he pushed to cast further than the target. The group worked on this, improving all the time until at around eleven they stopped for a break.

Unlike the previous day, rather than separate from the group for a vape and check his phone, Callum joined them as they converged on the tent. As he was pouring a cold drink, one of the group congratulated him on the trout he had caught the previous day. He thanked him but was distracted as Honor approached the tent, chatting with a beaming, energetic girl who was probably not yet a teenager. Callum stood tall on the edge of the grass next to the gazebo, appearing to be fascinated by the façade of the hotel. He feigned surprise as Honor joined him and asked, "How's your morning been?" Her voice was soft and her accent was different from that of his friends. Really different, exotic almost.

Without turning to face her, he replied, "OK, it's all a bit juvenile for me but I'm sure the kids are having a good time."

"Oh, I hadn't realised you were so experienced. My name's Honor." She held out her slender hand and he took it, quivering slightly. Why had he said something as cocky as that?

"Callum Anderson," he said. "I'm not so experienced, it wasn't meant to sound that way, just that it's not really my scene. I'm a bit more into adrenalin activities with people my own age." There, that sounded cooler.

"Ah OK. Did you manage to catch one at Raemoir yesterday then?"

"Yeah, now that was pretty sound, but most of the time it's a bit slow, right?"

"Maybe one day you'll make the perfect cast and feel the kick of hooking into a wild salmon. Believe me, nothing matches that adrenalin rush." With a gentle grin she wandered off to join Fergus, leaving Callum feeling rather small.

After the short break, they continued with their practice and Fergus showed the group a neat technique where the line was dangled downstream, then twirled upstream so that it was above the rod, ready to be safely cast out again away from the body. This took quite a few attempts before it was happening as planned, but it felt and looked really neat. Callum focused hard, determined to get this. "We call this the circle C cast, or some people call it a snap T," explained Fergus. "The line makes a C shape as it's looped upstream," he demonstrated again. "Then, with the line now upstream we can perform the roll cast like we did earlier."

It was soon lunchtime, and they had each managed some decent casts despite the challenge of using the two-handed rod for the first time, a pretty good achievement for a morning's work. Above all else, they had been having fun, though Callum was not ready to admit it.

There was a cheerful buzz around the group as they sat on the lawn enjoying their lunches just a few metres from the river. Callum had decided not to join the provided lunch; a walk into Banchory would give him a break from the group and he could avoid conversation. He hesitated, fearing for a moment that he would miss the chance to chat more with Honor, but he could see she was sitting with the other instructors, so he headed off.

In the public car park next to the supermarket was a kiosk selling burritos. Callum ordered one and sat on the wall keying his phone whilst it was prepared. There were a few vehicles parked near the kiosk with fishing rods attached to their bonnets. A group of men wearing waders chatted animatedly about their morning.

Surprisingly, despite access to his phone, Callum's mind was partly on what he had learned that morning, and he couldn't help himself eavesdropping on their stories.

Having finished eating he plodded back to the hotel, where he could see the group making their way down to the river's edge, so he quickened his pace to join them. He was looking forward to the chance to actually fish this river the instructors were making such a big deal about. If he could be in Honor's group, it would be even better.

He could hear Ross's address as he approached.

"So, this is it team. You've learned a lot in a short space of time, so much that you are each now going to get a chance to fish the Royal River Dee. Just look at her awaiting you! For this afternoon we are going to split you into groups of three – each group will be sharing a rod, but we are very grateful to our friends at Twin Peakes Fly Fishing who have kindly loaned us twelve pairs of waders, so in a few minutes each of you can put a set on. The waders each have a sticker with your name on and they are in sets of three, which signify the group you are in. The sizes are as on the registration forms you completed but it shouldn't be an issue if they're a tad too big, as we do have some spare pairs of thick socks if needed. Find your waders, put them on and your instructor will tell you what to do from there."

Callum followed the group as they excitedly located their waders and therefore their groups. He was again with the two younger boys from his school under the guidance of Fergus. They removed their trainers and started to slide their feet into the waders, all realising that without a support it was easier sitting down. The waders had rubber boots, like wellingtons, integrated into them, so the soles were firm. They were elasticated around the waist and had braces that sat over the shoulders when adjusted to the right length.

Pretty soon the three of them looked like proper salmon fish-ermen, ready for action. Fergus laid the rod down in front of them and drew a small box from his pocket, out of which he selected a fly. It was a bit bigger than the fly they had used yesterday for the trout, being about as long as Fergus's thumbnail and in beautiful silver and blue colours. He demonstrated how to tie it to the nylon, and after testing the knot he clipped the surplus off so that it looked very neat.

"This knot is very easy to use and one of the strongest," he said. "You can practise tying it for yourself when not fishing, but now I'm going to take the first of you into the river. Who's it going to be?"

Callum quickly replied, "Let the younger lads go first, I don't mind being last."

"OK then," smiled Fergus. "Marcus, why don't you show us how it's done? We'll swap over after thirty minutes. Please make sure you have your sunglasses on." And with that he thrust a safety collar to Marcus, which he slipped over his head before following Fergus.

The four instructors were spread along the bank, roughly a hundred metres apart, with Fergus being the third one going downstream and Honor the last one to the left. The instructors led their charges across the rocks and slowly into the water. As it was summertime and there had been only modest amounts of rain recently the river was not very high, so they only went in until the river was around the teenagers' knees before starting to cast. The instructors gave an initial demonstration, rolling line out, letting it drift in on the current and then casting back out with the circle C technique. It looked straightforward enough.

All those on the bank were watching closely as the rods were handed over, and after a few words of encouragement the lines began crossing the water again. Callum watched Marcus, who after a few messy attempts got his timing and was pulling extra line from the reel, so the fly went an impressive distance. The river's current then swung the line in an arc until eventually it hung directly downstream. At this point, Fergus led Marcus a step downstream after the line had finished its swing. Callum glanced upstream and could see everyone was now getting line over the river and clearly enjoying the experience.

He looked to his left and saw Honor patiently helping her younger pupil with the casting. For most of the remaining period he watched her, comfortable that to an observer he would simply appear fascinated by the fishing. She and her pupil were standing very close together and he could tell by her movements that she was chatting, occasionally using her hands to illustrate the point of her words. Her head snapped back from time to time, clearly from laughter, and periodically she looked back upstream to see how the others were faring. There was the occasional splash of a fish that stirred extra excitement, though nobody at this stage had managed to tempt one to take.

After thirty minutes, Fergus sent Marcus to swap over, and then continued the process again over the next thirty metres or so of the river. A cheerful Marcus sat down and chatted a little with Callum as they calmly watched those in the sparkling river. In formation, all the guides had moved downstream approximately the same distance, so they remained about a hundred metres apart.

There was a minor commotion from the next group upstream as the fly stopped swinging across the current and the rod bent on being lifted, but it was soon apparent that the cause was a snagged rock rather than a fish; it was dislodged with the help of the instructor.

Time slipped by as the haze that had grown over the sun warmed them and the river entertained them. There were a few people walking by, enjoying the footpath that ran along the riverbank. Callum had not yet been tempted by his phone this afternoon.

In no time, Fergus had covered another thirty metres of the river and was sending for Callum, who wandered down the bank and took the safety collar with a thin smile. After a few encouraging words and a brief demo, he was handed the thirteen-foot rod. He moved the rod too quickly initially, before it had flexed fully under the weight of the line, but within a minute or two and after some reassurance, he was into it.

His mind was no longer occupied with thoughts of what else he might be doing or where else he might be. He concentrated carefully on the feel of the casting motion and could tell when it was going to plan. Fergus gave encouraging comments as he lengthened the line until it was reaching the middle of the river. They began to step downstream after each cast, before flicking the line upstream in the C movement ready to thrust forward again. With Fergus's support, Callum took two further steps. Now the river nearly reached his waist, and he attempted to cast a little further, for there was clearly a wider pool below him.

"Take your time here," whispered Fergus. "See if you can cast towards that big boulder you see just breaking the surface below us."

The line went out nicely, landing five metres in front of the rock and smoothly swinging across the water. As Callum looked downstream, he saw Honor smiling as he drew in line, preparing to cast again. He felt sure her look was directed at him.

He stepped towards her and sent out another fine cast straight across the river. As it started to swing, he looked towards her, again admiring her grace as she helped her student to cast. He was hoping she would look back, but then suddenly his right arm was pulled forward. Fergus saw the line tighten.

"Shit!" said Callum. "Shit, it's a fish, I've a fish!"

"Slowly lift the rod, Callum, keep your left hand off the reel and gradually lift up," said Fergus.

Under instruction he lifted the rod, which now had a healthy bend in it as the fish moved around the pool. Just as Ross had showed him the previous day, he let the fish pull some line from the reel as it moved away from him across the current. The line loosened a little, allowing his rod to straighten, and then the fish swirled with a splash on the surface.

By this stage the rest of the group had noticed, and he could hear some of them gathering behind him. *Please stay on*, he murmured to the fish. This fish was fighting much harder than yesterday's.

After a few minutes, Fergus led him slowly back towards the bank, guiding the fish in the same direction. Honor was standing next to him now, net in her hands. He was bewildered and slightly overcome with excitement as he continued to walk from the water and up the bank, coaxing the splashing fish into the shallows. It now lay on its side and Callum drew it towards him before Honor's net scooped it up. There came a cheer and numerous shouts of 'well done Callum!' from his group plus handshakes from Fergus, Ross and Scott as he walked towards Honor and her net.

"A beautiful two-pound sea trout, pristine and fresh," she said.

"Can we please get a photo?" said Ross, and Callum crouched down before the camera. Honor gently passed the unhooked fish to Callum and much to his pleasure she crouched beside him, placing her hand on his shoulder. Slightly flustered, he looked at her for guidance and she helped him return the fish to the river. They held it facing upstream and waited for it to regain its energy before Honor took Callum's hand and gave both his hand and the fish in it a short push, which caused the fish to swim off towards the deeper water.

"Well done, really well done," she said, beaming at him. He smiled broadly and made his way back to Fergus.

"Nicely done Callum! Your casting was excellent, and you played the fish really well. I thought it was a salmon at first, but it was a lovely fish nonetheless."

"Thanks Fergus, it was really tense. A bit smaller than the rainbow I caught yesterday but it fought so much harder. What's the difference between sea trout and salmon?"

"In many ways they are very similar. Both are born in the river and head out to sea to feed before returning, but their migratory patterns are quite different and although some sea trout run to ten pounds or more, salmon in general are bigger. You could really feel the strength of it, couldn't you? Yesterday's trout was great sport to catch, but it had been bred for the lake, whereas this trout had faced many challenges living in a fast-flowing river, surrounded by predators and with a long journey to and from the sea. Not surprisingly, the wild fish had more power and resisted capture harder. Well done again. Let's give Marcus another try now and you take a seat back on the bank if that's OK?"

Callum nodded and walked back to the shade, where he sat watching the fishing, although it really meant watching Honor. His mind drifted to the girls he had met in the park a few days ago. He had so wanted to get with one of them, but he was nervous around them. Honor was in a different league.

Before too long they began leaving the river and were instructed to remove waders and leave them lying on the grass before convening back at the tent. Ross gave a summary of the two days and passed his thanks to the Banchory Lodge hotel and to the owner of the fishing for hosting them. In return, the group gave a round of applause to the two casting instructors. Ross told them how impressed all the instructors had been with the energy and ability of the group, and said he felt sure they all had many successful and enjoyable salmon fishing years ahead of them and that the future of the sport needed their generation to ensure it survived. He promised to email them all with some photos and information on other courses or fishing opportunities before wishing them well.

As the group headed towards the waiting parents, Callum went to each of the instructors to thank them. He purposefully left Honor until last. She smiled as he approached.

"Not too bad Callum, you picked it up really quickly!" she said. "Nice to meet you, hopefully see you again soon." He could do little more than thank her for netting the fish before, with as cheeky a smile as he could muster, he made his way to collect his bag and headed off to the bus stop.

On the journey home, Callum's mind was filled with the thrill of catching the fish and the image of Honor smiling as she netted it. He arrived home, calling to his mum as he opened the front door. He started to recount the story of his catch even before he had let go of the bike. Fergie, at his side, wagged his tail.

"Come through where I can hear you, Cal," Mary called from the kitchen

"I was the only one who caught one, Ma. It was epic, right in front of the hotel. There were loads of people watching." He wandered in.

"Ah that's grand, I'm never surprised by what you can achieve when you put your mind to it. Cal. Just there at the mouth of the Feugh, I bet?"

"Yeah, right there, let me show you." He reached for his phone and opened the photo. Then he led her into the sitting room, the mood totally different from the way it had been the last time they had been in the hallway together.

"You're a natural," she said, smiling.

"Maybe," he replied. "It actually felt quite familiar, maybe I dreamed it. You're not allowed to kill the fish in the river though, did you know that?"

"Yes I did, there are far fewer salmon and sea trout in the rivers now. You have to release all that you catch don't you?"

"Yeah, I had no idea. Actually Mum, I didn't even know there was a difference between a wild salmon and a farmed one."

They chatted more and his mum confirmed that having attended the course, his grounding was now lifted, but she was also very clear that no repeat of his recent behaviour would be accepted. Surprisingly, he wasn't feeling particularly eager to meet up with the lads anyway. It bothered him that he still didn't have a full picture of what had happened last week, but it was also clear that none of them had been particularly concerned and this irritated him. Jake in particular annoyed him; he was always so superior and full of himself. They had had some laughs, for sure, but Callum never really felt they were friends.

Callum helped clear up after dinner and found other things to do before eventually changing into his joggers and heading for the park, turning over his thoughts about a meet-up. He was only just through the gate when he saw the three of them heading in his direction. He kept Fergie on the lead as they approached.

"Hey man, you come for another sleep?" laughed Jake. "We're just heading back to the man-cave, you comin' with?"

"Nah, I've got strict instructions with the dog and besides I am so knackered," replied Callum. "I've been up before eight o' clock both days, so I'm not going to be good company."

"Well, no changes there then," smirked Rory. "See you around, dude." With very little further dialogue they continued towards the gate, and a relieved Callum was able to continue his walk. He wasn't really that pleased the course was over; if he was honest, he would be happy to attend a further day, most definitely if *she* was there.

Releasing Fergie, he began a full lap of the deserted grounds. A big bright moon was replacing the sun. He resisted the habit of the vape and left his EarPods in his pocket, content yet troubled. For the first time in months, without the dullness of a hangover, broader thoughts about life occupied his mind. He was mature enough to recognise that he felt best when he was driven to achieve a goal, whether that was success in rugby or even when he was trying to achieve something specific on his PS4. It never felt good to fill his days aimlessly flicking through his phone.

He resolutely clenched his teeth, certain he needed a new goal or purpose, something new. With Fergie at his side, he broke into a jog.

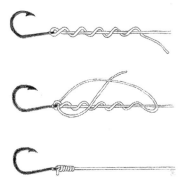

CHAPTER 6

Since his discussion with Mary, Donald had become very focused. Although he hadn't been in the attic for five years, he knew exactly where the items were stored. When Morag became ill, he had needed more space, but he had not been able to bring himself to sell or get rid any of it, even though much of it was outdated.

Removing the dust sheet as if he were uncovering a stash of ancient treasure, he unveiled the neat pile. It took three trips to transfer it all to the kitchen, meticulously placed like part of some ritual.

Over the next two hours he separated the items out. Some of them went into a large white bin-liner. Most of the older-looking items went back into an empty box that would be returned to the attic. Callum would get these, he thought, but not just yet. The remaining items were assembled on the work surface. He left the rods, reel-cases and landing net on the side, but took the canvas bag over to the table. Gently lowering himself onto the chair, he stared at the olive-green bag, his breathing laboured after the effort. 'IDA' were the initials embossed onto the leather patch; he vividly remembered the joy when it had been unwrapped more than forty years ago. For the following three decades it had been on every fishing trip but had remained indoors for these past twelve seasons. He unfastened the two buckles and lifted the flap back, reaching across to remove the nondescript containers from within.

There was also a hardback book, which he placed to his right on the table.

He opened the two exterior pockets. From the left-hand one he removed a bundle of photographs and newspaper cuttings bound together with an elastic band. From the other he removed two smaller books and a grey tin which had 'Anderson's Last Resort' handwritten on it. Donald smiled as he opened the tin, carefully removing the solitary grey fly and admiring it as if it were a diamond. With a soft sigh, he replaced it and closed the lid. His father had such recognisable handwriting. Come to think of it, he was confident he would recognise the scribble of his wife and his son, but he wasn't so sure he would recognise his grandson's. Everything was being digitised now, even greeting cards.

He shook himself out of the moment of sentimentality, for there was a job to be done. One pile was returned to the attic and the rubbish placed in the bin, while the remaining items were carefully placed on the table in the dining room next to an old pair of waders. With that done, he returned to the warmth of the sitting room.

The video cassettes hadn't been touched for a long time either, but he knew what he was looking for and diligently searched until it was located. He watched it twice, once more being transported to a different time and then snapping himself back into the present. The time had come, and he had to get this right.

When he was satisfied this was also prepared correctly, he reached for his writing set from the dresser.

Gina Rees

CHAPTER 7

Honor had Instagram, but Callum was too shy to request a following. He searched for stories and photos of her, finding some from when she had lived in the Borders. In one photo, taken maybe a year ago, her hair was full and bushy and she had no cap on. She was stood in the river smiling at the camera as she released a fresh salmon; he had never seen an image that was so captivating as he zoomed in and out. She swirled around his mind, even when he was playing on his game. Had he imagined her interest in him, or could it have been real? He had gathered that she was starting at Cult's in late August, but he couldn't wait until then. Callum wanted to see her again, and definitely before the other boys at school did.

An email had come in from Ross, who had hosted the introductory course, and among the photos was one of Callum holding the sea trout with Honor's hand on his shoulder. Initially, he didn't read the text, he just studied the photo of them together. When he did read the whole message, he saw that she would be co-hosting an intermediate fishing course in two weeks' time for under-eighteens who had mastered the basics. Ross had mentioned that at the farewell. It would be an ideal chance to see her again, but he was clearly still a beginner. How was he going to become proficient in two weeks without even owning a rod? If he tried to turn up without improving, it would mean a super embarrassing exit.

He turned to the obvious source of help and began to tap. 'Learn how to salmon fish.' Enter. Great, there were 130 million results, but he quickly identified a series of short videos from a tackle manufacturer and started to watch.

He knew from the past two days how to set the rod up, that was pretty straightforward. Connect the rod pieces, attach the reel and thread the fly-line through the rod eyes, then add a length of leader and a fly on the end. He could manage to get the fly out a bit using the 'roll cast' that Ross and Fergus had taught him, or the overhead cast he had tried on the trout pool, but it was nothing like what she could do with the line. It looked pretty simple on the videos and he could understand what the guy was saying about letting the fly swing round across the current when the line was tight. After every cast the demonstrator was taking a step downstream so that the swinging fly was also a yard further downstream, the idea being that you gradually cover the whole stretch of water to try and find where the fish are lying.

Callum had worked out that there were three areas he had to improve in order to cope with the intermediate level. He needed to learn how to attach the leader to the fly-line and how to tie a fly onto the end. He had to greatly improve his casting and be better prepared in case he were to hook a fish unsupervised. He had been given some instruction on the first one and could practise at home using YouTube. The second would need the help of someone experienced, and the third was a totally different challenge, for which any number of videos would not really prepare you. He was trying to think of anyone he knew who was into salmon fishing; certainly none of his mates, who were largely nocturnal these days.

He drifted into the sitting room with Part 4 of the tuition course playing on his phone, surprised he couldn't think of any anglers other than those he had just met on the course.

"So, tell me a bit more about the fishing course?" his mum asked casually. She had not pressed him on his return the previous night.

"Aye, not too bad," he coyly replied. "It's bloody tough, harder than you would think, but I managed OK." He looked across to her. "I thought I might give it another go; they have places free on an intermediate course running in two weeks. I just need to get some practice."

She could feel an emptiness appear in her stomach, but she controlled it by keeping her eyes on the newspaper. "That's good to hear, I'm not surprised you're good at it," she replied in a neutral voice.

"I'm trying to learn from YouTube but it's pretty confusing. I'll also need some of my own gear if I'm going to get on the intermediate course. Do you know anyone who might lend some to me, Ma?"

This was the defining moment she had hoped would happen and had rehearsed in her mind many times over the past week, but she was so nervous she could hardly speak.

"Mmm, folk just don't seem to have the time anymore. You could ask your Granda. He was regarded as one of the better salmon fishermen in the area in his time."

"Granda? Are you kidding, Mum? Had salmon been discovered back then?" replied Callum with a smirk.

"You know it wasn't that long ago. Why don't you drop him a message and see if he can help? He would dearly love to see you, he missed you during lockdown." She was relieved that his unexpected new interest was making her role easier and reducing the likelihood of an argument.

Callum cycled to Janesfield Manor mid-morning on Monday, much to his mum's approval as he had hardly seen his grandad since March. He used to visit most Sundays on his way back from a game and they would sit in the living room, Granda listening intently as every pass and tackle was relived. He was a relatively fit eighty-year-old, but since Morag had died he had lost some of the spark which Callum recalled. She had always been in charge inside the front door, while Donald in return had always been the worker, as was often the way with his generation. For more than forty years he had been a papermaker, following his own father into the Deeside mill at Peterculter until it closed in the eighties, when he moved to the Donside mill, until that too closed, in 2001. Donald and Morag had moved to Janesfield Manor in 2007, having fortuitously sold the house they had long owned at the right time following the big oil-led housing price rally seen in Aberdeen. This had created the nest egg they needed to manage on Donald's pension, and they loved living closer to their only child and being near the river. There was no chance of another job in papermaking with the mill closures, so Donald was able to retire relatively early, and he had planned to enjoy life.

Janesfield Manor wasn't quite the country retreat it sounded; it was a development of fifty-five retirement homes in South Aberdeen, conveniently just fifteen minutes' walk from Callum's home. Now alone, Donald had resisted moving to a care home and learnt how to cope.

As soon as Callum knocked, he heard soft steps along the hall and the door opened. He hugged his grandad for the first time in many months, then followed him to the sitting room and took the familiar seat opposite him on the grey sofa. The electric fire was off for a change – even in Aberdeen it was sometimes warmish outside – but the TV was reassuringly still on.

"How ye doing Granda?" he asked as he glanced around. The décor was unchanged, everything neatly in its place. His eyes fell onto the framed photo of Callum with the Granite City Colts team taken in April last year and the wedding photo next to it.

"Nae bad Callum, nae bad." He always said that. "How ye doing, back to training?"

"Nah, ma knee's a lot better but its still nae full strength, I need to build it up more before I can train."

"Aye, so *have* ye been building it up?" asked Granda, in a way that suggested he knew the answer.

"I've been doing some cycling and some exercises, probably need to step it up a bit soon," said Callum. He had loved mountain biking, but now he had pretty much given it up. The bike was now purely a mode of transport to hook up with his mates.

"Aye OK, well hope ye do, that team of yours has struggled since you stopped. What you been de'in instead?" enquired Granda provocatively.

"Well, that's one of the reasons I'm here. Of course I was keen to see you, but I'd really like your help with something. Mum enrolled me on a salmon fishing course last week and it wasnae too bad, but I'd like to get better at it. I watched some videos, but Mum said you'd fished a bit once, and I was hoping you could teach me something?"

Granda eyeballed Callum silently, preparing what he was going to say.

"Ah, salmon fishing, well you're in the right part of the world for that. There was a time when the city would buzz if a run of salmon was coming into the rivers. Many of us used to fish, it was a real source of food in those lean days as well as for enjoyment. Your great granda taught me when I was quite a bit younger than you are now and I used to fish a hell of a lot when I was working – nearly everyone at the mill did, as we were right on the banks of the river. I taught your dad in the seventies, we used to fish together in his school holidays, until he met your mum that is. Then both of us taught Finlay, around the time you were born, and we had some very special times. It's not as popular now, I know. I'm sure some of that might be because we have fewer fish in our rivers these days, but also probably because everything for youngsters seems to be electronic. Or maybe I'm just being old-fashioned, and times have simply changed. How serious about learning are you, Callum?"

Why didn't he know they had fished? Why hadn't his mum said anything? She clearly knew a lot more.

"I'm really serious Granda, even more so now," he answered. "I didn't know you were into fishing at all until Mum said. I would love you to teach me like you did my dad and Finlay." There was a brief pause before he continued, almost as if in respect, and his words had an earnest edge to them now. "There's an intermediate course being run that I really want to join, but it's aimed at kids who have fished way more than me. I did the introductory course but I only have eleven days to prepare for the advanced one."

"There's nothing I would like more to do," said Granda. "God knows I need a reason to get out of here and I can think of none better. But you need to be prepared to learn or we are both wasting our time, which doesn't do anybody any good. Your mum mentioned you might be looking for some help. I've had a think how best to get us started on the right track and I'd like you to take this bag away with you, take a look through it then let me know how you feel, is that OK?"

He handed the carrier bag across and folded the top down to make it clear it wasn't to be opened until later, then sat back with his cup of tea. Callum looked pensively at the bag, then back up to his grandad, nodding with a smile.

"So, have you decided what you're going to study next year, Callum?" asked Granda, changing the subject. They chatted a while, then Callum said a warm goodbye and cycled home with the bag stuffed up his T-shirt, his grandad's words going through his mind.

The house was empty, Callum sank gently into the sofa and opened the bag onto the coffee table. There were three items inside, a book, a photo album clearly from pre-digital days and an envelope bearing his name. It wasn't sealed, but he opened it as carefully as if it had been made of tissue paper and gently extracted a hand-written letter. He leaned back further into the sofa to read it.

Dear Callum. First, let me say sorry for not having had this discussion with you years ago, it was my intention to introduce you to fishing before you became a teenager in the same way as generations of Andersons before you, but the unfortunate timing of your grandma's ill-health prevented that. I have no doubt that were your father with us he would have done so with his usual huge enthusiasm as he did with Finlay, and you would have become a fine fisherman like them, but the responsibility is mine and I am very sorry. If you are serious about learning and can accept my apology, then I promise to teach you as well as any doddering eighty-year-old can. Please look through the enclosed photos, because it's important for you to see the connection fishing, and in particular the River Dee, have with the Andersons. I have also enclosed a book entitled 'Letters to a Salmon Fisher's Sons' which was written over a hundred years ago, because although the author was no relation of ours some of what he wrote could so easily have been written by my own Granda. Please read the first two chapters and if afterwards you are still interested in becoming a salmon fisherman, let me know and we can make a start. Much love, Granda.

Callum leaned forward and took the small photo album nervously, but without hesitation. There were twelve photos, and he viewed them one by one.

The first was a black-and-white photo which clearly showed three generations of the same family. The elders looked like they had been to church and were wearing ties, as was customary for fishing in those days. The youngest was about ten and only a little taller than the salmon he stood next to. Callum could see some ballpoint writing through the photo, so he turned over and read the caption: "Donald aged 9 with Da and Granda Anderson, 19th March 1949. 26lb cock fish, Culter."

He placed the picture down on the coffee table and viewed the second photo, which was faintly coloured. This picture was similar, but the faces were slightly different and the clothing less formal. The men stood with two impressive salmon held in that same nose-to-the-floor suspension. On the back of this photo were the words, "Ian aged 11 with his first salmon admired by Da and Granda Anderson, 11 May 1976. 14lb and 11lb, Garthdee."

Callum studied the child's face before exchanging the photo for the next, which this time was in colour and showed a teenager holding a lovely silver fish admired by a proud parent who he realised was his grandad. There were five more photos of these two fishermen, in colour, and they seemed to span about ten years, each with a weight, date and location. The most recent of these was at Parkhill on the River Don and dated August 31st 1987. It seemed to be a bright sunny day, a fresh salmon lay on the grass and next to his dad stood a pretty, smiling lady whom he recognised as his mum. His dad looked equally happy with both catches. There was such a sense of happiness in each photo, with broad smiles to match the beauty of the background flowers and the river itself. He looked through these six again, seeing images of his dad as he had changed from boy to a man.

The next photo was again on a riverbank. Granda and Callum's dad were standing next to a solid blond-haired man and in his father's arms was a baby wrapped up tightly. The caption read, "No fish but a white shark! Finlay meets one of the Grand Slam winners. 25th June 1990." Callum did not fully grasp the description, but he lingered on this photo of his brother as a baby, examining the faces of his family and that of the familiar stranger.

The colour was better on the next photo, which showed just one person in the frame, a boy waistdeep in the river holding a shining salmon that was being released. The boy was staring at the fish, not the camera, mesmerised. 'Finlay's first' said the writing.

The next photo featured Callum's dad standing on a tartan rug spread over the grass. He was smiling and his arm was proudly around a tall, young man next to him with a small messy-haired boy between his legs. On the back it said: 'Red letter day at Banchory Lodge, six silver grilse for Finlay, all caught on a Sunray Shadow (netted and carefully released by Callum!) July 2008.'

Callum looked closely at this. His brother clearly resembled his father, and that similarity had passed on to himself, even aged four. They were both handsome and healthy looking, and Callum was sure he resembled them. Sitting on the blanket were his Granda, Nanna and his mum, all smiling at the camera, which by this date could presumably have been someone's phone. This was the only photograph Callum had seen of his extended family before it happened. He stared at length before taking a shot of it using his own phone, enabling him to magnify and study it in more detail. He placed the photo face-down on the table, pausing for quite some time before retrieving the final picture, which was in its own brown presentation folder. Larger than the others and clearly a reprint of an official photo, it showed Callum's father shaking hands and receiving an award in front of a large group with Finlay standing next to him. On the floor in front was a sign which read "Aberdeen District Angling Association awards 2008, fish of the season". He must have been a really good fisherman, Callum thought; he looked so happy on all the photos.

Hypnotised by this picture, a wave of sadness washed over Callum and he turned to look through the open window at the blue sky. There was something different about photographs that weren't displayed on a screen. They were entirely original, and a pure representation of how life for those in the frame had been at that precise moment. Just being able to hold them made them seem more authentic and yet they were brittle. These pictures could burn, they could be washed away, they could be lost. They brought a different connection. He felt the hairs on his arms standing on end.

Before, when Callum had questions, he would ask his mother. For the past few years, he had completely blocked the past. But today, he decided to do something he had religiously resisted. He opened his phone and typed into his browser: 'Ian Anderson helicopter crash.' He hesitated, then opened and read stories from numerous sources, his jaw taut and his eyes clouding. Finally, he returned to the one titled, 'Father and son amongst 16 perished oil workers in tragic North Sea helicopter crash.' There on the front page of the *Evening Express*, below the heading, was the photo he had just been looking at of his father and brother from the award presentation. It had been taken just a few months before.

He gathered his thoughts and sent a message to his grandad. "Granda, I really want to learn to salmon fish. I want you to teach me to be like Finlay and my dad."

The reply came back immediately: "I will be happy to do that Callum. See you at 2.30 tomorrow afternoon."

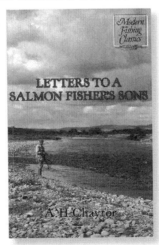

CHAPTER 8

When Callum arrived at 2.30, he saw Granda already at the door waiting. Callum waved as he approached, dismounted, and leaned his bike against the wall of the small house. Unlike last time, when there had been a long gap since they had last seen each other, Granda just gently put his hand on Callum's arm, guiding him inside. Callum kicked off his trainers, leaving them where they fell outside the door. He followed his grandad carefully through the hall, which now contained a tidy pile of fishing tackle, and into the small kitchen. On one work surface was an open canvass bag holding a number of pouches, as well as some storage boxes bearing pictures of fish. Granda picked up his tea and they both sat at the round table, which had been kept clear of everything other than what looked like a map.

"So, you opened the package? How did you feel?"

"I felt lost, like I was in a cellar without a light switch," said Callum, staring forwards. "Nothing quite made sense. But as I read the wording, it all became clearer, and I began to understand. All the faces were smiling, but they made me feel sad. Not because they are gone but because I felt closer to them after looking at the photos, like they were suddenly real people. It must have been really difficult for you and Nanna." He reached out to the map, placing his hands on it as if his fingertips were touching skin.

"It was terribly difficult Callum, you can't imagine. I so dearly hope you never have any experience like it. Your poor mother was devastated, and it was only looking after you that kept her going, I'm sure of it. I still think it was the shock of what happened that eventually led to the death of your Nanna. She was never the same after we lost our son, our only child. It has been a difficult time these past ten years."

Callum searched his face for more details, something personal or emotional but there was none.

"I do think we should try to talk about it some time, but today I don't want to dwell on it," continued Granda. "Even though I am biased, you had the most wonderful father, and I can see him now berating me for neglecting you. He worshipped you and your brother. I'm so pleased you are interested in learning to fish, and it would make me so happy to provide you with some help and tuition whilst I still can. It's about time we started adding to the library of photos of happy Andersons on the banks of the River Dee."

"I feel the same, Granda. I really want to catch a salmon and have my photo taken with you just like they did."

Donald stood and placed the now empty teacup in the sink. He placed a hand on the back of his chair for support, leaning forward slightly to emphasise his words. Then he began to talk about the salmon's life cycle and what makes it such a special fish. Sensitively and politely, Callum assured him he had learned much of this on the introductory course. Granda asked more questions about the course and Callum recited much of what he had been taught, clearly showing that he had picked up the basics.

"Right loon, so we have ten days before the intermediate course to get you up to scratch," he said. "Today we can spend some more time on the equipment and knot-tying because you have to be able to set the rod up by yourself. One day this week we can go to the green to do some extra casting practice."

Callum felt the energy of his grandad's words, reassured by them that he would be ready for Honor's course.

"I'll see if I can find a videotape I have from thirty years ago where you can see your father fishing," his grandad went on. "He was a terrific angler and it would be instructive for you to see how he could cast a line. Then next week, let me have a word with a few contacts and see if we can go for a practice on the river. Och Callum, I can't believe I'm hearing myself say that – we're going to fish the Dee together!"

He opened the map and spread it over the table. It showed the length of the River Dee and all the fisheries along it. For most of the next hour he talked Callum along the river, recounting special times when he had been to many of the beats, either with his son or his father. He showed him where the paperworks had been and the location of some of the photos Callum had been captivated by the previous night. Eventually he had worked upstream to the village of Braemar, where he showed Callum the Balmoral-owned water.

"That's where I have always wanted to fish," he said.

"Is it possible to buy a permit for there or is it totally private?" asked Callum.

"It is possible to get on but not very easy, and often you have to book a whole week or at least three days, up until late July at least. After that date the Queen is in residence, so all fishing is by the Royal Family."

Hmm, there has to be a way, thought Callum.

After studying the map, they spent some time talking through the tackle that Granda still owned, and it was soon five o'clock. They had covered lots of information but at no stage had it been boring. Callum was interested to learn more, both about fishing and his family. He left knowing that they would see each other the next afternoon for some casting practice.

Callum smiled as he rode home. He was going to get on this

intermediate course and he was going to spend the day with Honor. He had found his teacher.

That evening he opened an email that had been forwarded by Granda entitled 'Welcome to the Aberdeen and District Angling Association'. Granda had written, "Here you go Callum, you are now a junior member of this fine fishing club, just like the rest of us. I even managed to do it all online!"

He then opened the email he had received from Ross, and after gazing at the stunning picture of Honor mid-cast he clicked on the link to the intermediate course from the email and registered. No turning back now. Granda had given him another book called *Salmon Fishing: A Practical Guide*, which he now opened as he lay on his bed. His TV remained turned off and he had aired the messages from the boys; he was just not in the mood.

The next morning Callum awoke around nine and without much delay made his way downstairs and into the kitchen, surprising his mother, who had her hands in the sink.

"Good morning Cal, another sunny one, I just cooked some sausages – can I make you a bun?"

He brushed past her on his way to the fridge and removed the orange juice. "Aye Mum, that would be grand. I'm going to head out for a run with Fergie and if my knee's OK I'll do a few reps. I'll go before the park gets busy and it gets too hot. I'm back to see Granda again this afternoon, he's going to give me some casting practice."

His mum already knew that. She reached for the teatowel and dried her hands, smiling. "That's nice Cal, I really appreciate the effort you're making. I thought I could join you there after work and we could have a little barbecue with him?"

This was the pattern for the following few days. Callum spent all his time either reading his new book, watching instruction on YouTube or gaining it from Granda. He was really getting the hang of casting with the thirteen-foot rod he had been given. The fact that this rod, as well as the reel and other items, had belonged to his brother made it even more special.

The following week, two days on the river had been arranged ahead of the course on the Friday. On Monday they were heading just a few hundred metres away to the Garthdee stretch of the river, which was controlled by the Aberdeen and District Angling Association, and on Wednesday to the section at Culter, about five miles away. Granda would escort Callum on Monday, but on Wednesday he had a doctor's appointment so Callum would go ahead and start on his own. If these days went well, they were confident that he would be able to join the course.

On Saturday, Callum had arranged to meet with the lads in the park, but the weather had changed and it rained all day. After his dinner, as it had slowed to little more than a drizzle, he cycled over to Jake's house.

"Hey stranger," said Jake from behind the pool table as he walked in. "Mummy let you out again?"

Callum tutted and fist-bumped Rory before slumping next to Tomas on a beanbag facing the screen, then picked up a controller and joined him in the game. By the look of the empty cider cans and the full ashtray, they had been there for some time. Callum was more aware of the smell in the room than usual, a staleness.

Rory threw a full can to Callum, which he caught and opened. Some of the beer sprayed onto his jeans, raising a sneer from Jake. Callum took a modest sip whilst keeping his eye on the screen. Some time later, Jake celebrated beating Rory and they both took a seat in front of the screen around the low table. Rory, as usual, began to skin up and Jake started to needle Callum.

"So, did you catch any fish, Captain Birdseye? Or were you too busy playing with each other's flies?" he teased. Callum had seen him like this a few times when he was getting drunk. It was always directed at the perceived weakest in the group and often worse when there were girls looking on. Callum ignored him and appeared to be concentrating on the game, but his anger was building. *You wouldn't have a clue how to cast,* Callum thought. *You'd look a hopeless prick if you tried.*

Jake took the joint from Rory, inhaled deeply, and slugged back on his drink. The atmosphere had tensed a little.

"Too busy stroking your fishing rod to give your own rod any action, huh? You missed some proper fun when you fell asleep last week, you lightweight," said Jake.

Callum felt his jaw tighten, but his eyes remained focused on the screen.

"And where've you been this week? We had the Spice Girls round to play again, they were asking about your dog. Didn't seem bothered not to see you."

It was the mention of Fergie that proved too much. Callum dropped the controller and turned to face Jake.

"My dog Fergie, who you all abandoned when you left me unconscious in the park, you mean? He could have easily got run over. What the fuck is it with you Jake, do you really not care about anyone but yourself? You had no idea if I was going into a coma or what was happening to me, you just went off to do what you wanted with the girls. That's not friendship."

He stood up, expecting Jake to square up, and he was ready for him, but whether it was Callum's tone or Jake's own unsteadiness, he remained in the beanbag. Callum waited, breathing heavily and angrily, then left in silence. Outside he mounted his bike and heard mumbling and laughter from inside the garage. He sped home in frustration. It was no longer raining, but moisture ran down his cheeks.

CHAPTER 9

Granda was almost unrecognisable in his fishing clothes, as Callum could only recall seeing him in slacks and cardigans. He looked so different and seemed to have a real purpose about him, as if his world had got a little bit bigger.

"Aye aye, dinnae you laugh at me laddie and pick up those bags," Granda said with a smile before slipping his feet into the wellington boots that sat by the door.

The rain had continued all weekend but had stopped by Monday morning. Although there was a short walk across the university campus to the start of the Garthdee beat, they took their time, with Granda pausing to catch his breath occasionally and using the rod case as an improvised walking stick. They were soon walking past the university library, and as they passed the buildings, the trees appeared beside the river. It was a lovely scene, the far bank a deep green of grass and trees, a perfect place for a picnic on a sunny day, Callum thought, already with someone in mind.

They placed the bags on a bench under the horse chestnut and Granda asked Callum to set up the rod, using a slow sinking tip and fifteen-pound leader. It was a test, but Callum understood enough to set about the task. The weekend's rain had made its way into the river, which had risen quite a lot and had a brownish tinge to it.

"There's usually a shingle bar below us," said Granda. "But the river has risen at least a foot, so you can't really see it. This dirty water won't help the fishing, but it will make a perfect spot to

practise casting. When you've set the rod up, get your waders on."
He took a seat and surveyed the water. With the rod set up, Callum
sat next to him and began removing his trainers.

"This is where your father caught his first salmon," said
Granda softly. "One of the photies I gave you is of him just a few
yards from here with two lovely fish. Forty-five years ago, seems
like yesterday." There was a silent pause for reflection. "Of course,
we used to kill all the fish in those days, we could eat fresh salmon
almost any day of the year, but that has all changed. They are so
precious now we have to release them, which means your only
real chance of fresh salmon is farm-reared, and I'm not too keen
on that, thank you." There was a danger that Granda would go
on about his dismay with the salmon farming industry and how
it was responsible for terrible ecological crimes in Scotland, but
Callum stood up and pulled the braces over his shoulders.

"Right, shall we give it a go?" This wasn't really a question,
more a statement.

"Last thing we need to do is choose the fly," said Granda, still
seated. "Do you have any suggestions, Callum?"

"Well, I used a nice silver and blue one last week on the course
and caught a sea trout, do you have one of those?"

"Aye, I have one, but think how the water was that day, was she
as big and brown as she is today?"

Callum looked and realised the river was very different today
from the clear water of Banchory.

"I think we need something a bit bigger and easier to see,"
suggested Granda, picking up what looked like a red-bodied insect.
"Let's give this Red Francis a try. Can you see how these stiff
strands appear like whiskers? When it's in the water it creates a
very noticeable vibration."

As Callum tied on the Red Francis, Granda continued talking.

"The river can be a dangerous place if you don't respect it, Callum. Never put yourself at risk when you're wading. Although we aren't going deep, I would like you to wear this life jacket around your neck just in case. It will automatically inflate if you fall and it submerges." Callum was not convinced that it was necessary, but he decided against protesting and tightened the straps.

They stepped out into the river for a few metres until it was halfway up Granda's boots. It was shallow and shelved away very gradually. Granda asked Callum to show him his casting. The older man watched in silence as he began to lengthen the line and then, using the snap-C, retrieved it and recast. Callum felt he had done quite well, but there was one flaw that Granda wanted to correct.

"That's excellent, Callum, but see if you can finish the forward stroke of the cast with the tip of your rod pointing at the top of those trees opposite rather than the far bank. That will add a few more metres to your distance. It was good practising on the grass last week, but it's only really on the water that you see the results."

Callum practised this a few times, and indeed it did improve his distance. They went through some further tasks to help with line management before Granda took the rod from Callum for a demonstration.

"It's been quite some time," he said, almost excusing his attempt before he had made it. He drew some line off the reel and proceeded with the single Spey cast that Callum had tried during the course, but the effect was on a different level. Granda's small, willowy frame enabled him to send the line out twenty-five, even thirty metres, without appearing to take any effort.

"Whoa Granda, look at you!" said Callum, and they both began to laugh. After Granda had repeated this a few times, he handed the rod back to Callum and told him to begin fishing his way through the pool properly. Then he returned to the bench to watch. After a couple of casts, Callum took a few steps deeper into the water, then looked back at his grandad, who now sat, cup of tea in his hand, smiling back at him.

Callum continued casting, looking up the bank apologetically when the line landed clumsily but always receiving encouragement.

They tried using a different fly, though they knew they were unlikely to catch anything whilst the water was so high and dirty. Despite the slim chance of success Callum enjoyed the casting, just like a golf driving range he thought. They happily walked back to the house in time for some lunch.

As they were finishing the food in the kitchen, Granda spoke. "If you've time Callum, I found a few old albums and also the video I was talking about. We could take a look?" So they flicked through the two leather-bound albums, and Callum listened carefully as his grandad talked in detail about his father and the memories he still held.

When they had finished the photos, they moved into the sitting room.

"Granda, I can honestly say, I have never before seen a video cassette player," said Callum. "This is like some retro museum piece!"

"You know, it really wasn't that long ago when this was super hi-tech. DVDs only really started to replace VCRs in your lifetime. I can still remember your brother watching a tape recording of the 1982–83 season when we won the European Cup Winners' Cup over and over again. I've never got rid of this player as I have these family films I sometimes watch, though I could probably get them converted onto a disc, I guess. Anyhow, let's watch this one your grandma recorded of us fishing at Banchory in 2008."

Strangely, but it seemed appropriately, rather than sit on a separate chair, Callum sat on the floor in front of Granda and leaned back against his legs. The first tape was a shortish recording of two men fishing, wading waist-deep in the river. They watched and chatted about how well the casting appeared before Granda swapped tapes.

The new footage showed all six of them enjoying a beautiful summer's day centred on a picnic on the riverbank; Callum recognised the scene from one of the photos he had seen just a week before. There were clips of them sitting on the rug and some of them fishing. It was mostly his brother doing the fishing, and there were some recordings of him catching salmon and his father proudly netting them. The young Callum was clearly delighted to be given the chance to return them to the river as he paddled around in just a pair of swim-shorts. Whilst the picture quality wasn't quite what today's smartphones gave it was still very good, and the sound was also clear – so clear that for the first time he could remember, he found himself listening to his father's voice as he turned to the camera and described how Finlay, standing next to him, had just caught his sixth salmon of the day. A strong Aberdeen accent was recognisable in the gentle voice. "It won't be long before Callum's hauling them in," added Finlay, ruffling the hair of his younger brother. Finlay would have been just a little older than Callum was now, he thought.

As the camera panned upstream to other families bathing in the river, Callum rewound and listened to the scene again, subconsciously pressing harder against his grandad's legs, his eyes fixed on his smiling elder brother. Would they be friends now if he was still here?

"Thanks, Granda, I'd best be making a move now," he whispered when it had finished. "I'm really looking forward to fishing on Wednesday. I hope it goes OK at the doctors and I'll see you on the riverbank." He stood up and placed his hand gently on his grandad's shoulder, but he was feeling an urgent rush to leave.

His grandad remained seated and looked up at him with a

resigned sadness. "Aye son, Wednesday will be grand," he said. "The river will have dropped nicely. You take care, Callum lad."

CHAPTER 10

On Wednesday morning, Callum broke his usual routine by leaving both his bed and the house before 8 am. He had read another chapter of *Salmon Fishing: A Practical Guide* before turning his light off and drifting to sleep whilst imagining himself fighting to bring a salmon into a net held by Honor. He had been having different dreams lately; the recurring one was of him as a child, drifting down a river in a small boat. He wasn't crying but he was looking for someone, waiting for them to come back.

It was a simple ride to Culter along the quiet North Deeside Road, on a bright morning with scattered clouds. The rain from the weekend had largely run off and the river was much lower than it had been when he and Granda had done their casting practice at Garthdee. Callum found himself looking for the river as he cycled along, feeling a surge of excitement each time he glimpsed it.

He locked his bike in the lay-by and marched down to the river. He knew where he was going to start from the map on the website and could see the river below as he walked across the path, through the gate and down the steps to a bench, where he unloaded his gear. There was a familiarity to this place; he felt as if he had been there before but knew that wasn't the case.

He studied the layout of the water, absorbed in speculating where the salmon might be. There was much more routine about setting his rod up. He was no longer all fingers and thumbs and he felt as though he looked quite professional as he peered down the rod eyes to confirm that they were lined up. He attached his reel to the rod, fed the floating line and laid the rod down on the bank. Then, as Granda had taught him, he stripped three metres of line from the reel of nylon in his top pocket, tying a secure loop at one end and attaching that to his floating line. The final piece of his trap was the fly. He only had five of them in his fly-box and he had already agreed with Granda that he would be using one that had strands of black hair trailing from it and silver wrapped around the back of the hook – he had called it a 'stoat' or something.

Callum managed his knot first time and gave the hook a sharp tug to ensure it was set properly. Removing his trainers, he clumsily pulled on his waders. He performed a peculiar dance in which he removed his foot from his trainer, then placed it back onto the top of the shoe and repeated for the other foot. He then transferred his feet into the waders, trying not to topple over and get his socks wet or dirty. He looped the braces over his shoulders and slipped the safety collar on. He gathered his remaining belongings into his rucksack, which he stored behind a post next to the river. It was just after nine as he made his way nervously down the bank.

This was it; his first solo flight. His heart was thumping as he slowly edged towards the white water. It was as if he were stepping onto a stage on the first night of a show. He could hear the words of guidance in his ears, but gradually they were replaced by the feeling of water pressing against his legs and the tinkling sound of the flow, like a wave of applause.

He put his Polaroids on and pulled the peak of his cap down to reduce the glare of the rising sun as he looked downstream. Although the river was about as wide as a rugby pitch here, the current clearly narrowed into a channel about a third of the way across and he knew from what he had been told and had read that any fish would most likely be around the oxygenated area which extended downstream for about eighty metres. Such a stretch of fishable water was known as a 'pool', and each beat on the river was made up of several pools, many of them with names; this one he knew from the website to be Camphill. He stepped a little further into the river, but he knew not to go too far for fear of spooking any fish that might be close in.

He pulled three armfuls of line off the reel and began to slowly roll the rod so that the line flew forward. He was soon casting the line he had pulled out so that the fly-line was fully extending whilst in the air, then quite gently dropping onto the water and starting to swing in an arc across the current until it was dangling directly downstream of him. He pulled out another couple of armfuls of line and recast across the river with relative ease. His fly was now landing about fifteen metres away from him and took quite a while to swing across the current until it was directly downstream. He was managing this well, thanks to the guidance he had received and the videos he had watched, and it really wasn't too difficult on a pleasant day without more than a breeze to contend with.

He pulled another length of line off the reel, allowing him to cast comfortably across the ribbons of the current without having to strain too hard. It felt quite natural, almost like watching Stuart Hogg effortlessly kick a penalty from the edge of the twenty-two, all technique and timing. Once the line had finished swinging across again, Callum drew in three loops to keep the length of line on the water manageable, then took a step downstream and cast again across the current. He sensed a smile on his face as the line again straightened before gently dropping onto the water once more. It was working so much better than it had been just ten days ago.

He was casting roughly once a minute and stepping downstream about a metre between each cast, so he was covering about sixty metres of river each hour. This would have seemed unimaginably slow progress had he been walking along the bank, but Granda had explained to him the importance of this system to ensure the fly covered all the places a fish might be lying.

He continued fishing the water like this for some time, and soon found himself imagining the wispy tail of the fly as it moved through the water. He was willing a salmon to snap at it when, just a few metres directly below where his fly was, a fish belly-splashed in the current, catching the sun on its silver flank.

"Holy shit!" grunted Callum. He instinctively looked towards the bank to see if there was anyone else who might have seen it, but of course there wasn't, and he realised he was alone with the river.

The fish had jumped just downstream of where the current funnelled into a narrow turbulent zone before widening and calming again. Callum nervously took a step towards it before casting again, the cool water pressing gently against his thighs. He watched the floating light-green line swing a little faster across the stream and could almost pinpoint where the fly would be at any time. He tensed as the line moved through the ripples close to where the fish had jumped. It was surely going to happen, but the line continued to swing towards the bank untouched.

Next step, he thought, *this is the one,* and out went the line again. He was totally absorbed in the shimmer and tinkling of the river, every sense alert. The fly-line arced through the current and inexplicably continued without being intercepted until it trailed directly downstream; how could that be?

Without moving he cast again, covering the same lie to give the fish a second chance, with the same result. Irritated, he looked across the river and saw a car being parked on the south bank, another angler he guessed. As he studied the car to see if he recognised it, he had begun to draw in the line ready to recast when it quietly went taut.

Still looking at the car, he pulled a bit harder, imagining he had caught a rock. In return he felt the shock of a powerful opposing force juddering away from him.

In that magical moment when he realised that a salmon had taken his fly, the world seemed to freeze. Everything collapsed into two dimensions apart from him and the line that connected him to the salmon. His nerve-ends crackled as the line tightened and he felt the immediate strength of the fish.

Remembering what he had been taught and trying to get to grips with what was happening, he lifted the tip of the rod to forty-five degrees with a sense of nervous excitement. Feeling the resistance, the hooked salmon sped across the current, pulling the end of the rod towards the water. The line stretched until Callum removed his hand from the reel just in time. He could hear the unique sound of a reel in reverse as the fish fled. He lifted the rod tip again, creating an initial cushion to the efforts of the fish as it swam with the current downstream. It raced for a further twenty metres until, as if in protest at the resistance, it changed direction, leaping straight into the air. Callum saw the suspended silver before it landed back in the river with a sparkling splash. The initial excitement had turned to fear. This could not be compared with anything Callum had experienced before. He had played in some exciting rugby matches and experienced the thrill of mountain biking with his friend Alastair through Lairig Ghru last summer, but this was totally different.

The salmon did a U-turn and swam back upstream towards Callum, creating slack in the line. Now what to do?

"Reel it in as fast as you can, keep the line tight!" he heard a deep voice say from the other bank. He nodded and reeled in faster than an egg-whisking champion, clawing back the line until it started to tighten again. The circuit reconnected, and now the rod was bending hard again and pointing like a spotlight towards a point on the water about ten metres away.

The line juddered again as the fish aggressively shook its head, determined to resist. He slowly drew it closer in the hope of catching sight of it when, probably spooked by the outline of Callum, it twisted and made another dash for freedom. The tension suddenly disappeared and the line hung limp in the current.

Callum froze. He stared at the water, puzzled, and then reality came rushing back. He felt the river pushing against his legs again, the sun warming his face .

"Ah unlucky lad, she's off, lovely looking fish," said the man on the far bank.

Callum turned towards him, speechless and numb. The man was tall and wore a tweed flat cap pulled over grey hair. His eyes and nose appeared stern, but this was offset by a warm, narrow smile. Callum nodded, gradually reeled his line in and slowly, without speaking, waded back to land. He placed the rod facing up the bank and sat next to it. He lifted his knees and placed his elbows on them, peering into the water. After a few moments, he lay back on the grass gazing at the passing clouds, reliving what had just happened. That indescribable feeling of the initial contact as the line tightened followed by the scrap that had so nearly resulted in his first catch. Part of him was irate, so angry he had not caught the fish, but another part of him was bewildered by the experience itself. He so wanted to be able to tell Granda of his catch, maybe send a photo, but after the initial desperation he felt surprisingly calm. There was a sense of acceptance, like a boxer who knows he did his best but was second on the day, but also a concern he might not have handled it right, that maybe someone experienced would have landed it. At least his knot hadn't come undone; the hook had simply slipped out. As he relived it for a third time, he became even more determined that next time he would succeed.

He took out a chocolate bar, then sat up and ate it whilst

watching the fisherman on the far bank, who was moving downstream with a dance-like rhythm; cast, swing, draw and step, then repeat.

Another fish jumped further downstream, and Callum refocused, stuffed the wrapper into the pocket of his waders and stepped slowly back into the river at the point where he had been when the line had gone slack. He knew that the tussle could have disturbed any other fish there may have been nearby, but not those further downstream. The stoat-fly was intact, so he began to cast across the stream the same way as before, following the other angler, who was about fifty metres ahead and now approaching the bridge. Callum moved methodically along the bank, occasionally stepping over or around larger boulders that stood in his way, enjoying being part of the river. Time passed quickly. As he found himself approaching the tail of the pool he was fishing, another splashed just above the shallower water, but it could not be tempted by Callum's fly.

Resigned, he reeled in the line and began stepping up the bank towards the bench when he noticed that the man from the other bank had walked across the bridge and was sitting watching.

"Shame about that one you had on earlier, looked pretty lively," said the man in his deep but warm voice. "Don't think we have met before, are you a new member?"

"Yes, this is my first time fishing here. My grandad gave me membership just this last week," replied Callum.

"Och, that's nice. Great to have some new members in the club. Very nice to meet you, I'm Billy Grantham." He offered his hand.

"Callum Anderson, nice to meet you too." Callum laid down his rod and sat beside Billy on the bench.

"Ah, the Silver Stoat. That's a killer fly this time of year. You handled it really well, but it just wasn't meant to be this time. Remember to try and keep the line tight if you can and I'm sure ye'll have another before long. Whilst the line is taut the hook should remain set, but once they get some slack it sometimes comes out. It happens when they jump too."

"That's the first salmon I've ever hooked," said Callum, his hands on his knees, gazing downwards. "I'd love to catch one so I can show it to my grandad. They're so strong. It was amazing, whilst I had it on at least."

"Aye, it'll come lad. Enjoy the wonder of the river and the salmon will reward you. Who's your grandad, are you local?"

"Donald Anderson, we live in Garthdee."

"Och, no kidding?" said the older man, turning sharply to look directly at Callum. "I've known Donald for a long, long time." He paused before softly saying, "I knew your dad real well too. I'm a few years older but I worked on the same rig as him for some time and we often fished together. It should have clicked when you said your name. I'm real sorry Callum, I forgot Ian had a younger son."

Callum was looking directly back now. This connection he had felt with his father over the past few days was overwhelming, and he yearned to know more. He had lived alone with his mother for eleven years now. He had been too young to really remember anything up to to the day it had happened, and she had clearly shielded him as much as she could. But now, as a sixteen-year-old, he had a real urge to know more.

"What was my dad like?" he asked quietly. Sitting there over-looking the river, such a sensitive question felt right.

Looking directly but gently into Callum's eyes, Billy replied, "I can honestly say he was one of the friendliest, most hardworking and optimistic men I have ever met. Everything your dad did, he gave his all to, and he was admired for that. He would be there when the fishing club needed volunteers to cut the banks, there helping with the school fair and there whenever there was any challenge on the rig. He was the one person the younger guys would chat to if they were homesick or lonely and he would always make them feel better about life. He was so proud of your brother joining him at the company and I'm sure he would have been equally proud of you, Callum. He was a fine man and so very much missed. I am sorry."

Callum's jaw tightened, but he held himself together. Would his father really be so proud of him?

"Thank you, it was nice to hear," he said. "My Granda is hoping to head down after his appointment, so perhaps you'll see him."

"That would be cracking," Billy replied. He straightened his cap as he stood and said, "I think if your dad was here now, he would be saying we are missing a chance of a fish. Come on, let's have another go. You fish through this pool again and I'll follow after you. Maybe change your fly?"

Callum opened the fly box and showed him the contents, and Billy picked out what looked like a piece of clear drinking straw with long wisps of black hair trailing from it.

"Sunray Shadow. Give this one a chance now the sun's overhead, see if you can stir one up." They walked back upstream along the bank to where Callum's bike was tethered.

Before Callum had a chance to change his fly, his phone began to ring. "Sorry, you go ahead. I'll take this call and maybe fish after you," he said. He was already inserting an earphone into his right ear.

"Right OK then, nice chatting to you Callum, see you in a little while," said Billy, heading to the start of the pool and down towards the water's edge.

"Hey Ritchie, how you doing, what's up?" said Callum into the phone. He reached into his bag and removed sandwiches, crisps and a drink before taking a seat on the bench. He watched the older fisherman all the time he was chatting away to his friend. He defensively fielded questions about his morning, trying not to show too much enthusiasm, which would be uncool. "Yeah, yeah.

I'll be about later." But his attention was drifting away from the phone call; he soon ended it and hung up. He was more interested in the fisherman and how he covered the river with his line. Not only could he send the line, which was an orange colour, further than Callum, but he seemed to be working it as it swung back and it always lay very straight on the water. After each cast, Callum had let the current pull the fly-line straight and then swing like a pendulum towards the bank, but Billy adjusted the line after each cast, usually by rolling or flicking the loose line nearest the end of the rod further upstream. Callum studied this, trying to understand why, before slowly stepping down to join Billy.

"Do you mind if I watch a little?" he said. "I could do with some tips."

"Of course not, come and stand just here. I've fished this river for much of my life and it has brought me so much pleasure. I've travelled around Scotland and abroad salmon fishing, but to my mind there is no river more beautiful or more enjoyable to fish than the Dee. Some smaller rivers are bonnie enough, but they really need a spate of rain for fish to run up them, so you take your chances when you book fishing in advance. The Dee is fishable almost every day of the season if you can brave the weather. There can be times in February when she's iced over mind, and after very heavy rainfall she can swell to a fair old height, but that seldom lasts long as she drains very quickly compared to some other big rivers. Look how clear the water is, despite the rain at the weekend." He drew the line back in for another cast. He was right, it was like a mountain spring with no stain at all. "Gin clear, they call it," Billy added with a grin.

"Can I ask why you loop the fly-line after you've cast?" asked Callum. He listened as Billy explained how he 'mended' the line to speed or sometimes slow down the movement of the fly so it didn't swing too quickly past a fish.

It was at this point that Callum became aware of someone above them on the bank, and turned to see his Granda, who was now sitting on the bench. Unsure whether he had just arrived or been there for some time, Callum waved and began to wade out of the river towards him.

"Donald Anderson himself, well well, what a lovely surprise," said Billy. He followed Callum to the bank, where he laid down his rod and stepped up to the bench. Without thinking, Billy held out his hand, which Granda clasped with a smile.

"Billy Grantham, still plugging away are ye?"

"I've been having a lovely chat with your fine grandson here," said Billy. He's putting you to shame with his rod. He hooked into a cracker before, such a pity it managed to get off."

Donald turned to Callum. "Is that right, did you have one on?"

Callum recounted what had happened, the incredible excitement and the shock, then the disappointment of the escape. Finally, Granda turned to Billy.

"It's been a pleasure to see you, Billy, it must have been seven years since the last time. I'm going to take Callum up to try Greenbank now and leave you in peace. Tight lines."

"Aye, Donald. Might we see you down the Bothy on Friday?" asked Billy.

Granda paused, looking straight through him. "Aye, it's been a while since I went to the Pots & Fords. We'll see." With a nod and a raise of his hand, he turned. Callum gathered his belongings and slowly pushed his bike upstream to a new starting point, whilst Granda carried the rod.

"Ah Granda, I so nearly caught one, it was unbelievable."

"It's good that you got a take, it's a sign that there are fish around and they're active. The conditions are nice now that the river has dropped. This next pool is my favourite on this beat. I've known many a fine day here over the years, as a grandson and as a grandad."

They secured the bike and the bag and walked towards the river, where Granda sat on a vacant bench. Callum joined him, a little concerned. "Are you OK, Granda? Need a sit down?"

His grandad patted the bench next to him. "Let's just look over the water a minute, lad. Take in this wonderful scene, breathe it, become a part of it. Can you see where the pool starts and finishes and where the lies might be? Can you see through the surface?"

Callum looked onto the water, and after some thought pointed upstream. "That looks like the head of the pool, I would start there, and it probably finishes down to just there where there is a small rocky beach?"

"Not bad. With the river at this height, I would agree the fish would tend to mostly be lying between those points, but personally I would fish it a bit further downstream as it is deceptively deep, and you often find one right at the tail before the shallows. You don't have to cast very far at the head as the natural bend of the river helps you. Further down, a bit below where we are now, you need to open your shoulders a little and try to reach those big boulders you can see, there's always one or two there."

"Should we put the Sunray fly on?" asked Callum.

"I think the Silver Stoat will have a good chance here," said Granda, thoughtfully. "We can always try the Sunray after maybe."

Granda was not wearing fishing clothing, just his usual warm house clothes, but he had brought a pair of wellington boots, which he now put on. It had warmed up since the morning, but the cloud cover had thankfully stopped it getting hot.

"You go and get started, Callum. I'll watch from here until you have passed me, then I'll come and join you. Just take your time and remember, there's no need for a long line at the top, but make sure you let the fly come right round onto the dangle."

For some reason this amused Callum. "Aye I will. The one I hooked this morning was right on the dangle." He grinned as he made his way along the bank and slowly down to the water's edge about twenty metres above the bench. Although they had been on the water together on Monday, it had essentially been more casting practice. They were properly fishing today, and he wanted to make a good attempt. He remembered the videos they had watched the previous afternoon and how, encouraged by his father, his brother had made it look so easy.

Callum took two steps into the river, which was only ankle deep at the edge, before he began to cast.

"Perfect," said Granda, watching closely as the line went out and swung back towards the bank. The comment made Callum glow with pride and confidence.

The top part of the pool was proving quite difficult to fish, as a large boulder was snagging his line as it swung past it and creating a large eddy below which affected the fly's movement. Seeing this happen, Callum started to 'mend' the line when a loop appeared in it so that the line remained quite straight all the way to the fly, which appeared to move through the water as naturally as possible.

"Nicely done," said Granda. Callum was enjoying the praise, much as his brother had in the video.

As the path of the river straightened, the main current moved towards the middle, and Callum took a few steps deeper until the water was up to his thigh. He added a bit more line and was soon reaching across the channel. A couple of fish had splashed in the next section; this didn't mean they were necessarily likely to snap at a fly, but it was encouraging, nonetheless.

"This has always been the hotspot," said Granda. He had now joined Callum at the water's edge and peered across the water through his sunglasses.

With a longer line, each cast took more time to swing across the river. The fly was reaching all the lies where a fish might be. Callum's excitement and anticipation remained high and just as in the morning, he was imagining the fly as it moved. Where the current was fast, he tried to 'mend' it just as Billy Grantham had shown him, to slow it down. He felt he was covering the water nicely, and there was nothing more he could be doing. It was now all in the lap of the fishing gods. He just hoped they were smiling on him today.

"You see those big rocks peeking through the surface?" asked Granda. Callum nodded and sent the line out towards them. Although he was using a small fly and a light line, he could pinpoint where the fly landed on the water, and he knew it would be swinging nicely in front of the rock. He gradually moved downstream. His fly had now passed the first boulder and was covering the flat water in the gap before the second one.

As it came round, his line twitched as if it had met some resistance. It could have been a rock, it could have been something swimming into the line or it could have been a tentative take. They looked at each other and without stepping downstream this time, Callum cast again to the same place. Under his breath, Granda murmured, "Lovely, now come on ye beauty."

As the last syllable left his lips the line twitched again, then again and once more, until the line was tight. Callum raised the rod.

"There she is," said Granda calmly as the rod bent over. The reel began to shriek and for the second time that day, Callum found himself playing a salmon.

He fought anxiously to control the fish, determined to make no mistakes this time and desperate to impress Granda who calmly watched. "Try and keep her away from those rocks she is heading for, see if you can tire her in the main stream," said Granda.

Although Callum was inexperienced, he was learning fast. He

let the salmon run downstream, but when the fish halted, he reeled line back in and gradually drew it towards him. Firmly, but not so hard that the line might snap or the hook bend. Every moment was thrilling but nerve-racking, and that was evident on Callum's face as he took a few steps downstream to where the fish was heading with his lips pressed firmly together. He was nervous of losing the fish but felt slightly more aware of his actions than he had just that morning.

There was a shallow bank of gravel about twenty metres away and Granda slowly made his way to it, having already identified it as the best landing place. They had no net with them, so Callum would need to lead the tired fish into the shallows so it could be held and unhooked.

The rod was bending hard, and his arms were starting to ache. He was determined not to lose this one, but the fish had other ideas and again pulled line from the reel in its bid for freedom. This time, though, when the run ended the fish rolled on the surface, and they saw the whiteness of its belly.

Granda knew it was tiring. "Draw her down here, Callum," he said. "Easy does it."

Too tense to speak, Callum nodded. As he stepped backwards the fish allowed itself to be dragged into the shallows, where Granda reached down and gripped it around the 'wrist', just above the tail.

"Well done, Callum!" came a familiar voice from the bank. It was Billy Grantham, already making his way down to join them.

Callum looked down at the pristine shining creature that lay at his feet. The salmon's underside was almost white and its broad back dark grey, but its flanks were shining silver. Callum's heart was still thumping as he stared in shock. His grandad removed the fly from the corner of the salmon's mouth, then pointed to something behind the gills.

"Look Callum, those are sea lice. That means the fish has only been in fresh water for a few days, because they drop off when they leave the sea. What a stunning fish."

Callum nodded, regaining composure he ran both hands through his hair, a broad smile now stretching across his face.

"Mr Grantham, would you mind taking a photo please before we return her?" asked Callum.

"Of course not. What a beauty, must be an eight pounder. But she is actually a he. Look how its lower jaw is starting to develop a hook."

A beaming Callum took out his phone and opened the camera with trembling hands. He handed it over before crouching next to Granda and with both hands, lifted the fish slightly above the water for the photo. Under Granda's guidance he then quickly replaced the fish in the river facing upstream whilst the flow of water over the gills helped it regain strength. Within a few seconds the salmon began to wriggle, and as Callum released his grip it sped off back into the main current. Callum watched it swim off, then turned to face his grandad and took a few steps towards him. "Oh my god, yes!" he cried as they embraced.

Eleanor Seougall

CHAPTER 11

The rear door of the green Land Rover slammed shut and young James Tippen hurried round to the driver's seat to escape the drizzle. It was about a thirty-minute journey to Banchory, so it would be tight, but James connected his phone and launched his playlist as usual before moving off. He reached almost sixty before braking as the end of the drive approached, then turned right onto the public road. He raced along, banging the top of the steering wheel in time to the beat. As he neared his destination, he pushed his preppy hair back to put on his sunglasses, despite it being overcast.

Then his phone rang, and he nervously answered it. "Hi dad, everything OK?"

"Yeah, yeah." He heard the clearing of his father's smoker's throat. "I was just a bit tied up with work, sorry I didn't see you. You know it's very impressive that you're attending this course today. Chance to show them how it's done. I'll come down and see how you're getting on later afternoon. See you then." And he abruptly hung up.

Relieved that there was nothing more to the call, James relaxed. His exam results would be out this week and he knew he had to create a good atmosphere at home before they arrived. Signing up for the fishing course had seemed an easy way to curry some favour, given how passionate his dad was about salmon fishing.

Once he knew *she* would be there, it was a no-brainer.

The music kicked back in and as he passed over the bridge, he could see the white lodge to his right and the river running past it. The gravel crunched under the heavy tread of the tyres as he skidded to a halt outside the hotel. He stepped onto the car park and sauntered towards Ross, standing at the hotel entrance, who raised a hand in greeting.

"Morning James," said Ross, in a slightly flat tone. "Straight into the conference room please, everyone else is there."

James put his shades in the pocket of his khaki shirt, pulled the brim of his cap down a little and walked through the hallway and into the large room at the rear. There were five males and two females of a similar age to himself, none of whom he recognised, standing chatting by a small table. He approached and picked up a paper cup of coffee, nodding acknowledgement to the others but without making an introduction.

Turning to the rest of the room he saw, with relief, that Honor was there. As he started towards her Ross closed the door, asking them to take their seats at the tables. It was all very classroom-like.

Disappointed at not having the time to chat to her, James took the seat closest to the door. Embarrassingly, they each had to give a short intro on themselves to the rest of the group, with their fishing background as well as their respective schools. All the others were from around Aberdeen and most went to Cult's Academy. He was the only one from Fettes. He listened intently as Honor gave her background, and she smiled back at him when she spoke about her time on the River Tweed.

The first session he found pretty dull; it was all about fly presentation. There were some underwater videos showing how salmon reacted to the presented flies depending on whether they were just under the surface or weighted deep. Another filmed their reactions when the fly swung slowly by compared to when it was moving fast or jigging up and down. He couldn't help thinking that if you could see what was happening under the water, catching them would be much easier.

At mid-morning they stopped for a break, and he headed straight to her, narrowly heading off one of the others.

"Hey, Honor bella, how are you?" he said.

"I'm fine, nice to see you," she replied.

They chatted until it was time to reconvene. All the time he was conscious of another athletic-looking guy circling in the background until they took their seats again.

The next session focused on different casting techniques and was hosted by Honor, guaranteeing James' attention. She explained the concept of selecting the style of casting to suit the conditions, sometimes casting from the right hand and sometimes the left. He was familiar with this already from his past private tuition, but he remained interested whilst she demonstrated, losing his focus when the videos were shown.

Just before lunch, Ross gave a talk on salmon conservation. James was aware that their numbers had been falling, as his dad banged on about it every time he failed to catch anything, but he hadn't realised it was so severe in Scotland. They would just have to travel to other countries to catch them, he thought.

The students had formed small groups to eat their lunch, and James took a seat next to the instructors, directing most of his dialogue towards Honor, though little was on the topic of salmon. After twenty minutes they broke and the instructors asked the group to put up their rods and get into their kit. James was the first to achieve this and he stood waiting in his expensive new waders, his sunglasses on again.

There was very little instruction directed at James during their practice time. Some of the attendees were struggling with the more complex techniques, but he had no problem. With the water so high there was little chance of catching, but that wasn't why he was here. He was good at this and knew he could show it.

He delayed handing over his spot in the river to his partner, and when he looked up towards the hotel again, he saw his father had arrived. He was standing on the grass bank, talking animatedly to Honor's father, who diverted their attention towards James. "Go on son!" yelled his father, and James swapped the rod to his other hand and executed a perfect but difficult cast. After the line had swung out, he reeled in and headed up the bank to them, smiling broadly.

"Hi Buster, great to see you. How are you settling in?" he said to Honor's father.

"Afternoon James. Everything's going well, thank you. Lovely casting there."

James could see Honor saying goodbye to one of the other attendees, and whilst they were waiting for her, Ross, the other instructor, came to introduce himself.

"Well done, a good day and glad you could join," said Ross, who then introduced himself to James's father.

"He seemed to be top dog from what I could see," said James' father.

"Ha ha, yes, he did very well, but there were no prizes today. We are, however, hoping to announce a competition for under-eighteens next year with some very generous sponsorship and a big first prize. We have an exciting year ahead on the Dee."

"Hear that, James? One for you, I think. If you win the prize, I'll match it myself! Here she is, the instructor herself. Maybe you can get a bit of private tuition James, know what I mean?" James' dad warmly embraced Honor before she politely stepped back to her father's side.

Smiling at his dad, James inched closer to Honor. Lowering his voice, he said, "Hey, that wouldn't be such a bad idea, I'd like that.

Maybe we can arrange to meet up?"

Honor smiled back at him. "Yes, maybe," she said, but her eyes were looking over his shoulder back towards the hotel.

"Cool," replied James, and moments later he was following his father back to their cars.

CHAPTER 12

A fine drizzle remained from the frontal system that had nearly passed through; it had been raining quite hard the night before. The buzz of Callum's catch remained with him into the following week, and he had spent a lot of time practising with Granda or reading at home. He loved being in Granda's small home, which was like a sanctuary where he could ask any questions without hesitancy. With every instruction there was usually a family story that went along with it, a connection of energy established between them.

Callum wanted to share his success, but there were few of his friends who would appreciate it. He skipped over his Snaps, but the memes didn't hold his attention. He stepped off the bus, remembering the kit he had to take this week, and jogged across the car park, carefully avoiding the puddles. He was nervous as he approached the terrace of the hotel. Nervous about the intermediate course but also about seeing her. There was no gathering outside, but in the doorway he saw Ross, who beckoned him over.

"Morning Callum, nice to see you. We're all in the conference room this morning. Hope you're going to enjoy it today, it will be quite a lot more technical and advanced than the introductory course, so see if you can keep up."

Callum returned the greeting but was a little irked by the final comment. He was determined to keep up, and to do a lot better than that if he possibly could.

He walked through the hallway, down the corridor and into the large room at the rear, where he saw Scott, four young men of similar age to himself and two young women, neither of whom was Honor. Concerned by her absence, he ambled towards the two he recognised from rugby and fist-bumped them with a 'Sup'. They were twins and although they weren't at Cult's they had met at district youth matches a year before. He also raised his head in acknowledgement of Alastair, a good friend he had lost touch with over the past twelve months, but then he was distracted by a voice to his left saying "Hey Callum". He turned and saw, with relief, that it was her. He took a couple of steps towards her, unsure of the right way to engage her. It was not appropriate to embrace or kiss on the cheek, but he would have loved to be that close to her. Instead, he gently raised his hand and smiled.

"Hey Honor, hadn't expected to see you here," he lied.

"I hope it's not a disappointment," she said, with a flirty smile.

"I might need a bit of guidance today," he said. "My grandad has been helping me with some extra practice, but I don't want to embarrass myself."

"I'm sure you'll be fine, you did great on the last course. Today is all about learning and enjoying."

They both turned as the door was closed. Ross was following the final participant into the room and asked the eight of them to take a seat. It was all a bit classroom-like, not what Callum had expected, but he took his seat as Ross ran through the usual fire and safety drills before giving an outline of the day.

"This morning is all indoors," he said. "We feel it's important for you to understand some of the technical aspects of salmon fishing, and we also want to discuss some more conservation matters. This afternoon we'll be back on the river, where we'll be pushing you to try new fishing techniques which may be necessary when you face more challenging weather, or when the river is running high and fast. Our first section is going to be on fly presentation. We know you can all cast out the line, but how the fly behaves once it's in the water is critical, and different conditions require different approaches."

Over the next ninety minutes, they watched instruction videos, then discussed what they had seen. It all made sense to Callum and he felt comfortable in the group. What was clear was that salmon fishing required thought. It wasn't like the mackerel fishing he had done in the sea, dangling a string of feathers and waiting for them to find a school of fish. The fact that salmon stop feeding when they enter the rivers created a totally different challenge as most fishing involves presenting food, or a representation of food, with a hidden hook. They saw clips showing fish lying deep in the water and ignoring flies that swung across the surface above them but were irritated and snapped at those that crossed right in front of them using weighted lines. They also saw clips where a very slow-moving fly was ignored, but once it was twitched and animated, it provoked a reaction. Callum was really into this, it was all helping him understand how to fish better.

They stopped at this point for a break. Callum took his time; he knew where he was heading. But as he approached Honor, another young man squeezed through, virtually pinning her to the wall. He was tall and wore a confident smile.

"Hey Honor bella, how are you?" the other lad said in a loud, confident voice. Callum swerved away immediately and headed towards the coffees on the table. He instinctively collected one of the paper cups and began to blow on the surface whilst peering over at the two of them.

"How's Buster?" he heard the lad ask. They were soon deep in conversation and seemed to know each other well. Honor seemed slightly reserved, unlike the boy. He waited his chance to replace him and opened his phone to appear occupied before ambling over to chat with the twins, but as he did so they were asked to retake their seats.

In the next section they focused on different casting techniques to match fishing conditions. It was Honor who presented this topic, following up the video with some footage of herself using different casting techniques to overcome such challenges.

"We'll be trying some of these after lunch," she said to a very attentive group.

Ross thanked Honor who took her place at the front of the room "I'd now like to take a few minutes to discuss the current status of the wild Atlantic salmon and the recent trends," he began. "You will be aware that the number of salmon being caught in the River Dee has seen a sharp fall over the past thirty years, but you may not be aware to what extent that is local or a more global trend. All of the five main countries where wild salmon run have seen such declines, though they have been more pronounced in Canada and the United Kingdom. Total salmon numbers can be estimated at around eight to ten million in 1985, but this number is probably closer to three million today. Back in the 1970s it is recorded that more than 3.5 million salmon were being netted each year. We are not far from the point where there are more red squirrels in Scotland than there are adult salmon, for the first time ever." He went on to show some slides to explain the many pressures on salmon and their effects, from climate change and salmon farming to hydro-electric schemes and intense farming methods.

They then broke for a thirty-minute lunch. The hotel had provided a packed lunch, and as Callum collected his, he was joined by Alastair. "Hi Callum, you were one of the last people I expected to be here, but it's good that you are," he said.

"Hey Al. Yeah, to be honest it came about quite quickly for one reason or another. Bugger all else to be doing. You been fishing much?"

"Aye, I've done a bit this summer with my dad. As you know, we used to get to the river when I was younger but hadn't managed it for a few years. It's been good, we've even managed to catch a couple, but I'd like to get a bit better and I'm really interested in the conservation aspect. How's your mum doing?" he asked with genuine interest.

"She's not too bad, she's pleased I'm here today rather than doing what I have spent most of the rest of the summer doing. Wanna grab a seat outside?"

They walked out to one of the tables and chatted until it was time to rejoin the group that was now forming around Honor and Ross.

"OK, let's see if we can add some variety to your casting techniques that will give you that ability to safely cast the line out in different situations," said Ross. "As you can see, the river's running quite high, and it has a brown colour to it due to the rains we've had, but thankfully there's only a gentle breeze. It looked quite easy on the video but who thinks they can do a double-Spey cast?"

A hand went up.

"James, great, would you come and give us a demo?"

The tall young man with hair like curtains who had been chatting up Honor made his way to the front. He took the rod and following a few words with Ross, stepped to the edge of the water, which had now effectively become a stage. He proceeded to cast as requested to a small ripple of applause, but rather than stop there he swapped hands on the rod, now gripping the top of the butt with his left, and performed the cast from the other side of his body.

"OK James, thanks very much," said Ross as he stepped forward to take the rod.

Impressive, for a dick, thought Callum.

"OK guys, split yourselves into pairs and we'll get you practising," said Ross. Callum turned to look at Alastair, who nodded, confirming the plan they had made.

A tap on Callum's shoulder was followed by Honor's soft voice. "Come with me guys," she said. They both followed her to the water twenty metres downstream. She talked them through the casts slowly and clearly, then took turns under her supervision and encouragement, now extremely attentive. Honor was teaching them how to cast left-handed, which was taking some time for Callum to get used to. At one point she stood very close so she could help him with the action. They were almost touching, and he was aware of her perfume, which did not help his concentration.

After some time practising, the young anglers began to fish the river properly, though with the water so high, they did not venture very deep. When it was Alastair's turn to fish, Callum sat on the bank and checked his phone in between watching the others. He could not help admiring James as he executed each cast perfectly.

"Mind if I take a seat?" asked Honor.

"Hey, sorry I was just watching the others."

"He casts well, doesn't he? He fished with my dad on the Tweed and he had a coaching guide with him all three days."

"Aye, a proper hero," said Callum, unable to hide his sarcasm.

"I think they live towards Montrose. How about you, Callum, what's your story? I was a bit surprised you'd come back for more punishment."

He explained his background, and how he had been the bad boy before he took up fishing. He felt he might have overdone this, as she did not seem impressed. Then he spoke about his grandad, and how sharing their angling experience had brought them closer, and how this had led to him joining the intermediate course.

"Does your dad not fish with you?" she asked. Over the past

few years, pretty much everyone Callum had interacted with had known what had happened, so this took him aback.

"My dad died when I was young," he replied flatly.

"Oh I'm so sorry," she quickly replied. "I didn't..."

He cut her off. "How about you, Honor, how has Aberdeenshire been able to get you here?"

She tapped his arm. "Come on, let's swap over, we can chat and fish there." They stepped down the bank, where Callum took the rod from a grinning Alastair. Callum rolled out the line quickly and turned his gaze to her.

"Well?" he smiled.

"My mum's in the oil industry, I guess coming to Aberdeen was inevitable once we had decided to return to the UK."

"How did you learn to fly fish, was that abroad?"

"Not really, my dad's been a ghillie on the Tweed for the past five years and just took a job near here, which is why we have moved. It's closer to Mum's work. I learned from my dad here in Scotland."

"What's a ghillie?" asked Callum.

"Oh sorry, a ghillie is basically a fishing guide, a river-keeper," she replied.

He nodded, then sent out a nice cast left-handed and smiled to himself. "Which school are you going to?"

"Cult's Academy, do you know it?"

Callum was delighted to hear this confirmed. He reeled in the line and they headed back to to the hotel. "Nice to have you in the 'deen," he said. "I think you'll like Cults. Maybe I can have your Snap in case you want to ask any questions about school?"

"Sure, it's salmon dot honor." She smiled, and he smiled back.

The course had felt very different from the last time; there had been a greater educational element and more specific detail on certain aspects. It was like going from a snowplough to a parallel turn on the Aberdeen dry slope. The others on the course were probably better than Callum, but maybe not for long. He just needed more practice, and in Granda he had the best teacher he could wish for.

He strode confidently over to the group as they gathered for the final briefing. Alastair and two of the others were engaged in a discussion about the plight of the salmon and how little seemed to be done. "I'm not eating that shit they call salmon you buy in the supermarkets," said an emotional Fay, to nodding heads. "Have you seen *Seaspiracy* and videos of the fish in the cages being eaten alive by sea lice? It's disgusting and it causes huge issues for the environment. I can't understand how they get away with it."

"Teach a man to fish and you've fed him for a lifetime," added Alastair. "What bullshit, there's not going to be any wild fish left."

They gathered round, cheerful and buzzing from trying new cast techniques as Ross gave them a summary of the day, congratulating them on their performance and wishing them luck in their fishing endeavours. The group gave a round of applause for all the instructors before drifting towards the car park.

"Watch out for some big news in the coming days," added Ross. "It'll be on email."

Alastair was collected by his father, who had been watching the boys cast from the bank. Callum knew him well, as he had stayed over at their house numerous times in the past and even joined them for a long weekend near Fort William a year earlier.

"Hi Callum, nice to see you, it's been quite a long time. Are you well?" he asked.

Callum shared what he had been doing the last few weeks, avoiding the months prior to that for obvious reasons. Callum was explaining how his grandad had been helping him when they were distracted by a commotion to their right and turned to investigate. It became apparent that Honor's father had arrived, as had James's father, whose booming voice was advising all onlookers how pleased he was to see him. Callum was sure Honor rolled her eyes at him, and he gave a faint grin back.

Alastair suggested they try to meet up the following week, to which Callum immediately agreed. They parted, and as they reached the car Callum drifted towards the path at the front of the hotel which would take him to the bus stop. He paused in the sun that shone on the top of the lawn and took out his phone, opening the app before glancing back to the remaining group. Honor looked stunning, and Callum couldn't keep his eyes off her. He typed her username in and a single message, 'Hey, thanks for the help today' and sent it before he could change his mind.

CHAPTER 13

Callum had not had any discomfort from his knee over the past three weeks and was feeling in good shape. The fishing seemed to have helped his core strength, for keeping his balance in the swirling river whilst casting was like low-intensity yoga. He wanted to reclaim his place in the Granite team and had restarted his exercises and jogging, much to Fergie's enjoyment. Pre-season training camps had been limited, but he was hopeful that they would soon be able to restart. It was going to be a good season, he was sure of it.

There was less than two weeks of the holiday left and he was intent on making the most of them, given how little he had done in June and July. He had not seen Jake and the others for over a week. He was loving the precious time he was spending with Granda and seeing how much it meant to him too. He felt each day had a purpose: he wanted to get better at fishing. It had reached a point where he felt compelled by it, feeling that he would be letting his father down if he didn't succeed.

The discovery of the link between his family and salmon fishing had brought mixed emotions, as until recently he had rarely thought about his father or brother. Hearing others say their names out loud – Ian and Finlay – felt strange and it took Callum a moment to realise who they were referring to. He had been only four when the accident happened and he couldn't really remember them but the photos, the video and the conversations had stirred something. Initially it had been a deep sadness, but this had been replaced by a drive to experience the river in the way his father undoubtedly would still have been doing had that helicopter not crashed.

On the Sunday, Callum rode over to his grandad's and they chatted in the front room about the intermediary course. Granda was very interested in the conservation discussions and to hear Callum's thoughts on the course. For sure he had enjoyed learning more about fly presentation, using sinking lines and the introduction to different casting techniques. He had particularly been interested by the discussion around dwindling wild Atlantic salmon numbers and what the reasons for this might be. There was growing concern about human activities at sea and the lasting effect they were having. Like most of his contemporaries, Callum was passionate about the natural environment, but he had not heard anyone talk about this issue before. Reconnecting with Alastair and then of course spending time with Honor were what really stood out.

He was now in touch with her through social media. She had replied to the message he had sent as he left on Saturday and they had exchanged a few more since, although Callum was trying really hard to remain cool. As well as some direct messaging, he could see posts about what she had been doing this summer and before, mainly fishing by the look of it. He had also been back in touch with Alastair, diverting his attention away from Jake, Rory and Tomas.

It was thanks to Alastair that he was now preparing for another fishing trip, this time to an estate called Sluie. Alastair's father, Sean, had booked a beat for Tuesday and had invited Callum to join them. Although it was for two rods, they would be able to share and take turns. Callum felt guilty towards Alastair; they had been good friends, but he had prioritised spending time with

Jake and the others this year. Admittedly this was partly due to their proximity during the restrictions, but that did not justify him blanking him. He was pleased and also relieved they had been able to pick up again. He had missed his friend, and spending time together on the river would be cool.

Callum had described to Granda how limited the fishing had been the previous day due to the river being high and murky before asking him his thoughts on Sluie.

"What tends to happen is that the fish are hard to find and tempt when the river is rising and the water's cloudy," Granda explained. "It's not impossible but it's difficult, and the odds are much more in your favour when the river is dropping and clearing. You watch the catch numbers that get reported each day and invariably they are highest in the days that follow a good rise in the river's height." He reached for the iPad, turning the open webpage weather forecast towards Callum. "As it looks like being dry for the next few days, the river should be settling down. That should make it very promising for Tuesday."

"I just hope I don't embarrass myself," said Callum, though he felt confident that he could handle it.

"You'll be just fine lad. You've made huge progress in just a few weeks. It's a nice open beat too, if I remember correctly. Some of it is usually casting off the bank as the deeper current is close in, then there's a nice wade where the current crosses to the far bank. It's the left bank of the river, so you can cast from your right shoulder. How about I see if there's any space at Garthdee tomorrow and we can go have another few hour's practice? The river's closed on a Sunday, but I'm sure my friend at the club will be happy to check for us."

This was the ideal scenario for Callum, and he sat patiently as his grandad picked up his ancient mobile phone and made a call to the Angling Association. He heard with disappointment that the bookings for Garthdee were full but was relieved to discover there were two rods available at the adjoining Banchory and Devenick. Whoever was on the other end of the phone obviously knew Granda well, and they chatted enthusiastically for some time. Callum overheard the other man say, "Great to have you back on the water, Donald. Best of luck to Callum and yourself tomorrow. See you down the bothy." Granda placed the phone on the table and turned to Callum in triumph.

"We're in luck laddie, there's space on the South Bank," he said.

"Why is salmon fishing illegal on Sundays? I don't get the logic," enquired Callum.

"It's a historic thing I believe, back to the times when very little apart from churchgoing happened on the Sabbath, including fishing, shooting and hunting,"

Callum had been thinking about this. "It just seems so out of date. It's OK to trout fish on Sundays, it's OK to canoe down the river on a Sunday, but it isn't OK to fish for salmon on the same water the canoe is travelling down. To be honest Granda, I think it's unfair for younger anglers and anyone working full time. It's taking away fifty per cent of the available days for people like me outside the holidays. Shouldn't it be up to the fishery owner which days they want to fish?"

"I'm not sure, but I do tend to agree with you. It's more relevant now than ever, I would say. We need to get more people into salmon fishing, it's their passion that will wake the world up to the trouble the salmon is in. Anything that can be done to help ought to be done, especially where there seems to be no real downside. I appreciate that by opening on a Sunday you may remove the day off the ghillies that work on the river usually take, but many beats don't employ a ghillie. Some might feel Thursday is a better day off to allow fishing all weekend when more people are free. It's legal to fish for migratory species on Sundays in England, you know."

"Maybe we need a campaign or a petition. There seems to be a petition for pretty much everything else. I'd love to be fishing with you today." Callum was thinking to himself that he was going to look into this.

"I'm just so pleased it matters so much to you, Callum. Before long it will be too late for us. At least we have tomorrow to look forward to. Can you get here for ten? I think I'll drive us there, as it's a bit far to walk."

"I'll be here on the dot, and I'll bring my tackle along too. Is there anything else we need?" Callum was rising from his seat as he spoke.

"If your kind mother can make us a couple of sandwiches, we will be just grand. See you then lad."

Callum arrived as promised the next morning, laden with fishing tackle and lunch. Thankfully the strong wind was blowing from behind him. Before long they had loaded Granda's car and placed Callum's bike safely in the front hall. The short drive took them across the Bridge of Dee and in ten minutes they were parking on Leggart Terrace, with the river just twenty metres away. It was dry with a fresh breeze, and although the air temperature still reflected the fact that it was July, the strong north-easterly wind made it feel colder.

Callum set about putting up his rod, using the car as a windbreak.

"What fly do you think, Granda?" he asked.

"I was thinking we might try something with a bit of colour, as the river still has a tinge of stain to it. Here, this is called a Cascade, I think a size ten should be about right." Granda held out a fly with two black hooks that was largely coloured yellow and hot orange. "It's supposed to look like a shrimp in the water, let's give it a go."

They made their way down to the start of the pool, which, frustratingly, was very open to the wind. Callum, who was wearing his waders, took a few steps into the water and looked forlornly at his Granda. They were on the right-hand bank of the river and with the wind in his face, Callum knew his favoured Spey cast would not work. If he wasn't careful the line, and potentially the hook, would wrap around him. He needed to get the line safely above him, and that meant casting using the snap-C but left-handed. This was going to be tricky.

He started to lengthen the line and was managing to cast reasonably well to about eight or nine metres, but any longer and the wind forced the line back towards him so that it landed on the water in an ineffective heap. Seeing Callum's frustration, Granda took over the rod and demonstrated the need for more punch in the cast to try and get the line under the wind. It was an improvement, but it was still proving difficult. Callum persevered for half an hour, but without conviction. When a gust caused his line to become tangled in a messy knot, he waded back to the bank and sat on a rock next to Granda, who helped to unravel the bird's nest of line.

"It'd be a lot easier downwind from the other bank," said Callum.

"Yes, I think we are doing what's known as pissing into the wind," was Granda's surprising response. "I don't think we're doing anyone any favours continuing like this. You need specialist equipment to handle casting a fly into such a strong wind, I think our best option is to make a complete change of tactics. Over to the dark side!" He winked.

They walked back up to the car, attached the fly rod to the roof and drove a few hundred metres upstream to another car park next to the Banchory Devenick church. Granda reached into the boot and removed another rod tube, which he handed to Callum. "Let's set up the spinning rod," he said. This rod looked more like the one Callum had used whilst sea fishing. It was shorter and carried a fixed-spool reel. There was no fly-line, just nylon, and after they had threaded it through the eyes of the rod, Granda attached what looked like a miniature silver shoehorn with a hook attached. "It's a spinning lure," he explained. "Nowadays, most of the estates on the River Dee restrict fishing to fly only. The river is renowned for having idyllic fly-fishing water, it rarely gets too wide or too deep and maintains a nice current, so the fly works well. It's generally believed that a salmon released after being hooked on a fly is less damaged than one that's had the bigger hooks of a spinner lodged in its mouth." Granda held up the spinner, and Callum could see that the hooks were quite large. "But there are some circumstances where, in my opinion, spinning for salmon is perfectly acceptable. Dragging a spinner through a crystal-clear pool in low water that's holding a large number of fish is definitely not on, but a day such as today when it's windy and the river is carrying some colour make fly-fishing almost impossible, so it has to make sense.

"The pool we're going to now is called the Manse pool, and you'll see it's very slow moving. This makes fly fishing almost impossible, as there's no natural movement of the fly, so it's much better suited to a spinner."

Granda led Callum down to the water, where he spent ten minutes demonstrating how to deploy the spinner across the pool. It was possible to cast upstream and retrieve the spinner quickly or cast downstream and retrieve more slowly as the current of the water created the movement in the lure. It took a while to get used to the different reel design, but pretty soon Callum was reaching all corners of the pool and finding it much more enjoyable than attempting to cast a fly into the wind.

"There are a number of different lures you can use for spinning and they all require skill to use properly and successfully," said Granda. "Not the kind of practice for tomorrow I had in mind, but the wind is forecast to drop overnight, so I'm sure you'll be fine."

Callum covered the water thoroughly over the next hour, after which they stopped to eat the lunch that his mum had prepared. They seemed to chat solely about fishing these days. It used to be rugby, but now Callum wanted to hear more about the history of the river and of memorable catches, especially when the stories included his father. He really did love this river and fishing on it.

Granda recounted a story of when Callum's father happened to be walking along the riverbank at Garthdee and noticed that a lady angler had hooked a fish that she was struggling to control. He had walked down the bank and it became apparent that it was a very large fish, so without a second's delay he ran home to grab a landing net. The round trip only took him ten minutes, and it was another fifteen before they got the fish in the net. It was a true lifetime fish for the angler, well over twenty pounds. She was extremely grateful and hearing the story twenty-five years later Callum felt very proud.

They tried another pool with the spinner but were unable to tempt a take, so they decided to head back to Granda's, where they chatted through tactics for Callum's trip to Sluie the following day and made tentative plans to try again together before Callum returned to school.

Next day, Alastair and Sean, his father, picked Callum up at 8.15. He was already standing outside with his fishing gear when they arrived. He was excited to have the chance of fishing again, but there was another reason for the smile on his face. Alastair, given a slight nudge by Callum, had asked Honor if she would like to meet, as she lived just a couple of miles from Sluie. Callum had played it down, suggesting her fishing ability would be a help, and he thought Alastair had believed him. Honor had offered to head over around twelve and bring a contribution towards their lunch.

Callum was determined to show how much he had improved, and if at all possible to catch a salmon in her presence. He had this crazy notion that if he did, she would be so impressed she would not be able to resist kissing him. Or had he dreamt that? He got the impression that Alastair liked her too but hadn't said so. Callum had put on his half-zip sweater which he thought looked good and had bought some new fishing sunglasses with dark lenses.

The three of them talked animatedly during the thirty-minute journey. Sean was optimistic about their chances, as the owner had caught two on the beat the previous afternoon. He had advised using floating lines and quite small flies now the river level had dropped.

They were soon parking next to the hut, which sat ideally positioned on a bend in the river. Callum was already getting the sense that most fishing huts were positioned close to the most productive water, and the pool in front of the car looked really promising. It was also clear that a bench on the bank was usually a good sign of a hotspot.

"Right, you guys, get yourselves set up and you can have a go first," said Sean. "Maybe I'll wet a line later." Within ten minutes they had both assembled their kit, just as they had been taught on the course, and were changing into their waders. They had agreed to try different flies, and Callum had plumped for a Cascade again.

"Alastair," said his dad, "you've fished here before, so why don't you give the Hut pool a go and I'll take Callum up to the Jetties. You should be fine wading, just put one of the safety collars on." So Alastair headed towards the river as his father and Callum went back up the track. They walked a few hundred metres with the river on their left, then cut across the grass and down to the water's edge. There was still a breeze, but much less than the day before, and thankfully it was blowing from behind Callum this time.

"OK Callum, there are three pools here but they pretty much run into one another so you can fish all the way down this stretch," said Sean. "You can see the current generally runs to this side of the river so you don't need to cast any further than midway, and you'll see on the bottom pool the river is very deep against this side, so you fish that from the bank. I would suggest you wade out just two metres to make the casting a little easier, then make your way down until you need to get onto the bank just there by that large boulder." He pointed to it, then moved downstream and sat on a flat slate rock where he could look over the river without crowding his guest.

Callum was fishing nicely, the breeze from behind helping the line to extend fully before dropping onto the water. He could see the bottom of the riverbed in front of him through his new polarised sunglasses, making it easy to step down after each cast. There were glimpses of sun through the clouds, and it was warming up quickly. As he reached the place where Sean was sitting, he removed his fleece and tossed it onto the bank.

"Getting ready for some action, are you?" said Sean cheerfully. "You're fishing really nicely Callum. It took me a lot longer to get to your level when I started."

"Thanks Sean. I really like the casting, it just feels good sending the fly out well. When did you start salmon fishing?"

"My story is a bit different to yours. I'm from a military background and went straight into the Guards, so we moved around a bit. I'd done some coarse fishing as a boy, but not fly fishing. It was after returning from Afghanistan that fly fishing as an activity was organised for a bunch of us to help us through a few problems we were having. I was a little sceptical, but the research and data show that fly fishing can be good for your mental health. To be honest, at the time I would have tried anything as things were quite tough and I guess I was lucky to be given the opportunity."

Callum turned towards him. He hadn't known about this. They had not really spoken about anything other than sport before.

"It's not just PTSD it can help with," Sean went on. "I've found time spent fly fishing just clears my mind of any negativity or downbeat thoughts I might have, so it's become an important part of my life. Having seen the challenges your digital generation is facing, I'm keen to get Alastair out as much as possible too. With mixed success!"

"It doesn't have the sexiest of images, does it?"

"There's still a perception that it's the realm of middle-aged gentry, but that really isn't the case now. It has become much more dynamic with huge technological progress in both equipment and clothing. Even David Beckham loves his salmon fishing. And your friend Honor, what a great caster. I follow a few of the high-profile angling guides on social media and I swear the ladies are the best. You are all essential for the future of the sport."

The image of Honor effortlessly casting in her waders leapt into Callum's mind, momentarily interrupting his ability to reply.

As he was about to speak, Sean's phone began to ring, and he raised it to his ear.

"Aye, good stuff. Just hold on, I'll be right there," he said to the caller. He rose to his feet. "Alastair's hooked one, I'm going to give him a hand."

"Me too!" said Callum excitedly. He stepped out of the river before laying his rod carefully down on the bank. "I'll come back and carry on with this pool after."

Back at the hut, they could see Alastair's bent rod tip poking above the bushes. It was a thrilling sight. The river rushed towards the far bank and Alastair's tall, athletic frame stood like a statue. The muscles of his forearms strained as the fish made another run for freedom. He was now only knee-deep in the river but was unable to bring the fish closer as it tore downstream, line streaming from the reel.

"Let her go," said his dad calmly. "Keep the rod tip up, you're doing well." They both moved downstream towards where the fish was.

"Can you grab the net Callum please?" asked Sean.

"This is the third run it's made, my arms are killing me," groaned Alastair. There was pain and anguish on his face. But gradually the fish began to tire, and he was able to coax it in. It was just ten metres away when it rolled under the pressure from the line, and they caught the first real glimpse of it.

"Holy smoke!" said Callum in a loud whisper and handed the net to Sean.

"You try and walk slowly onto the bank Al, and see if you can bring her to me," said Sean.

As Alastair slowly stepped backwards, the fish followed him until it was scooped up by his father's net. For a moment there was silence. Alastair shook his tired arms and stared at the net. His dad looked up at him, Callum too, and suddenly all three of them started to laugh in amazement and disbelief.

Sean kneeled down beside the net and removed the hook, then pulled the in-built scales from the net's handle and lifted it from the water to measure the weight.

"Nineteen pounds, a hen fish. What a beauty. It's the biggest I've ever seen, and caught by my clever son." Alastair threw an arm round his father.

"Here, let me get a photo of you both," said Callum, already with his phone out. "I was able to video the last few minutes too."

They both kneeled beside the net and Alastair eased it to the surface for the picture, then held the fish facing into the current to regain its strength. After a minute, with a gentle waft of the big paddle-like tail, the salmon disappeared into the deeper water as if it had all been a mild inconvenience.

Callum shook a beaming Alastair by the hand. "Congrats Al, that was something pretty special. Best see if I can catch one too, I've left my rod upstream a bit. I'll be back for lunch in an hour."

"Aye thanks Callum, the photos look ace too," said Alastair. "Go get one and see you in a bit. Dad, why don't you fish the rest of this pool? I'm still shaking."

Callum trudged back to where he had left his rod and made his way down to the water's edge. He paused, watching a dipper bounce between the boulders showing in the middle of the river. He was delighted for Alastair, he really was, but he had been imagining Honor arriving to hear about the big fish he had caught, not his friend. He tried that little bit harder to stretch his casts, methodically covering the pool without response, and before long he was making his way along the track to the hut.

Alastair was sitting at the table with his phone. The photo of him with his nineteen-pounder would have gone global by now. He turned with a smile as he heard Callum shuffling towards him. Callum sat beside him and they both chatted as they watched Sean fishing the tail of the Hut pool. A few minutes later he made his way towards them. "Looks like we have company, lads," he said, and they turned to see Honor arriving. Her tousled curls were drawn back into a ponytail, the sun highlighting her dark features, smiling as she cycled towards them. Both lads stumbled to their feet. Welcomes and introductions followed, until Alastair could wait no longer and showed Honor the photo of his incredible catch.

"That's one of the best-looking fish I've ever see," she exclaimed. "Look how deep it is, it's shaped like a tuna!"

They chatted about the morning's excitement whilst laying out the lunch items on the picnic table. It was a serious feast, but they made a big dent in it as they chatted and laughed.

Honor recounted the story of her own biggest catch, coincidentally also nineteen pounds, from Islamouth on the Tay. It was only five miles upstream of there that the UK's largest-ever rod-caught salmon, weighing sixty-four pounds, was famously landed by Miss Georgina Ballantine nearly a hundred years ago. Two years later another huge fish of sixty-one pounds was caught, also, intriguingly, by a woman, and this time using a fly. "There's no denying that women are very successful salmon anglers, they reckon it's to do with female pheromones," said Sean, smiling. "But I think it is because they are less aggressive and they listen to the advice of the ghillies!"

Callum joined in the banter, but his impatience was building; he needed to catch one. He rose from the table and collected his rod from the nearby rack. Then he unhooked the fly and presented it to Honor. "Here, Honor. Can you roll this in your hand for me and I'll see if it brings me luck?" She happily obliged and with a theatrical bow, Callum headed to the start of the Hut pool.

"Don't forget your safety collar," said Sean and tossed it to him. "I might go and have a cast at the top of the beat whilst you two finish eating."

"Aye dad, good luck, we'll be fine here. See you in a bit," replied Alastair. He stretched back just as the sun began to shine through the clouds.

"I'm going to boil some water and make coffees," announced Honor as she made for the hut.

Callum could hear them chatting, but he was occupied in his desire to catch one whilst she was there. A twenty-pounder would be just fine, and she could land it for him and throw her arms round him to congratulate him. He was getting frustrated by the regular splashing of salmon at the far side of the current, only a few yards in from the opposite bank and just out of reach. He had quietly waded out to his waist and was sending a nice line across in their direction but couldn't quite get the fly that far.

He wasn't feeling entirely confident in the fly he was using. Carefully he reeled in and managed to change it despite the pressure from the water against his body before casting again. He took another step forward, feeling the water rise above his waist and cast as hard as he could. This time the fly landed close to the far bank and began to swing back through the current precisely where he had seen the activity. The sense of anticipation rose and he took a small step downstream and cast again almost to the far bank. With the rod in his right hand, he held the line with his left and very slowly retrieved it, accelerating the fly's movement as they had seen on the course last week. He knew he was fishing well; it was about to happen.

He took another small step forward, but as he did so his right knee met a submerged rock. Instinctively he moved his left foot forward to regain his balance, but it too hit the rock and in a split second he was toppling forward with nothing to hold on to. His arms stretched out, still holding the rod, and launched into a form of involuntary breaststroke. The cold water rushed into the front of his waders, collecting around the waistline constricted by the belt as he scrambled to find a footing that would enable him to stand, but the current and the depth of water made that impossible, and he toppled forward again.

It was then that the safety harness automatically inflated. Instinctively, Callum clutched the rod and as the water was still only waist-deep he began to push himself towards the bank with his feet.

By this time, Alastair had seen what was happening and was running down the bank towards him, shouting to Honor. For a few seconds, Callum was in real trouble, but once the harness inflated, he had more control and was soon regaining his feet and stumbling onto the pebbles.

"Shit Callum, you OK man?" asked Alastair as he took his rod from him.

"Yeah, yeah I'm fine," Callum replied tensely. He saw Honor approaching, and the fear was quickly replaced by embarrassment. "Just fancied a quick dip," he said, attempting a smile.

"Here, remove the harness, take a seat and we can get those waders off," she said.

"I went a bit too deep and clipped a rock, my own stupid fault. Thankfully I had this on." He removed the safety device, then peeled off his boots, waders and polo shirt, uncovering his bare, broad chest. Wearing just his trousers, he made his way back to the table whilst Alastair hung everything up to dry. Callum was grateful that it was a warm day; he was blushing with the attention he was getting.

He pulled on his fleece and was wondering whether he was brave enough to sit in his underpants when Alastair threw him a dry pair of jogging bottoms. "Borrow these Cal, whilst yours dry out," he said. Callum plodded into the hut to change into them. Within five minutes he was sitting dressed at the table as if nothing had happened and Alastair took his place on the river but Honor was concerned.

"There are horror stories about fishermen falling in the water in waders," she said. "It can happen so easily and the consequences can be dire. If you're going to wade that deep again, please use a wading stick to give yourself some extra balance."

Callum found an intimacy in her concern, probably imaginary, but it felt nice nonetheless.

"Aye, I definitely will do. I'll not be going anywhere near the river in this fancy-dress outfit, mind." He smiled, flicking water off his hair at her.

"Shall we take a walk and see if we can see how Sean is getting on whilst your stuff dries?" she suggested. Callum felt self-conscious about the over-sized trousers but pulled on his trainers, and with a wave to Alastair they headed upstream.

At home that night, he didn't say too much about his swim to his mum. It had shaken him up a little, but he soon put it behind him. His clothes had dried pretty quickly, so he returned home the way he had left. He had really enjoyed the day, though he wasn't sure quite why. Getting out and being by the river definitely beat another day in front of a screen.

Fishing was becoming a bit of an obsession. He thought about it a lot during the daytime, and every night when he saw what fish had been caught, he imagined catching every one of them himself. He strove to improve how he fished, aiming for straighter, longer casting in particular. And for sure, there was some subliminal connection he felt with his missing family members. But today, it was the people he had been with that occupied his mind most. Watching Alastair land that special fish in front of his own dad and the joy it brought them would have made anyone happy. Of course, there was a nagging jealousy about the fish, and subconsciously maybe even the fact that Alastair's father had been there to share it.

All of this was secondary, however, to the way he felt about spending time with Honor. They had laughed and joked as they had walked to see Sean, partly at his expense, but they just seemed to get on, and he was sorry when she had gone. He couldn't wait to see her again, and through fishing he hoped it would be soon.

CHAPTER 14

Starting a new school in Kelso five years before had been nerve-racking for Honor, but exciting at the same time. Although she had visited her Grandparents in the UK before, leaving Montreal for good was a much bigger deal. She had very little recollection of those five years living in Nigeria; most of her childhood memories were of Canada. She was nervous of the change. Initially, it had been an adventure to this strange, green and often wet land they now lived in. Their stone cottage had a large garden and was close to the river. They had spent three weeks together making it into their home and getting to know the area, but more importantly for Honor, they had got a new puppy. Any spare time she had would be spent playing with Nelly on the riverbank. It had been the best summer. But the big adventure wasn't quite so much fun to an eleven-year-old once the holidays ended and her parents started work. Life in Scotland was so different, the people were so different, she was so different. Making new friends had proven difficult, and there were times in the first term when the other pupils had made her feel unwelcome in a way only children can.

With her mum establishing herself in her new role, Honor spent more time with her father at the river. She accompanied him every Saturday and during all school holidays in that first year. Her inquisitive nature gave her a growing knowledge of salmon fishing. In the mornings, she enthusiastically and diligently set up the rods for the guests precisely the way her father had shown her. The rest of the day she patrolled the bank armed with a landing net, desperate to help. It wasn't long before this enthusiasm earned her the chance to fish when the opportunity arose, often when the estate owners were in town, or sometimes when a group could not be tempted back onto the river after the pleasure of a long lunch.

The following summer, her passion firmly established, she was becoming a very able fisherman and had caught her first fish. A photo of her adorned a prime spot on the wall of the fishing hut. As she entered her second school year, she had become more accepted and built a group of friends, but it was by the river that she felt most comfortable. This pattern continued as she became a teenager.

The previous year, Honor had worked with her father every day of the summer holiday. She had been too young to help him on the Cascapedia when they had lived in Canada and spent most of the summer in the city whilst he was based at the river camp. But in Scotland it was different, and when Billy, the head ghillie, was on his holiday, they collectively took the decision that there was no need to bring in extra cover; she handled it. To everyone's amusement, the group of guests caught more fish when with her than with her father, whose pride just about outshone his embarrassment. She was building strong relationships with the anglers, most of whom came on the same dates each season.

When, earlier in the year, her parents had first spoken about leaving the Tweed for a new opportunity near Aberdeen, she had resisted, not wanting to discuss it. But later that month, she had been persuaded to join them as they made the three-hour drive to visit Cairnton. Up until then, only Buster had visited the estate as part of the interview process and had not impressed his views on his family; he had simply said they would take a drive together. There had been little conversation during the journey, the radio providing a welcome distraction until they had passed through the estate's main entrance and followed the sweeping driveway. Honor's eyes were initially drawn to the stunning contemporary white house that reflected the bright, clean spring sunbeams, but once out of the car a gentle rumble drew her attention to the Dee behind. They had walked straight down to the river, ignoring the house, her resistance quickly dissolving as she slipped her arms through those of her parents.

Two hours later, having circled past the oil company offices to the west of the city, the car stopped at the gates of the Cult's Academy. Their excited discussion had continued until they were back in the Borders.

As it had been five years previously, the first few weeks in their new home were a delight, although Honor had a much bigger part in the packing and unpacking this time. They had set a rule that no unpacking was to happen after five o'clock, which meant the warm evenings were occupied with walks, barbecues and of course fishing, right on their doorstep. The retiring ghillie was carefully preparing Buster for the role, showing him and Honor each pool and each lie after the guests had left. It was he who had suggested that Honor might help with the beginners' fishing course that was being run, knowing they would be grateful of her expertise.

As Honor had nervously walked through the school gates, wearing her new uniform, most people had cast a glance but avoided eye contact. Cults wasn't the closest school for her, but it had been their preferred choice with her mother working nearby. Approaching the sixth form block, she recognised the two girls who had attended the intermediate course, which slightly reduced her nervousness. But it was the smiling approach of Callum that made the real difference. He had greeted her and chivalrously escorted her to the registry, introducing her to a few peers as they went. The whole occasion became less daunting. Perhaps his kindness was due to his embarrassing dip last time she had seen him. Whatever the reason, he had helped to make her first day easy and enjoyable.

The first few weeks had been uneventful. She had studied hard and had been helping on the river each Saturday. She had suffered no discrimination this time and was gradually feeling a part of the community, particularly with a group of girls who were also studying sciences. As well as socialising in school she had joined a couple of fun evening gatherings too; being at school in a city was making a big difference, at least whilst it was still summer.

She had been chatting more and more with Callum, sometimes in person and sometimes by phone. He had asked her to join him fishing on the first Thursday during half-term and for them both to go on to a birthday party in the evening. This was the very last day of the fishing season on the River Dee for the year and it had felt like a gentle way to ask her on a date, though she couldn't be sure; perhaps he was just being friendly to the new arrival. After clearing it with her parents, she had casually accepted, but for the first time in her life she had asked her mum's input on what clothes she should wear.

Honor had busied herself helping at home and on the river for the first few days of the school break. The days were shortening and becoming cooler but remained pleasant for now. Callum had met her off the bus and insisted he carry both bags back to his house. They'd dropped one off, collected his fishing gear and cheerfully made their way down to the river. The fishing seemed purely to facilitate their interaction. They had taken turns; sometimes she had given him instruction and some of the time they had just sat on the bank. She felt he was interested in her but never intrusive, and they were relaxed in each other's company.

During the afternoon she had been introduced to his grandad and they had together light-heartedly critiqued Callum's casting. The purpose of their fishing had little link to catching; it was the reason for spending time together in a beautiful location. The perfect reason.

On the journey home that evening, perhaps slightly energised by the drinks that had been provided, she had excitedly recalled it all to her father. She told him how much she was enjoying visiting and fishing different estates on the river; she had known every inch of their beat on the Tweed, but new water presented a challenge. He had gently asked about school and the friends she was making, and her positive reply seemed to be avoiding mention of the person she had last seen. "Not many are into fishing but there are a few," she had said. "Maybe we could ask one of them to come and fish with us next season if there is ever any opportunity?"

"Yes sure, dear, that would be lovely. It would be nice to meet him," was the soft reply. She smiled and looked out of the window.

CHAPTER 15

With the fishing season over for the year, Callum's attention was on rugby. He had spent much of the remaining October holiday training with the team, and as was often the case he had stopped in to see Granda on his way back. Usually, Callum would knock on the door and Granda would call him into the sitting room, but this time as he slipped off his shoes, Granda appeared in the hall, enthusiastically clutching the day's post. He bubbled with excitement.

"Have you seen this?" he asked waving the letter,

Callum had received an email the previous evening, but had yet to open it, so he shook his head.

"It's Win the Fin 2021, another new initiative from the Dee Trust," explained Granda. "Just like the introductory courses you have been on, they are launching an award for next year to encourage more fishing amongst under-eighteens. They seem to have good support from the owners and some sponsors, which has enabled them to offer a really impressive prize to the young fisherman, or woman of course, who catches salmon on the most River Dee beats throughout next year." He paused, as if to compose himself, and his smile suggested he was aware of his own exuberance.

"The winner and runner-up in the under-eighteen and under-fourteen groups receive new rods and reels from Loop, the tackle company, but the overall winner also receives a golden trophy in the shape of a salmon fin and a cheque for five thousand pounds. Now I'm not really one for competitive fishing, but this seems like a damn good idea for encouraging the youngsters off their screens and onto the river. You know how passionate I am about that, laddie."

Callum took his usual seat in the front room and accepted the letter from his grandad, reading it through carefully. As he lowered the paper he asked, "So a beat's the same as a fishery, right? How many different fisheries are there along the river, Granda?"

"Well, a fishery may have more than one beat but often they are interchanged. The contest is how many different fisheries and there must be over forty from Aberdeen all the way up to the Mar Estate above Balmoral. I've fished quite a few of them in my time and caught fish in many of them, but that was over a long period. You have to remember that the fishing can be very different between them, and each is a unique stretch of water. Take for example the Association water at Garthdee. You would have much more chance of catching fish there in late summer when the river is low and there's a stock of fish building waiting for some rain so they can continue upstream than in the spring, when they would likely swim straight through. Salmon can be fickle, but they're quite predictable in some ways. If you look at the statistics for a river you can see which parts of the river and even which estates tend to catch fish at a particular time of the year. The cost of the fishing will usually reflect this. It's quite an initiative."

"Five thousand pounds?" said Callum. That was a big number.

"Yes, it's a lot of money, but I imagine the idea is that it creates a lot of buzz through the whole season, and they must have found a supporting donor because it isn't coming from the Trust's funds. Currently there are less than fifty youth members of the ADAA, but there used to be a waiting list when I was your age. I don't know anyone who isn't keen to encourage their grandchildren to give it a go. The more people your age who get to appreciate how rewarding and relaxing fishing can be, the more awareness of the threat there is to the salmon's existence. We sometimes don't realise how we're affecting nature until it's too late – look at the damage we've caused with all the plastic in the oceans. It's only your generation that can make this change, Callum, I won't be here to do it."

"Granda, to be honest I took it all for granted," replied Callum. "I was happy walking Fergie round the park and meeting my mates there until I was forced to try fishing. Crazy that only now can I see what's pretty much on the doorstep. I've met some cool people and seen some really neat places right here in Aberdeenshire, but I also really like the fishing itself, I'm not sure why, but I feel calm when I'm in the river. I'd really like to give this competition a go."

"I would love to help you with that in any way I can," replied Granda. "The more of your age group take it up, the better for everyone. I wasn't sure about the prize when I first read about it, but now I'm starting to understand what's behind it."

"You know, you can become a millionaire just from playing video games," said Callum.

"Aye, and you can earn big money winning a TV talent contest too, that's for sure. There are also money prizes for other types of fishing, so maybe it does make sense. If it brings salmon fishing to more people's attention, that can only be a good thing. The Trust is going to run more of the learn-to-fish courses, including some specifically targeting females, and they're linking up directly with local schools too. A new series of videos will help the social media marketing campaign to draw special attention to it."

"But won't the winner just be the angler who can afford to fish the best beats at the best times?"

"Well, and I think this is incredibly positive, at the same time, they have also announced that on Saturdays in July and August next year, many of the estates are going to offer free fishing for youth members of ADAA when they have untaken rods. They're going to set up a new members' section on the ADAA website for availability and bookings – it'll go live in the new year. They're calling it the Twilight Programme and they're planning to offer it on Saturdays to ensure there's no overfishing. The river can get a good rest on a Sunday even if some beginners have been fishing on Saturday. It'll help to make up for no fishing being allowed on Sundays – it evens it up for those still at school. And don't forget, this isn't about the total number of fish caught, it's about fishing all along the River Dee. So being on a prime beat at the best time for a whole week doesn't really give an advantage."

Callum's mind was racing to process this. He was going to miss his new sport over the close season, and of course it had also been a way to bring him nearer to Honor. The chance to win such a prize added a new dimension. He started to think about the money and what it might mean, his own car even. Then he started to wonder who else might be interested by this and how great the competition could be. Would Honor take part?

"This might attract a lot of new people into trying," he said.

"Yes, but I know what you're thinking, and they've addressed that. To be able to take advantage of a free day's fishing you need to have either attended one of the Fly Fish 50 introductory courses or an ADAA one – they're going to run some of their own with special focus on safety for junior members."

At home, Callum studied the email that had come in and as he read it, he noticed another link, which was to the annual auction run to raise proceeds for the River Dee Trust. He looked through the prizes, some of which were very special, but there was one which stood out. It was the chance of a day's fishing at Balmoral for two 'rods', which he now knew meant two anglers. He looked at the photo, which showed the river beneath the famous castle. He knew exactly who he wanted to win that for. He went to speak with his mum.

Gina Rees

CHAPTER 16

Callum read the email that had been sent to junior
members of the ADAA:

The River Dee salmon fishing season opens each year
on February 1st and closes in October. The dates are
not the same for all rivers but were established historically to reflect when the salmon spawn and when new
fish usually enter the river from the sea. The Tweed,
for example, also opens on February 1st but the season
continues until the end of November as in the past fresh
fish have continued to arrive into autumn, although
this pattern has changed considerably in recent years.

For the larger rivers there is usually some form of
fanfare to mark the opening, and the Dee is no different.
In normal years, a celebrity such as Billy Connolly will
attend a gathering on the banks of the river, and a
piper will play as the celebrity tosses a dram of whisky
into the cold water and then makes the first cast.
Early February can be pretty cold in Scotland and this
year was no different. But sadly, due to the pandemic
there will to be no gathering this year to launch the
new season. All fishing is subject to very strict social
distancing restrictions only for those staying locally.

Callum had always cycled to school, even in winter, but it was dark and often treacherous in cold weather. Remote schooling meant he had avoided cycling in the recent harsh weather, but he was spending the majority of his day in front of a screen either studying or an attempt at socialising. With such short days he made use of lunchtime to get outside for exercise with Fergie in daylight.

Tuesday 2nd February was much the same as other days that year, but when Callum took his lunch upstairs to eat at his desk, he clicked his inbox and saw a new mail from the FishDee group. He read that the first fresh salmon of the season had been caught on opening day. The first fish came with a welcome trophy for the captor, who was seen releasing a sturdy salmon into the jet-black water contrasted by the snow-covered banks. The brave angler also received a bottle of malt whisky.

In addition, there was the exciting headline 'U18s TO FISH FOR FREE', and Callum read an email outlining another initiative to encourage younger anglers on the River Dee:

> As some travel restrictions are likely to continue until at least the end of April, it is anticipated that the river will be more lightly fished than normal. A number of estate owners have decided to offer the chance for anyone 18 or under to accompany an adult angler without charge. Similarly, any 16- to 18-year-old angler fishing on their own is to be offered a 50% discount for the same period. Speaking over the phone, a spokesperson said: "We recognise how difficult a time it is for younger people, unable to participate in many of the energetic sporting activities they are used to. Fishing, being a non-contact activity, is generally more socially distanced and is allowed to continue. We feel some time on the river could be valuable to the mental health of the area's youngsters and this is a small step to support them.

Callum decided to call Granda, who despite cancellation of the opening event on Monday 1ˢᵗ February, had been invited by one of the estates to join them on the opening day and to fish himself, but he remained largely isolated by himself indoors.

"Hi Granda, just seen they caught a fish at Park yesterday, that could have been you!" said Callum.

"Hello there Callum. Aye, it could have been twenty years ago when I didn't mind losing the feeling in my feet standing in that icy water. How's the home schooling?"

"Aye it's OK, but just so damn monotonous. I seem to be looking at a screen all the time I'm awake, and unlike last summer it isn't because I'm gaming. I'm really looking forward to this Saturday. There's no rugby training at the moment, so fishing is one of my only outdoor pleasures. I've just seen the announcement that many of the rivers are offering discounted fishing for under-eighteens, which is great. It's a shame you can't join on Saturday, but it is definitely best you stay indoors. Hopefully we can get out together soon. What set-up do you think I am going to need for Saturday?"

"Ah dinna worry about me, you get on and have an enjoyable day outside, I'll be watching the rugby and waiting for you to tell me all about it afterwards with some photos! Early season is very different to how you were fishing last year. Fish that enter the river system in the first few months of the year are known as springers and they're very special fish. It's without doubt when the salmon are in their finest condition and they certainly are revered. The UK is about the only place in the world where you can fish for Atlantic salmon at this time of year and normally passionate anglers from all over the world will visit Scotland in the hope of catching a springer. The River Dee has long had the reputation of being the best spring river. In 1980 there were ten thousand salmon caught by rod on the Dee, of which seventy-five per cent were before July, incredible huh?

"If you bear in mind that in 1980 most of these were killed so no fish was caught twice and that there were also thousands of fish being netted near the estuary, then you get an idea of how many fish were in the system. Last year, with no netted fish and all caught fish released, the total number was just three thousand, and only thirty per cent are caught February to June. That's a change from seven thousand five-hundred to nine-hundred in a single generation, and as I said it's probably even more extreme than that, given the catch and release programme. If they aren't successful and the numbers continue to fall it will be like a blocked artery for the region. The salmon are the red blood cells that surge upstream and to the mountains above Balmoral."

Just then he was overtaken by a fit of coughing, and it took him a few moments to clear it before he could continue.

"Anyhow, how are you going to catch your first springer? Let's think about that. Well, the water is real cold, which keeps the fish deep – you very rarely see them jumping until it warms up. This means you need to get your fly down to them by using a sinking line. The ghillie will no doubt help you, but you do have some sinking lines in the tackle I gave you. Casting a sinking line is a bit trickier than using the floating lines of warmer weather so you'll need to practise – maybe you can try in the park before you go. Then you need to select a fly that's also going to sink so it gets down to where the fish are. It'll need to be easy to see even if the water's a bit cloudy and be the right shape to tempt a springer. The most reliable spring fly is known as the Dee Monkey and there's one in your kit. How does that sound?"

"That all sounds OK and I don't think there will be anyone daft enough to be in the park this week, so I'll try and practise as you suggested. Thanks Granda, I'll be in touch soon."

Callum did practise in the park that Wednesday, in a strong easterly wind and some sleet. Once he had got the hang of the heavy line, he tried practising into the wind, knowing that a similar wind on Saturday would be right upriver, making casting difficult. Although it was different from fishing on water, when the drag of the water on the line forms an anchor, it was still good practice. The first cast he tried, the line came back and almost wrapped around his upper body. Thankfully he had no hook on the line. Gradually he adjusted his technique and kept the rod tip a bit lower, forcing the line forward under the wind. It was neither elegant nor artistic, but it worked, so he felt more confident as he returned home to thaw out.

That evening as they sat down to her cottage pie, Mary placed a photo of Callum's father on the table. Again, he was beside a river.

"It would have been your dad's fifty-fourth birthday today, son," she said softly. "Hard to believe it was nearly twelve years ago. He would have been so excited at the start of a new season and the chance to fish with you both. For many people, late January's the toughest time of the year, but if you're a salmon fisherman there's the excitement of a new season, no matter how foul the weather. We would always get together for a Burns supper and all the chat would be about the start of the season, it was the same for your Granda too. Your dad was born on a Friday and was a couple of days late, and that was a huge relief to Granda as he was nervous that he might miss opening day, although I'm pretty sure he would have made it to the river at some stage even if his only child had just been born! Let's give him a call after we have eaten, he would appreciate that, I'm sure."

Involuntarily, Callum placed his hand on her wrist. "Are you OK talking about him and Finlay, Mum? We never really did until recently."

"Yes dearie, I'm OK and think I should have done more talking. I wouldn't have counselling, just cocooned myself with you, Granda and Nanna until the pain got a little better. Sometimes I still cry, but the closer you and I are the less that happens."

He squeezed her arm with a smile, which she returned, and they ate, occasionally glancing at the photo in an awkward silence.

On Thursday and Friday the snow was so bad that Callum only left the house briefly to take Fergie out. It was boring; he got his work done easily and watched a new Netflix series and some YouTube videos. He didn't even have a sibling to mess about with, so the days passed with virtually zero contact. He had been really struggling in January; he felt he ought to be with his mates and was desperate to see Honor. They had been chatting more and more and their friendship had grown, but he wanted to take it further. They had become close, and their chats seemed more intimate. Fishing was a crucial distraction for him, and there was no knowing when school would restart, let alone when he would be able to have fun again. He was not alone in this; his whole school year felt lost, but at least he had his fishing and the contact it gave him with her.

Honor had said she was going to try and meet him at the river on Saturday. The Invery and Tilquhillie fishing hut was a few miles outside Banchory. It was a decent bike ride, even in good conditions, and it would be even trickier with the snow on the ground, but he would have walked it if it had been the only way to see her. A few hours fishing in the freezing cold was such an adventure, and the fact that she would be with him made it seem crucial that he should get there.

On the Saturday, as the days were still short, he was able to have breakfast and a hot drink with his mum before leaving at first light as she had agreed.

"You be careful on that bike, it's icy out there and the gritters may not have covered all the roads," said his mum. "Please be sure to leave before four o'clock Callum, I really want you home in daylight, love."

He tightened a scarf across his face and put on a bobble hat and gloves for the journey. It was really cold, yet it was such a release to be off on an adventure rather than facing another monotonous day indoors.

Thankfully the roads were clear of snow and although he had lights on his bike they weren't really needed. Before long he had passed the Academy and was onto the North Deeside Road, where there was very little traffic, which was probably the result of a combination of lockdown and the wintry weather. He felt strangely alive and energised, a feeling amplified by the occasional excitement of his back wheel skidding in the slush.

He crossed the Dee and pedalled along the south side until he got to the fishery entrance, then freewheeled down to the stone hut. Despite the cold and a strong breeze, it wasn't too unpleasant a morning, as there was some sunshine. He leaned his bike against the rod rest, placed his rucksack with the rod attached onto the floor and tapped on the door of the hut. He could see smoke coming from its chimney.

"Morning, morning Callum, good to see you," said Colin, the ghillie, as he opened the door, and they did an awkward bumping of elbows in the absence of the traditional handshake. "You're the only one brave enough to come today."

"Morning Colin," replied Callum. "I'm not sure about February fishing!" he said with a smile and a theatrical shiver.

"Aye, and I'm afraid you probably won't get fishing for a while yet as there's so much grue on the water." Callum eyed up the rafts of slush and ice that were floating downstream, clearly due to the extreme temperatures. "With this sun, it should be a bit clearer in a couple of hours and we'll be OK, but it's not worth it now as it'll just get under your line."

Callum was a little shocked. He was now stuck where he was until the river warmed up a little. If it hadn't been for the chance to meet Honor he would have called it off; she was getting a lift to

Invery mid-morning when her mother was doing her grocery shop.

Noticing his dilemma, Colin said, "You can sit in the hut and watch me tie a couple of flies if you like? I've a fire going, so you'll nae freeze at least." This sealed it and they moved inside and sat at opposite ends of a large table, with a funny-looking vice between them.

Colin proceeded to talk him through the steps to tying a salmon fly. It was extremely intricate, each piece a work of art. As he proceeded with his creation, their conversation widened, with Callum sharing the background on his introduction to salmon fishing, and before long he had discovered another link to his father and Granda. There seemed to be an ongoing fabric between many individuals and families knitted by the river and the salmon that ran it.

As he listened intently to Colin's reminiscing, they heard the approach of a car along the gravel and Callum dashed outside to see Honor arriving.

"Mrs Garba, pleased to meet you," he said to Honor's mum through the car window as politely as he could.

"And you too Callum. Now have a good catch-up you guys, I know you've hardly seen anyone all year. I'll be back in about an hour and a half. Try and stay warm!"

As the car left, Callum introduced Honor to Colin, then informed him that they were going to take a walk along the riverbank and would be back to try and fish in a while. They set off, slightly awkwardly, heading downstream towards the bright sun. As they crunched through the snow their conversation was a little stilted initially, but before long they became more relaxed. The river appeared to be carved in black through the white landscape, and theirs were the first footprints on the snow.

They walked for over a mile and as time passed the conversation flowed more easily, Callum's humour came through. Responding to one comment, Honor pushed him in jest, and he threw his arms round her in retaliation. She did not withdraw, and he kept his arm round her as they continued their walk, eventually reaching the end of the beat, where they leaned on the fence and looked across the river to the sunlit far bank.

Honor turned towards Callum and without a word he kissed her, just as he had imagined he would since the day he had first seen her six months before. She tugged his jacket towards her as they separated, looking up at him with a smile. Then she put her arm through his and they began to walk back to the hut. The angst of the previous month had disappeared for a while, but they did not want to think about how much longer it would go on; they were simply enjoying this chance to be together.

"Fishing is allowed," he said. "It's a form of exercise, same as walking. So, if we fish together, we can see each other. Maybe we can try and do that on Saturdays?"

"I would love that. We just need to keep the kissing out of sight!" giggled Honor as they approached the hut. As she still had a little time, she helped Callum to set up his rod. After chatting with Colin, they attached the heavy sinking tip to the line that he had discussed with Granda and the Dee Monkey fly.

"Good luck," she whispered with a smile as she made her way to the waiting car. "Bye Colin."

"She seems like a nice lass," said Colin. "Her dad's the new ghillie at Cairnton, you say? I'll look out for him at the next ghillie meeting."

With the car out of sight, Callum's focus returned to fishing, and after putting the safety float over his head he followed the ghillie to the river.

"Right Callum, the water's much clearer now," said Colin. "Let's see if we can get you your first Dee springer and make a start in the Win the Fin competition. This lovely big pool here flows straight into another one with the river at this height and you have them both to yourself. You know what you're doing, no need to wade very deep here, keep the fly moving and I'm sure you'll find him." Having given this advice, Colin said goodbye and made his way back to the hut, his vice and importantly, the fire.

There was a strong wind, but it was no worse than it had been when Callum had practised in the park. He began to roll out the big fly on the heavy line, adding more line each cast until he was rolling out about two rod lengths. He was excited and focused to the extent that he was not feeling the bitter cold on his hands, and he felt the happiest he had been for months.

After about twenty minutes the line went taut, and Callum's pulse raced for a moment until he realised the heavy fly had caught on a rock. He was able to detach it from the snag and continue. The February sun had just about made it above the treeline, which began to warm both water and angler, and it was beautifully peaceful with just the sound of the current and occasionally a gust of wind.

Callum had now got into a nice rhythm with his casting and was enjoying the tranquillity of being there to such a degree that when the line tightened again, he was mildly irritated at the interruption. But then he recognised the tell-tale pulse of live resistance, and without thinking he slowly lifted the rod in opposition. He was in.

Fish and angler were matched for a few moments, and then the fish made a break for it across and downstream. Callum allowed it to pull some line from the reel, but it did not go far and he was able to reel it back to the original lie quite quickly. After another tussle, he was able to draw it gradually towards him. The fish stayed quite deep, not splashing on the surface like the one he had caught in August, nor did it shake its head quite so vigorously, which no doubt reflected the low water temperature. After a few minutes he felt he was in control and began to guide the fish towards the shore.

Thankfully, just then Colin arrived by his side with a net, which he slid under the fish in a single motion. Callum laid his rod on the bank and crouched down to see the fish in the net.

"See how slim the fish is compared to usual?" asked Colin.

"Yes, it's head looks almost too big for the body," replied Callum, "but it's nice and silver, the autumn mating colours are gone."

"Aye, this one spawned a couple of months ago and it's now on its way back to sea. We call such a fish a kelt. It's a nice, well-mended one but unfortunately these are not considered the same as a fish that is yet to spawn and is heading upstream. We often catch kelts in February and March, both male and female, as they can be quite aggressive takers when they're rebuilding their energy before returning to the sea. Let's pop her back and see if there's a springer in here. We've caught a couple this week from this pool."

The kelt swam sharply off, seemingly unaffected by the previous five minutes, and Callum continued. He was pleased to have connected with a fish but determined to get his season properly off the mark, especially after he had braved such conditions.

After ten minutes, they reached a place where the river turned towards the left, which created deeper water on Callum's bank.

"This can be a hot spot," said Colin. "Let it swing right the way in here, he might just be waiting by that big rock." Not a single fish had moved over the past two hours, in contrast to last autumn. It was like a different river in a different land.

"Just give the line a little mend now, slow it down a little," said Colin. Callum did so and the line swung straight and slow until it was nearing the bank, when it happened just as Colin had predicted. Clunk, then another clunk as the line tightened up.

"Kelt again?" said Callum in nervous excitement, but before Colin could answer the fish twisted and steamed across the current and downstream, and he heard the wonderful sound of line being torn from the reel. The fish fought well, tirelessly tearing across the river like a dragon with fins.

Just when Callum believed it was ready to be netted, as if reading his mind, it made a strong and steady break downstream and charged off round the bend into the next pool. Callum followed it, desperately trying to keep the line away from the prominent rocks. He longed to see the fish, but it remained low in the water as he carefully pursued it. This pool was open and wider, and the fish surged to the middle, making a desperate break for freedom. Callum's heart was thumping, his focus acute as he kept the pressure up. Slowly the fish began to weaken. As Callum reeled in line, it finally rose to the surface and they caught a glimpse of it in a silvery-white swirl.

"Now bring him to me," said Colin through his smile, and Callum stepped back, drawing the fish to the net. As the water was quite deep, the ghillie gently placed the net onto the snowy bank. Callum looked down on the iridescent salmon, which was shaped like a torpedo and almost seemed to be snarling as it thrashed its tail. The background of snow emphasised the fish's beauty.

"That, lad, is your first spring salmon, and a cracker at that," said Colin. "Ten pounds of pure muscle that has just arrived in the river. Fresh as paint he is, well done." He drew the hook from the fish's mouth. "Now gently get him back in the water and I'll take a photo."

Nervously and carefully, Callum stepped into the river, then lifted the fish with both hands and lowered it to the surface, where he paused briefly for the picture. Then he held it facing into the current and gently released his grip, watching its gills pumping. Despite the coldness of the water, he could have knelt there for hours, feeling the firmness of the salmon against his hands. But after a few seconds, the salmon was ready and with a flick of its tail it shot back towards the deeper water.

Callum felt slightly high as he stepped back onto the bank and smiled at Colin, it seemed almost surreal. There was a perfect silence as they both absorbed the moment.

"Time for another?" asked the grinning ghillie.

"No, I think that's the ideal time to finish, and I can make sure I'm home for the game if we pack up now," replied Callum. They chatted about rugby and Scotland's chances as they walked back to the hut. Callum took his rod down whilst Colin made a hot drink and shared the photo with him. Before setting off, Callum sent the photo to Honor with the message, 'The perfect day x'.

Safely back home, he hugged his mum and mischievously placed his freezing fingers on the back of her neck. She squealed. "It's fresh out there, Mum," he said. "But guess what?"

"You got to see Honor?"

"Not only did I get to see her, but I caught a springer, a real Dee springer! I can't wait to tell Granda!" He headed upstairs with a huge smile across his face.

"Well done, son!" his mum called up after him.

The first thing he did was to log into the website and record his catch by uploading the photo and a few details. He then saw his name appear in the summary table at the top: 'Callum Anderson – 6/2/21 Invery.' He opened his phone and Facetimed his Granda, finishing just in time to watch the England v Scotland game on the TV. Scotland had not won at Twickenham for nearly forty years and despite having a strong team they were not expected to do any better this year.

Two hours later he sent another message: 'OMG Honor, it got even better!' Almost instantly he received a reply: 'Well done!'

Gina Rees

CHAPTER 17

Callum spent most of the following day either reading about the Scotland team's victory or looking at the photo of himself holding his springer. He had decided to post it on his story and was surprised how strong the response was. Maybe it reflected how little people were currently doing, but there was a long string of messages of encouragement.

The Win the Fin contest had attracted a lot of interest, no doubt due to the prize, with articles in all local and many national publications. There were links across social media to the many courses being run and with this first catch, Callum's season was under way. And so, vicariously, was Granda's. He made Callum recount the whole experience twice, and there was a childish, excitable tone to his questions. There was certainly no resistance from Callum as he provided all the details of the take, the fight and the landing.

The weather forecast was bleak for the coming week, with lots of snow and lower temperatures. He had been chatting with Honor to arrange another get-together, but they agreed that the coming Saturday would be impossible and were focusing instead on the following one. They were trying to decide where would be the best place to try and fish. Park could be ideal, as it was pretty much equidistant between their homes. There was always a chance to catch on that estate in the spring, and the price was not too high. They could return to Invery, but Callum wanted to make further progress in the competition. Although early-season salmon fishing was not extortionately expensive it still added up, especially for sixteen-year-olds. As a member, he could fish the ADAA water for free, but that was too far for Honor to travel and anyway most salmon would pass straight through the lower part of the river in spring.

They could try and take advantage of the two-for-one spring fishing promotion, but Honor had a plan. Many of the regular February bookings had cancelled this year, which created the unusual situation of there being very few people fishing at Cairnton over the coming weeks. Honor's father had suggested that she should invite Callum and his Granda to fish as his guests on Saturday 20th February. Granda knew all about Cairnton; it was one of the most famous estates on the river, not least because it was generally regarded as the home of modern salmon fishing. A hundred years ago, Arthur Wood had perfected new techniques in the process of banking over three thousand fish. Granda had offered to drive Callum, as cycling just wouldn't be an option this time.

That week the weather was even more extreme than forecast. The whole region was hit by two feet of snow amidst sub-zero temperatures. In Braemar, the temperature fell as low as -23°C, the lowest in the UK for twenty-five years. The weather created a lockdown of its own, and it was not until Saturday that Callum braved the conditions to take lunch for Granda as they watched Scotland narrowly lose the rugby.

Apart from all the snow lying outside, the following week started as all others had that year with Callum studying from his bedroom. He was so looking forward to seeing Honor again on the coming Saturday and excited about fishing at Cairnton that he applied himself to his studies with extra energy. They had been chatting regularly, and by Wednesday Callum could think of nothing else.

He checked the river levels and could see the height was similar to when he had fished at Invery, so he assumed he would be using the same fishing approach. He had discussed this with Granda the previous Saturday and sent him a message to say that was his plan.

The reply caught him completely off-guard. 'Have you taken a look at the forecast, Callum?'

He quickly opened the weather app on his phone to see that for Friday and Saturday there was an amber warning for rain in the area, which he knew meant the river would flood. He nearly threw his phone at the wall. He called Honor and told her that he didn't think Saturday would be possible, not only because the river would be high, but because he didn't feel he could ask Granda to drive him out in such bad weather.

Out of their frustration, Honor hatched an idea. Neither of them had lessons on Tuesday afternoons as this would normally be for sports, so maybe Callum could head over when he finished at twelve and they would still have a few hours. She would check with her father when he was home from work, and at the same time Callum would check if that would work for Granda.

With huge relief, both answers were positive. They were going to be able to meet, if just a couple of days later than planned.

By Saturday, as they had expected, the river was in flood. The rain didn't stop and not only was it racing off the hills into the main river, but it was also melting the lying snow. On Sunday morning, photos were appearing on social media of the river reaching heights in excess of thirteen feet. Boats were damaged and huts flooded. When the rain finally subsided and the river began to drop a little, tree trunks were left stranded on the banks where the high water had reached. Some of the scenes were difficult to comprehend.

Callum watched a video from the Banchory beat where he had

attended the courses, and it looked more like the Amazon than the Dee. Whole trees were floating past and the raging torrent had risen close to the level of the hotel car park. He wondered how much damage such a flood would do; would it scoop out pools and change all the usual salmon haunts? What about upstream, where the eggs were hatching in the redds, those nests the female digs? Would they all get washed away and add further pressure to the salmon's survival? Only time would really give the answers. At least the rain had been replaced by blustery sunshine which looked like it would hold for the coming days, and slowly the water was escaping into the North Sea.

Callum could see Granda's black Fiesta parked in the street below his bedroom window as he impatiently awaited the end of the online lesson. Bang on twelve o'clock he turned off the screen, ran downstairs, shouted goodbye to his mum and collected his bags from the hallway. He put the bags on the back seat and bounced into the front with a broad grin.

"I've never seen anyone so excited at the prospect of fishing a flooded river before," said Granda as they headed west along Auchinyell road. He very well knew Callum's real motivation. "I checked this morning, and it's still six feet, might be more like casting practice today. But it's a treat to be out of my front room and to get some fresh air by the water. Our own fishing bubble."

"What are the tactics if the river is really high, Granda?"

"When the river's higher, the current flows much faster, which can push the fish towards the slower, sheltered water closer to the bank. The higher the water, the more they will seek protection or risk being flushed downstream. But as well as the water height, the colour in the water is very important. I don't mind fishing in high water if it's running clear, you have a good idea which pockets the fish will be hiding in and they can see your fly. But when you have cloudy, brown water, it's a real challenge to get the fish to see your fly. You have to go big and bright or use a spinner, if allowed of course."

Callum nodded thoughtfully as they drove on along North Deeside Road past Crathes Castle. There was only the odd patch of snow remaining, but all the fields looked very wet.

Granda knew exactly where they were going and a few minutes past Banchory they turned off the A93. The drive took them between grand estate gates and through immaculate grounds. As they passed the main house, they could see the river in front of them, swollen and angry. Much of the debris Callum had seen on the photos had been cleared up, but a clear line of smaller deposits proclaimed the high-water mark.

They followed this further upstream before arriving at the main hut. Buster's truck was parked outside, and he stepped out to greet them from across the car park. His broad frame was quite imposing, but there was a warm smile on his kind face.

"Good afternoon gentlemen, lovely to see you, so pleased you could still make the trip. I've had nobody here for a few days, understandably. It was a serious flood, not quite as big as Storm Frank five years ago from what I'm told, but still a proper one. It's going to take a bit longer to clear it up. I nearly lost my boat too – it had been lifted from way up the bank and was bobbing in the middle of the deluge on Sunday morning. I'd have lost my job if it had ended up in Aberdeen." He gave a deep, friendly laugh. "It'll take a bit of luck to find him today, but you know what they say, you can't catch fish if your line isn't in the water.

"It'll be fishing from the bank only, it's too dangerous to get in the water just now and not necessary anyway, so there's no need for waders unless you prefer them. Honor has suggested Callum try in the Grey Mare first as she's going to head up from the house and meet you there shortly. Donald, you are most welcome to give the Ferrochs a go, probably start with the middle as it's too high for the upper. It isn't nearly as cloudy as it was yesterday, and it's dropping quite fast, so you never know. Heavy tips and a big, bright fly would be my suggestion."

"Sounds great," replied Callum and opened the rear door to grab his bags.

"You know, Buster, I think I'll just take a seat at the table outside the hut with a cup of tea and enjoy the scenery," said Granda. "Maybe I'll have a go later, but I'm a most contented chauffeur for the time being with my tea and my newspaper. I'm saving myself for the trip to Balmoral in April that the lad has kindly arranged. Hopefully the snow will have gone by then at least."

"I don't blame you at all, Donald. Once he's set up the rod, I'll take Callum down to the Grey Mare, then I need to head to the other side to cut up a tree that's blocking the bank. I'll soon be back and it'd be lovely to have a chat with you, I understand you've caught more fish on this river than most." He turned to Callum, who was trying to choose the right fly. "How about that gold-bodied Willie Gunn?" he said. "That's bright and sparkly for sure."

Once Callum had secured the fly, they attached his rod to the holders on the truck roof. "You'll have to jump in the back, Callum," said Buster. "We're doing all we can to limit contact, so the hut's closed and no passengers in the cab." But there was no opposition as Callum said goodbye to Granda and excitedly leapt into the open back of the truck.

It was only a four-hundred-metre ride down to the start of the pool, and he bounced out once they had parked and retrieved the rod. Buster led him down to the river's edge and talked him through how to cover the river with his fly. He was to make sure he let the line swing right the way back in before retrieving. It was a nice long pool, so he could work his way down and they would meet up again, with Honor too, at the main hut around two o'clock.

Callum began to cast, with supportive encouragement from Buster before he departed. It was a bit different casting from the bank as you needed to make sure you didn't hook the grass behind you, but without the need to cast very far, he mastered it quickly. It was comfortingly warm in the sunshine, and he was soon absorbed and gradually making his way downstream until his concentration was broken by a call; it was Honor's voice. He turned to see that she was close; the sound of the rushing river had hidden her approach.

He reeled in the line just as she arrived. She lifted her head to kiss him, but only succeeding in bumping his forehead with the brim of her cap. They laughed, and she threw the cap on the floor theatrically before trying again. Neither of them wanted it to end.

"Here, leave the rod against the tree and come with me, I've got something to show you," said Honor. She took his hand and led him back the way she had come. They chatted cheerfully as they strolled along the bank in just their trainers. As they rounded a left-hand bend in the river, they arrived at another hut that was near to the main house, and Honor opened the door.

"This is the famous Cairnton rod room," she said. "You can see here all the instruments and records from Arthur Wood's years. It's been closed to visitors for some time, but I know where the key is." She removed her sunglasses and raised just one eyebrow. This drove him crazy, and they embraced passionately. Their kisses were deeper, their hands explored further. Callum's cold hands reached the strap of her bra before she withdrew smiling. She guided his flustered attention to the items in the room, but he could not concentrate. Fascinating as they were, Callum's attention was on Honor, and they kissed again before she led him reluctantly back to the river.

As they walked back to the Grey Mare, Callum plucked up

enough courage to ask the question he had practised. "So, are we together now?"

"Does that mean you are asking me out, Callum Anderson?"

"Yeah, I guess it does."

"Then yes, we are together," she said. She kissed him again briefly and then ran ahead to collect the rod. "C'mon then, show me how you cast this." She thrust it back to him before walking twenty metres downstream, sitting on a rock and looking back at him like a judge at a diving competition.

It was the left bank, so he could cast right-handed, and for the next fifteen minutes he did a pretty decent job rolling the heavy line out just ten metres and letting it swing right back in.

"Very good, student," Honor commented. "Keep the rod a bit higher as you finish the cast, but that's enough for now, let's go and see how your grandad is." They walked back to the hut, where Granda had now set up his deckchair and was looking very settled.

"Just been watching those courting goldeneye ducks, funny things they are," he said as they approached. "Hello Honor dear. Have you been lucky, lad?"

Callum knew he was referring to the fishing and felt it would be safer not to mention the rod room. "Nah, we gave it a go in the Grey Mare but no contact so far. I'll just get our lunch Granda, you chat with Honor and please behave," he said with a smile.

As Callum was returning with the lunch-bag from Granda's car, Buster's truck arrived, and he joined them on the terrace outside the main hut. They chatted as they ate, and before long the two adults were passionately discussing the current state of Atlantic salmon, particularly in the Dee.

It was at this point that Honor's phone rang and as she stood to take the call Callum asked Buster if he might have another cast. Buster encouraged him to start about a hundred metres downstream in a pool known as the Middle Ferroch. He pointed out the starting place and suggested he should tie on something even bigger from his fly-box. Callum lifted out what looked like a large Dee Monkey, but with the long tail of a Sunray Shadow. "Let's give that a go, with a size eight double hook, if he's there, he ought to see that," said Buster with a chuckle.

Callum quickly changed the fly and headed down to the pool. There was a single tree with an inbuilt seat that marked the start of the pool, and Callum was straight into his casting, trying to adjust the rod position a little, as Honor had suggested. He really liked wading in a river and feeling the water pressing his legs, but it was quite liberating to fish in normal clothes from the bank for a change. The line was going out nicely and the big fly was making quite a splash when it landed, but with the river so full it probably didn't make much difference.

After a few minutes, he walked along the bank and stepped onto a big rock that formed a small point next to the water's edge. He made a short cast and let it come back into the bank, then pulled out another arm's length of line before casting again. He liked the angle the line was moving across the current, but it felt a bit too fast, so next cast as the line landed at forty-five degrees, he gave it a mend to slow it a little. He looked up the bank to see if anyone was watching, but the men seemed engrossed in conversation and Honor had her back to him, still on the phone.

He was still twisted round and looking upstream at her when the rod was nearly yanked from his hand by a huge take. He turned as the line momentarily loosened again and a split second later the line tore from the reel as the fish moved away from the bank into the fast current. He lifted the tip and felt the power and pressure through the tight line as the rod bent over in a savage arc. He could do very little other than maintain the pressure as he watched the end of his fly-line heading straight downstream. The force was relentless, and Callum knew this wasn't sustainable; he was going to run out of line. He turned and shouted towards the hut but could not get their attention as the river drowned his call.

Moving downstream, Callum applied more pressure to try to resist the fish's run, and after some time, thankfully, it seemed to take a breather and hold in the current about seventy metres away.

He held the rod with his left hand and lifted his phone from his pocket. "Hey Siri, call Honor Garba," he said. He watched her as she lifted the phone from her ear to see who was calling and instantly looked downstream, recognising what was happening as he waved to her.

After replacing the phone and with both hands on the rod, Callum slowly walked towards the fish. Each step allowed him to retrieve some of the line, until when he was about thirty metres away it started to move towards him, so he was able to reel more line in without moving. Despite the strength of the current, the salmon steadily motored upstream past him until it was close to where he had hooked it. He walked upstream towards it, gaining line as he went. He was close to the fish now as the junction of the sinking line was running through the rod eyes. Feeling confident, he applied extra pressure on the fish he had now been fighting for ten minutes, but it bored away again into the murky flow and went quickly back downstream. Callum's reel shrieked again in reverse and his arms were starting to ache.

"Well, I never," said Buster as they arrived. "Look at him go!" They slowly stepped back downstream whilst Callum tussled with the salmon. "It's not going to be straightforward landing him with the river this high, but let's see if we can get him into this little bay and I'll try and net him below," said Buster.

Callum looked at Honor. She gave a wide, confident smile and clasped her hands as if to say 'finish the job'. Next to her, with a scarf wrapped tightly round his neck, was Granda, brimming with a look of pride that Callum had never seen before.

Callum slowly lifted the rod towards the upright position and pulled the fish gradually towards him. In his mind, he wanted to show the salmon that the fight was over, that he was the stronger and it was time to surrender. At first it was like trying to budge a sofa, but it became easier and he built up a little momentum. As he wound the line in, the nylon leader emerged from the water and he knew the fish was almost in sight. Then they saw the stunning chrome outline appear as the fish's handsome head broke the surface. At last Callum steered it to the ghillie's waiting net in a single movement.

"Good lad!" cheered Granda, and Callum carefully laid his rod on the bank. The big fly looked like a cigar draped from the corner of the salmon's mouth as Buster smoothly unhooked it. Callum crouched down next to the recovering fish, speechless. Buster quickly weighed it at fourteen pounds. It was certainly his biggest but catching it in these circumstances felt unreal and dreamy.

He stared at the brown pectoral fin, as big as a scallop shell against the chalky white flank. Then he glared at the mighty paddle of a tailfin that had propelled it on an incredible journey since it had been born in this very river just a few years ago. Maybe it had even been an egg that survived Storm Frank five years ago. All the angst of the previous few months was dissolved by the wonder of the moment as he reached down to the fish. With one hand firmly round the wrist of the tail and the other gently supporting its belly, he lifted it for Honor's camera and then placed it back into the net so Buster could safely release it away from the bank.

Callum sat down on a large grey rock a metre up the bank, flexing his aching arm and watching the fish disappear into the cloudy water. Honor joined him, placing an arm round him and kissing his cheek. It might have looked like a friendly gesture to an onlooker, but there was much more to it. Communicating through their computers was one thing, but nothing could replace physical, social contact and these last two meetings on the river had meant so much.

Granda looked over. "You're a lucky bugger, Callum lad," he called, and they all knew he was not just referring to the salmon.

Buster could not stop himself laughing. It started as a chuckle, then erupted into a guffaw. "Talk about finding a needle in a haystack. That's the biggest fish we've had all year and the river's six feet high," he said. "That's one to remember, Callum. Well done, there's plenty of folk wouldn't have even tried."

Callum felt intoxicated with happiness and grinned in delighted disbelief. "That feeling, when you get the first pull from something on the end of your line, there really is nothing like that," he said. "That's the bit I imagine when I'm fishing and the bit I remember before sleep."

"The tug is the drug, that's what they say," replied Buster.

"Ain't that true," was Callum's reply. "I'm addicted!"

They stayed chatting by the Middle Ferroch until the sun dipped behind the tops of the conifers, by which time the temperature had dropped sharply, then made their way back to the hut. Nobody had felt motivated to try for another fish; lightning wouldn't strike twice today. For a moment nobody spoke; the only sound was the rushing water.

"You'll be top of the board I would think Callum, won't be many more fish caught this last week," said Buster as they loaded their bags into Granda's car.

"Maybe Buster, all thanks to you. I'd be pretty happy if every Tuesday afternoon was like this, it beats geography homework." He couldn't help opening his phone once more. "I've got a new picture for my profile." He tilted the screen to show Buster; his face held an expression of the kind that usually accompanied someone showing off an image of their newborn baby. Honor squeezed between them, and Callum gave her an awkward farewell embrace. "My turn to arrange fishing next time," he said, and he reached for the passenger door handle.

On the journey home, the conversation turned to their trip to Balmoral. With a lot of help from his mum, Callum had been successful in the auction. Although it was still two months away, they were both already excited. What would the weather be like, how high would the river be, would there be fish that far upstream by then? Salmon fishing had very quickly got under Callum's skin. He was swiftly learning the language and all the peculiarities that came with it, including the habitual checking of weather forecasts, river heights and recent catches that infect so many.

When the weekly email came out the following Sunday, he had moved ahead in the competition, as his fish had indeed been the only catch of the previous week. Catching two in February was no mean feat. If he could keep this up, there really was a chance.

CHAPTER 18

It was natural that John would become a ghillie on the River Dee. He had spent much of the previous fifty years either fishing or helping others to fish on the Dee and the Don. Having completed a full career as a policeman, he had become the part-time ghillie at Crathes Castle, where he worked from February to July. This suited him perfectly as it left him the second half of the year for his own fishing, although it was apparent to all who knew him that he took more pleasure in helping a newcomer to catch than in landing one himself. Whilst there were more experienced ghillies on the river, there were none more respected, despite his humble nature.

The owners of the Crathes Castle fishing had generously made the beat available for three days of Easter fishing that targeted specific groups. On Thursday they had hosted the 'Dee Damsels', a group set up to encourage more women to fish the Dee, and it had been quite a party, as usual. The group had been on great form, listening to the instruction carefully, practising diligently and enthusiastically putting it into practice to great effect. That one of them had caught her first-ever spring salmon was the icing on the cake. Netting that fish had given John huge pleasure. But within twenty-four hours, it had been topped. The previous day they had hosted a group of under-sixteens whose enthusiasm had been at times uncontrollable. Everything about the day had involved excitement; whenever a fish had splashed there were yells, and when twelve-year-old Evie Kemp had hooked and landed a nine-pounder from the Birkenbaud pool just after lunch the whole group had shared in her success. This made her equal top of the under-sixteen Win the Fin trophy, and John was certain she was hooked for life.

Today was dedicated to the under-eighteens, and John knew by the messages he had been receiving that there were some experienced fishermen amongst them. Several of the registered names matched those on the Win the Fin leader board too. The conditions remained favourable; there was a good height of water with a pleasantly warm air temperature and very little wind. With the clock change, he was still able to arrive and take that first walk with Tweed, his confusingly named Golden Labrador, along the bank as the sun awoke. It would be a couple more weeks before the sun started to beat him to the river but by then a huge variety of wonderful wildflowers would be coming through. It wouldn't be long before the swifts arrived, swirling around the river surface scooping up flies.

There was no need to provide equipment today, just instructions and guidance, so there had been no rush to prepare. He placed the urn of hot coffee on the outside table just as the first car approached along the track to the hut. Within ten minutes there were six cars, all at various stages of unloading as the teenage anglers deposited their bags and rods in front of the hut.

After introductions and welcomes they set about assembling their rods whilst the parents chatted over coffee. John spoke at length with Callum's grandad, whom he knew well, whilst Alastair's father introduced himself to Honor's mother. After a few minutes, John called the group together, but just as he was preparing to address them, they were interrupted by the arrival of a green Land Rover Defender containing James and another lad. He waited for them to join.

"Right, you're all here now," began John. "Welcome to Crathes Castle, one of the prime spring beats on the river. Delighted to have you here. I know you'll be keen to get started but let me run through some details." He explained the safety guidance and gave a broad outline of the day. "We have eight here and ye'll be fishing as pairs, so if you want to couple up that would be good. Say goodbye to your parents and I'll start to deploy each pair on a different pool spread along the bank. We have more than two miles of fishing, so there is plenty of space. Once you've each fished through a pool you'll then move downstream to the next. All clear? Nothing too complicated for you experts, there's plenty o' fish about, let's see if you can find them."

As the parents departed, John approached the two latecomers, who were in conversation with Honor. "Morning James, this must be Tyler? Glad you could make it. As you have a vehicle can you two start at the top of the beat and work your way down? I'll get everyone else going and come and see you in a couple of hours. Try and get the flies down a little."

"Morning John, yes that's no problem," said James. "We'll get the rod set up when we get to the top. Is it just you ghillieing today?"

"Aye, just me this morning, but I have some help this afternoon. Will you be OK, or d'ye need anything?"

"No no, nothing, just wanted to check. Many thanks, see you later." James smiled to his friend and they turned and made their way back to the Defender.

John returned to the remaining six anglers, who had divided themselves into pairs. "Alastair, you know this beat, could you and Carl head upstream and fish the Floating Bank? Sarah and Jade, I'll start you both at the Birkenbaud. Callum and Honor, if you can hop on the back of the truck, I'll take you a short way downstream.

You all have my number, just call if you need any help, I am always within five minutes."

With everyone under way, John drove slowly back up the river, Tweed carefully watching from the open window. At the top of the beat he could see James wading part way into the river, Tyler was sitting downstream on the bank of the river and appeared to be hunched over his phone, which he put into his rucksack as John arrived.

"How're you getting on?" asked John.

"Nothing so far, but there are a few around," Tyler replied.

"Do you not have a rod?" enquired John.

"No, I use James's. It's fine, he's much better than I am. He's caught two this week already," he boasted.

"Ah good stuff. When he's finished the last few metres of this pool, skip this shallow stretch and drop into the next pool. I'll be back around eleven."

John ascended the bank and turned to watch them for a while. James was a very good caster, but it was a bit strange that his friend wasn't keen to take over, as that was the only way to improve. Tyler seemed more interested in what John was doing than anything else. John waved and made a mental note to help him later, but for now he was going to check on the others.

By mid-morning John had rotated the rods and as it approached lunchtime, he was preparing to collect the anglers from the top and bottom of the beat. Part way to collecting from the top pool, he pulled the truck over and looked down the bank. There were many floating bank pools along the River Dee, all of them signifying where in years gone by the timber had been rolled into the river and transported downstream. The one at Crathes Castle was particularly productive, and for a while he watched James, who seemed very focused on covering a particular spot. After a few casts he changed the fly and tried again.

John stepped out and began to scan the bank to see if he could locate Tyler. Moments later he saw an excited Tyler appear from under a tree. Meanwhile James was on the move back towards the bank, and there was a big bend in his rod.

James expertly played the fish until after a few minutes the bar of silver was drawn to the net, held by John, who had now joined them. Like the others caught that week it had sea lice clinging to it. Tyler photographed them as it was quickly returned, bolting straight back into the pool.

"Well done James, you seemed convinced you would get one there. Just behind that big rock I'll bet?"

"Yeah, we knew there were two there," said Tyler excitedly.

"Ah, had they been showing? You would never know they were there at this time of year, but they are, and once the water warms up, they start jumping all over."

"Erm yeah, splashing just there by the rock. Right where we hooked it," said Tyler.

"Excellent, I'll see you back at the hut for lunch. I'll just go and collect the others."

There was a lot of friendly chatter over lunch, with praise for James, but John also sensed a touch of envy. As they cleared away and prepared to restart, he approached the successful pair. "So, Tyler, your turn to catch one this afternoon then? You'll be starting just in front of the hut."

But before Tyler could speak, James replied. "Ah John, afraid something's come up and we sadly aren't going to be able to stay. Really sorry, thanks for your help this morning netting my fish." He held out his hand to John, who realised that it contained a twenty-pound note. Caught off guard, he shook his hand and took the tip but was taken aback.

"I hope all is OK, real shame you can't stay with the rest of the group," he said.

"Yeah, all OK, but my dad needs some help with something, thanks again."

"Well done with your catch James, keep well and hopefully see you guys again."

The young men headed to their vehicle, leaving John feeling slightly perturbed. But the friendly impatience of the remaining rods soon shook him into action, and he directed them to their new fishing points. Another fish was caught that afternoon, interestingly from the very same pool as the earlier one, by Honor. John passed on his congratulations to her proud father when he arrived to collect her and her boyfriend.

When everyone had gone, before locking up the hut, John took another walk along the water's edge. There was something special about Easter; it was a time of hope and positivity. After a cold winter of restrictions, there was a real sense of promise in the air. These past three days had been the same. A kingfisher skimmed across the river and landed on the bench just ten metres away, cocking its head towards him as if in agreement. He smiled and turned back.

The following evening, John opened the email which gave the latest standings in the Win the Fin competition. He was delighted to see that Evie Kemp remained equal top in the under-sixteens group but was surprised to see that James Tippen had caught four in the past week, taking him into the lead of the under-eighteens. What bewildered John was that not only had he added a fish at Crathes Castle yesterday but he had also caught one at Birse. It didn't add up.

CHAPTER 19

Toward the end of the Easter holidays, Callum had arranged a day with Alastair at a beat called Commonty, a little upstream of Cairnton. Like all beats on the major rivers, in the past when there was an abundance of fish and the cost of fishing was higher, it would have had a full-time ghillie. Nowadays, with lower prices, some of the ghillies had gone. Anglers were typically shown to the river and provided with detailed instructions, and such was the case at Commonty.

Despite being April, it was another cold day, but thankfully dry. Winter seemed to be dragging on and on. They were met by Ian who showed them the beat before leaving them to roam along the bank alone. He and Alastair rotated between the interestingly named pools, stopping together for hot soup at lunchtime. After a quiet morning, without explanation, they both hooked fish at the same time in adjacent pools, having to land them without help. Was it coincidence, or had something in the weather at that time created the urge to take the fly? Neither of them knew the answer.

As evening approached and they prepared to leave, they compared photos of the fish lying in the shallows next to their rods. They looked identical, both 7lb and even lying on the same side of the rod. Callum's had been taken from the Suicide pool and Alastair's out of the Otter Trap.

This was the single fish Callum managed during the holiday.

Only Honor had found a fish at Crathes Castle, other than James, and she wasn't taking part in the competition. She had rightly decided it was not aimed at qualified instructors. Callum felt some relief about this, as there was a chance that a competition between them might not go well.

Despite his limited access to the river, James had hit a streak of good luck, but Callum knew he was now back at boarding school. If Callum could continue to add to his total through the spring he could build up a lead ahead of the summer holidays. As the prize was based on results from a number of different estates, it paid to fish throughout the year, as some beats were more prolific in spring than in summer. Even though James had the means to access the costly beats, through the Twilight programme Callum was still well positioned. He also felt sure that James would not have a chance to catch on Balmoral.

Granda collected him at 7.45 on the morning of Saturday May 8th; they were to be at the castle gates for 9.00 to meet the ghillie. The Balmoral estate lay in the upper reaches of the Dee valley, some forty-mile drive from Aberdeen. Although the road was a good one, they did not want to risk being rudely late.

There was a real sense of adventure and excitement as he waved goodbye to his mum and they set off. Callum noticed how talkative Granda was, almost nervously so. He knew fishing the Balmoral beat was a dream he was delighted to achieve, but there was something extra special about them doing this together.

Spring had just about arrived in Deeside and as they made their way inland, they were surrounded by the evidence of it. Huge swathes of daffodils brightened up the roadside, but it was the mustard-yellow gorse bushes that were most impressive as they stretched up the grassy banks.

Callum could see the river for large stretches of the journey and found himself providing a commentary. "Ooh, that's Borrowston there, water looks lovely, it's a nice height," he said.

This increased the sense of anticipation and Granda usually recounted some story of another time he had been in this location. They passed through Aboyne and once they reached Ballater, the scene became even more beautiful as the snow-capped Munros were accentuated by the blue sky to the west. The largest of these, Lochnagar, rose majestically above the surrounding grouse moors like whipped cream on a chocolate brownie.

Their conversation slowed as the countryside sucked their attention, until they saw the sign for the castle and turned off the main road. An old iron bridge crossed over the river, and they approached the main gates ten minutes early. They were prepared for a wait, but were welcomed by David, whose truck awaited them. They made brief introductions before David asked them to follow him as he drove along the Southside Road towards Birkhall, the home on the Balmoral estate where Prince Charles lived.

Leaving the road, they followed a track that passed between two grass fields, both containing stocky, shaggy Highland cattle, before branching right and into the forest. The vehicles moved slowly, wheels rolling over a blanket of pinecones.

David pointed from his open window. Granda and Callum followed his indication and just a few metres into the trees they saw a roebuck, its wide eyes stared nervously back at them until they had passed. The Fiesta crept cautiously along the track, manoeuvring around large rocks, until they arrived at a small clearing, next to the tumbling river. They stopped directly outside an idyllic-looking log cabin, turned off their engines and slowly stepped from the vehicles. The setting, the sound of the crashing water and the smell of pine were intoxicating. David walked over to them.

"This is Polvier, the Queen Mother's hut, much loved by all the family," he said. "It's a wonderful base for fishing, but it can be used for entertaining as well. There can't be a more romantic place for dinner on the whole estate."

Callum and Granda were both momentarily lost for words. It was truly magical, and as they turned to study the pool in front there came the splash of a fish. Granda was full of questions for David, asking which of the royals were keen anglers, if it was true that the ladies were better than the men and if the children were still taught to fish. He received courteous but measured responses.

Callum opened the boot of the car and removed the rods and tackle bags, which he placed on the outdoor table.

"Och, I could talk all day but that's not what ye're here for is it Callum?" said David. "Let's get you started." As Callum erected his rod, David described the beat and how he thought it would be best to fish it.

"There are some good fish about," he said. "They caught a few at Crathie this week and the water is still a good height with the last of the snowmelt whenever temperatures rise a bit. We are generally shallower here than in the lower section of the river, so quite light tackle and you don't need big flies. If you use a slow-sinking tip that would be fine, and I quite like a fly with a tail and a bit of blue in it."

That was all Callum needed, and in a couple of minutes he was all set whilst Granda was still chatting away, animated and happy. It was only when Callum had finished putting on his waders that they remembered him.

"Sorry Callum, got a bit lost in reminiscing then," said David. "Right, let's get you going now. Follow me."

"I'll get myself set whilst you take the lad,' said Granda, watching them walk down the bank towards the river.

"There are three pools here, each connected by rapids," said David. "I'll start you at the top one as it needs deeper wading, it's not a huge stretch of water but it always holds fish. Then I'll start your grandad a bit lower down in the larger middle pool, which is mainly shingle bedded and you need only wade to your knees. You'll still be able to see each other. That's the pool where I caught my biggest fish a few years ago, twenty-three pounds. I can still feel the ache in my arm after that one! After you've done the top pool, leapfrog past Donald into the lower pool in front of the hut. That pool was much loved by the Queen Mother, she landed many a fish there. By the time you've fished that one I should be back from visiting the other beat, but you can always fish through them again with a different fly if you have time. The real hot spot is by the hut, so take your time when you get there, just small steps, start with a short line. Good luck, I'll see you at lunchtime."

Callum thanked him and slowly waded into the water as instructed. When he was confident that he was at the right starting point, he began to cast. It was quite easy with the light tackle and they were sheltered from what breeze there was. He was casting at an angle such that the fly was moving nicely across the current, swift but not too fast.

Before long he heard a call from Granda and turned to get his first sight of him wearing waders as David slowly led him to the start of the middle pool. Laughing, he waved and yelled, "Good luck Granda, don't you dare catch one!" The response was a gentle wave of the hand.

It was close to ten o'clock now and it had warmed up a little. Callum continued to cover the water systematically, but as the line swung across the current, he was distracted by the stunning scenery. The opposite bank was essentially a sheer cliff that plunged straight into the river, the current hugging it closely. Further upstream, on the edge of a shallow stretch of water, a red squirrel was working the forest edge as it searched for food, seemingly ignorant of Callum's presence. It rummaged through the tussocks, disturbing branches and rocks in its search. Callum moved gradually downstream as the squirrel scampered away into the trees with its bounty. High above the glistening water he had seen the circling silhouette of what was either an eagle or a very big buzzard.

He eventually reached the end of the pool, having covered the water nicely but without any response. He reeled in, then made his way along the bank, stopping next to where Granda stood about halfway down his pool. "Isn't this magnificent?" said Granda with a twinkling smile from beneath his worn fishing hat.

"It really is something else. I'm pleased the weather's OK, Granda, but my feet are pretty cold from standing in the water. I'm going to try the lower pool now, join me when you've finished." He trudged the hundred metres to the neck of a deeper stretch that ran beneath the sheer stone cliff, splashing energetically past Polvier and opening into a wider bay.

He looked over the pool before stepping into the river, deciding on how he was going to cover it. Only two steps in from the bank, he began to present the fly across the top of the main current as the same soaring bird drew his attention a little downstream. He felt blissfully relaxed, and so pleased to have been able to arrange this special day for them both.

Two simultaneous splashes near the hut, where they had seen one jump when stood by the cars, regained his attention. Moving downstream, he put a mend in the line as the water was running through quite quickly, and as he did so there was a noticeable twitch. He cast again from the same place, and again felt a slight pull on the line. This time it persisted. He paused, letting the fish come to terms with the unexpected resistance before it turned downstream as if making for the sea. Line rapidly departed from the reel. He lifted into the fish and felt a solid pressure.

Confident it was on, he called "I'm in!" and turned to see that Granda was already heading his way. He let out a cowboy-style whoop that was more suited to an eight-year-old than an eighty-year-old. "I'm on my way, son!" he shouted.

The fish had turned back upstream, and Callum wound in line to keep the pressure on. It zigzagged across the deeper part of the river with steady power as his grandad reached him and placed his hand on his shoulder. Somehow Callum found himself imagining it was the hand of his father, looking on proudly as he played this wonderful fish.

"I'll get the net, take your time with him," said Granda after gathering his breath. Gradually, the runs the fish was taking shortened and Callum started to step backwards towards the bank, increasing the pressure a little. As the fish tired it rolled, and they could both see the shine in the clear water. "Beauty!" whispered Granda.

The fish was still near the middle of the stream, but it was succumbing to the pressure and turning its silver flank upwards. Granda stepped into the water, lowering the net in anticipation.

Then, as Callum reeled in the last few metres, a great dark shape flew in over his shoulder and struck the water with a huge splash, right above the resisting salmon. In a fraction of a second it had returned to the air and was heading towards the clifftop on the opposite bank.

It was only at that point, when he could clearly see the fish suspended in the bird's immense talons, that Callum grasped what had happened; an eagle had grabbed his fish. He instinctively began to reel in the loose line, and in an instant the line was taut again, swinging the fish back towards him and drawing the bird back with it.

Granda stood fixated, unable to react. "Holy shit!" gasped Callum. He had just got the words from his mouth when there was a sharp crack and the bird began to regain height and speed away, still with the fish in its grip. They both watched in amazement as it climbed over the trees and out of sight before turning to face each other.

"What the hell was *that?*" gasped Callum.

It took a moment for Granda to regain his composure. "That was a white-tailed eagle," he replied. "We have just seen something quite incredible. That huge bird just seized the struggling salmon."

"*My* struggling salmon!" was all Callum could say.

They were sitting at the outdoor table by the hut when David returned. Callum waved as he bounced out of his truck towards them. He stopped in front of them and thrusting both hands out, palms upwards said, "Well?"

"I'm not sure you'll believe this, Dave," said Granda. They proceeded to tell him the story of the sea eagle and the salmon as if it were a fable.

"Well, well, I have to say that's the strangest 'one that got away' story I have ever heard," said David. "There's no way anyone who wasn't here is going to believe you. I'm not sure I can report this story to the family, they'll think I've lost it and I'll get the boot! To be fair, there is a pair of eagles up on Mar Estate, quite close to here, and we see them from time to time. They have even been spotted with fish along the river, but I've never heard of any bird of prey taking a salmon that was hooked by an angler. There are lots of stories of other predatory fish taking a hooked fish, even seals have been known to do it, but to my knowledge never an eagle. That is some story. Lucky for the eagle but not so lucky for you, Callum. I'm not sure what else to say. Anyway, let's take a look at the next pool, that should give you the best chance of hooking another, and hopefully this time even a pterodactyl won't steal it." He made for his vehicle, still shaking his head.

Callum fished through the afternoon in the new beat without success, his enthusiasm now a little abated. He was standing partway across the river fishing the main current as it passed close to the far bank below a pretty white pedestrian suspension bridge. Granda had fished a little himself straight after lunch, but after an hour he gave up and was now contentedly cradled in his folding chair at the water's edge, sipping tea and giving the occasional advice to his only grandchild. It was advice which would have arrived possibly ten years earlier had things been different, so there was perhaps a little more urgency to pass it on now.

Granda's comments became less frequent and then dried up entirely. Callum turned towards him and saw his eyes were now closed, the sun warming his wrinkled skin. He appeared wonderfully peaceful, resting to the river's lullaby.

The shallowing river signalled the end of the pool, so Callum reeled in and returned along the bank. Granda beckoned him to take a seat on the rock beside him. He laid down the rod, then sank onto the pale grey stone, facing the river.

"There they are," said Granda, and they both watched two huge eagles circling high above the gothic spire of Crathes kirk.

"They don't look very hungry," joked Callum, as they watched them curl away and disappear behind the forest.

A short while later, Callum and his grandad were passing the castle gates, crossing the river, and pulling onto the A93.

"I would swap five landed fish for the experience we had today," said Granda as they passed Ballater. "I know it doesn't help you in the competition, but you'll make up for this another day this season, I'm sure of it."

As Granda pulled up outside the house, before Callum moved, he reached across and tugged his shirt. "You know Callum, that was one of the finest days of my whole life. To be on the beautiful Balmoral estate was always an ambition, to do it with you was a blessing and to have witnessed that incredible creature do what it did, well, that was a miracle. Promise me you'll never forget it and you'll talk about it with your own children one day. Won't you, son?"

Callum smiled back, not sure if being called 'son' was intentional.

"I promise. It was very special, Granda." And he opened the door.

Inside the house, Callum dropped his bags and went into the living room, where his mum was watching TV. He walked over to her and knelt beside her armchair.

"So, how was it?" she asked.

"Mum it was awesome, I don't think we could have ever done anything that would have made him happier. Thank you, I know it was a lot of money." He opened his phone to show her a photo that David had taken of him and his Granda standing outside the Queen Mother's hut.

"I'm so pleased Cal. Send me that photo and I'll get it printed for your Granda. Did you catch any?"

He paused and broke into a broad smile. "That's a long story, I'll tell you over tea. Let me change, Ma. Thanks again, it was epic." He headed upstairs.

Kitty Shropshire

CHAPTER 20

A year earlier, one of the last things that would have been on Callum's birthday gift list would have been a day's fishing at Banchory, but this year it was second only to the driving lessons he had received from his mother. Granda had booked the day some months before, knowing it was often sold out during the summer. Aware that Callum wanted to make an early start but not being able to drive him, Granda had also arranged a taxi, which had just arrived outside the house.

Callum quietly closed the front door behind him and sat in the back seat with his bag and rod. The previous day he had spoken to Jordan, the ghillie, who had welcomed the early start and told Callum he would be on the south bank lower section in the morning as part of the rod rotation. This suited Callum, as he knew that was where the River Feugh, a major tributary, ran into the Dee and at times large numbers of salmon would hold in that area awaiting a spate so they could swim up to the spawning grounds. They could then be seen leaping the waterfalls, and the Falls of Feugh had become a tourist attraction as a result.

Callum directed the taxi along South Deeside Road and within twenty-five minutes they had arrived at the Banchory Fishing hut, which sat opposite the imposing Banchory Lodge Hotel where he had attended the beginners' course less than a year ago. With his rod set up, he made his way down the steep, dusty slope towards the path running along the bank. Wisps of mist hung over the river, which tinkled like a wind charm. It was wonderfully peaceful, though he was surprised to see another angler already on the opposite bank.

Callum had a wading stick with him to help navigate the large boulders that created a form of causeway across the mouth of the tributary. He edged forward into the stream, leaning on the staff for extra balance. The sun was rising over the river as it raced away to his right, and he began to cast out the fly on a short line. They had been consistently catching on this beat, so as he lengthened the line, each cast was loaded with expectation.

About thirty metres downstream, right in front of the hotel at the point of juncture, was the famous and appropriately named Hotel pool. Some fish were already showing there as he slowly approached, announcing their homecoming with each leap. His orange and gold fly landed gently on the surface at the confluence with the main stream, and he was surrounded by the sound of running water.

He had reached about halfway across the mouth of the Feugh, next to three very large rocks that must have been deposited during a huge flood, when he felt a gentle take. It was soft, like a small trout, but then persistent and powerful like nothing else.

The scream of Callum's reel alerted the angler opposite that a fight had begun. For the following fifteen minutes, Callum never really felt he was in control, but thankfully the fish remained in the pool and did not try to escape downstream through the rapids. It bored deep, but he was patient, keeping up the pressure until its runs became shorter.

Then he realised that landing this fish was going to be a challenge. He had no net, and as he was standing in the middle of the river there was nowhere practical to beach the fish. The only suitable spot was a small sandy bay thirty metres downstream, but to get to it Callum would have to cross the deep part of the tributary whilst still playing the salmon.

Anyone in the hotel opening their curtains to take a look at what the day held might have thought they were still dreaming. With the clock not yet past seven, a seventeen-year-old boy was walking across a river with a stick for balance in one hand and a bent thirteen-foot salmon rod in the other.

Despite the efforts of the salmon, Callum made it to the bay and was able to guide the tiring fish ashore, where he unhooked it and took a quick photo. At Crathes Castle, John had suggested they placed some coloured tape marks on their rods that enabled quick measurement of the fish's length. Callum had placed different coloured tape at the approximate lengths of 5lb, 10lb and 20lb fish. Lying in the shallows next to his rod, this hen fish was a few centimetres above the 76cm mark, which made it around 12lb. He held her facing upstream whilst she regained enough strength to continue. The last time this fish had been at Banchory it had almost certainly been in a cohort of adolescent smolts, racing downstream like a shoal of uniformed children towards the school gates. She had probably been at sea for two winters gorging on small fish and building herself into the powerhouse that had taken twenty-five minutes to tame. She had survived the perilous journey and given him such excitement; with a flick she was away.

Callum decided to wade back across the Feugh and start again at the top of the pool. He took his time, just pleased that the risk of not catching anything was gone. When he restarted casting he realised he had a knot in his line. He had barely finished unravelling it when something took the trailing fly with a bang, and entirely without warning he found himself playing another fish.

About an hour later, Callum was sitting on the bench outside the hut nonchalantly eating a flapjack when Jordan arrived. "Morning

Callum, you're looking pretty pleased with yourself," he said with a grin.

"I was trying to put on my best poker face," Callum replied.

"You might have got away with it if Mr Leith on the opposite bank hadn't already told me. Two before breakfast? Well done you!"

Callum could contain his delight no longer and smiled broadly. "Yeah, unbelievable. The first was a beauty, a good twelve pounds, and she took me on a proper ride. The second, well, better to be lucky than good they say, don't they? A grilse took the fly when I was unravelling a knot in my line! A very special morning, two on the board already."

"Aye and it's always nice to know you won't blank," said Jordan. They chatted whilst Callum proudly showed Jordan the photos.

Surprisingly, perhaps, no more fish were hooked in the morning, but for once Callum was keen to leave the water promptly as lunchtime approached. The second part of his birthday treat awaited him on the far bank, and as he crossed the bridge, she had come to meet him.

They kissed, then continued towards the town and turned into the hotel drive. Callum excitedly recounting the success of the morning as they walked in the shade of tall trees. Cutting towards the river, they soon reached the picnic spot, where Honor spread out the feast on a blanket she had brought. As well as food, she had brought chilled beer. After recounting, in great detail, the success of the morning, Callum lay down and placed his head on her knee. He looked up at her and calmly said, "This is the place Honor, I've been here many times before and seen it on photos and video. This was where the family felt tightest to my dad, I know it was."

She smiled back and gently ran her fingers through his hair. "And now you've fished here too."

"Yes, I have. Look, you have a go now, while I call my Granda and clear up lunch. You don't need to wade here, you can fish from the bank." But instead of standing up Honor sat on his chest, caressing his cheeks with her heavy locs and slid down his torso until her mouth met his. He held her, he was happier than he had ever been before.

A few minutes later, they reluctantly separated and she picked up the rod on her way to the water's edge. Callum called Granda but could only leave an animated voicemail. He sent a message too, which contained a photo of the hen fish, knowing Granda would reply as soon as he saw it. He messaged Alastair as he had promised to and couldn't resist telling his mum too. Then he paused, looking over the river towards the point where he had fished that morning. It was without doubt the same background as that family photo Granda had given him last year.

Eventually, he rose and stepped slowly down the grassy bank to the water's edge. Deep in thought, he headed back upstream towards the Holly Bush pool where Honor was fishing. His eyes refocused, but it took a moment for the bend in her rod to register. Then he abruptly zoned back in and quickened his pace. He called Jordan, who was just above the bridge, and asked him to bring a landing net.

Honor stood on the bank holding the rod firmly with both hands, the butt clamped against her waist for support. From the tip he could now see the line stretching like a zip-wire until it met the surface of the fast water twenty metres downstream. The toned muscles in her bare forearms were clearly straining.

"Am I glad to see you!" she gasped without turning round. "I couldn't even reach for my phone. Feels like a good fish by the power of the runs." The reel screeched as more line was pulled from it, and the point where the line met the water moved a further ten metres downstream.

"Try not to let it go much further," instructed Jordan, who was beside her now. "It gets shallower and there's way too many big rocks for it to wrap the line around."

Honor tightened the drag on the reel and anxiously applied even more pressure. She knew that if there were any frays in the line or substandard knots, they would be exposed by this tussle. But the equipment held, and after a short stalemate the fish turned back towards them. Callum was sitting on the grass taking occasional video clips of Honor as Jordan carefully stepped down the bank. They still hadn't seen the fish; unlike smaller salmon the larger ones often don't break the surface when hooked but remain deep.

Finally, after an incredible twenty minutes, Honor worked the fish closer and they saw a long grey back above the pale rocky riverbed. Believing the fish was almost ready, Jordan lowered the net into the water to receive it, but on seeing it the salmon bull-dozed away again. It was another few minutes before it finally succumbed, turning onto its shining side and being drawn into the net. Honor virtually collapsed with relief and placed the rod on the ground.

Jordan kept the net in the water, stepped in besides it and unhooked the fish with his forceps. He called Honor to him for the release, but he also wanted to show her something. On one side, the fish was magnificent, the perfect image of a salmon of around 16lb. But on the other flank were two deep, ugly gashes.

"Seal?" asked Honor.

"Aye, this one had a lucky escape. They must run the gauntlet these days when they get close to the coast. Let's take a nice photo of you with her, Honor, but on her undamaged side. Then we can get her back, she's a precious mother-to-be."

Callum took a short video of the release and Honor's high five with the ghillie as the fish swam towards the deeper water.

"Chance of another, I reckon," said Jordan optimistically, but they were both making their way up the bank and returning to the picnic blanket.

"Come and have a drink," said Callum, beckoning him to follow. He wanted to share with Jordan what the beat meant to his family and therefore what it now meant to him. Of how perfect the day had been, and how he had accomplished what they had done before him, following in the steps of his father's waders.

As they sat chatting, Callum's phone announced the arrival of a text message. He looked and saw it was from Granda. When he opened it he couldn't believe what he read: 'Lovely fish – WTF?'

He was taken back. Such a crude expression was not Granda's usual language. Perhaps he was excited because he had paid for the day, or maybe Banchory held a special place in Granda's heart too. Callum was just about to reply when he figured it out and burst into laughter. He texted, 'Yes Granda, I'm now leading the Win the Fin, thanks to you.' Amid laughter, he told Honor and Jordan what had happened.

Eventually Jordan had to leave to check the other anglers. Callum expressed his gratitude and hoped they would meet again soon.

After he left, Callum and Honor remained sitting on the blanket together until nearly eight o'clock. He just made the bus, inebriated by the experiences of the day – that mystical start when he had hooked into the twelve-pounder whilst the mist swirled over the river like dancing ghosts, the real connectivity he had felt with the time he was here as a toddler, and of course the closeness to Honor. The summer holidays started in two weeks, and in contrast to last year he felt far more positive and energised about what they would bring.

CHAPTER 21

Although Callum had not stopped to consider it before, Royal Deeside in the summer was a pretty special place to be. He had been able to get a part-time job at the hotel for the season, but he still had four free days each week and Honor seemed to have an unquenchable desire to explore the area, not just to fish. They had been all the way up to Braemar, hiked around the back of Balmoral, then on to circle Loch Muick. With such good weather they had spent a day in the dunes at Balmedie beach. Despite the suncream, Callum still ended up with an embarrassingly red nose, as always happened.

The weather had been so good that it had made the fishing difficult. With drought conditions the river level had dropped away, and the water heated up to an extent the salmon had become stressed. This was the case across all Scotland, and the longer it went on the more concerning it became for the welfare of the limited fish stock in the river.

But the low water level had led to a build-up of fresh salmon that were only now entering the river, especially where the tidal water ends above the Bridge of Dee near the city centre. This had given Callum the chance to catch on the two ADAA beats at Garthdee and Banchory Devenick. So far, summer was going really well.

The Lower Woodend fishery lay directly upstream from Cairnton, stretching round a long bend for about a mile in a very secluded position. Honor had messaged Callum on the Tuesday evening to see if he was free the following afternoon, as the owner had offered her father a chance to fish, an opportunity to build relations with their new neighbouring ghillie. Buster would be busy looking after guests on the Cairnton water but had gladly accepted when the offer was extended for both rods to his daughter.

The owners were aware of Win the Fin and keen to give an opportunity to have Lower Woodend feature on the board. Even better for Callum was the news that Honor's father had offered to give him a lift home afterwards, so they could stay into the evening.

Honor messaged: 'cld u get 1:10pm bus dad will come pick u up 1:50 ish, jus bring a hoodie and towel.'

Calum burst into the kitchen. "Mum, Honor has invited me to fish tomorrow afternoon at Lower Woodend, next to their place," he said. "I'm heading over straight from my shift, and her dad has offered to give me a lift home after. Would it be OK?" he asked, as if she had a choice.

"How lovely, you're a lucky lad. Just make sure you take plenty of sunblock, it's going to be hot again. Have you caught one on this beat?"

"No, I've never been there and didn't think I would get a chance. I'm going to try and see Granda in the morning on my way to the hotel to get his thoughts."

"What a real treat. Actually son, I got a message from Granda saying he was struggling a bit with a bug and it might be best to let him get over it before you visit, so maybe just email him."

"OK, I'll do that. I hope he shrugs it off as we are planning to fish together before school restarts. I'm going to take Fergie out for a walk now, see you in a bit, Ma." With that he headed towards the front door, followed by the spaniel.

They headed towards the river, Callum's regular route now. He seldom went to the park any more and was no longer in touch with that group. He stopped to watch the few fishermen who were probably there after avoiding fishing in the bright afternoon sunshine and opened the browser on his phone to research on tomorrow's beat. They had caught a few so far in July, and Callum read how certain pools held fish when the river was low. The dry, sunny, warm weather was being enjoyed by nearly everyone apart from salmon anglers, as a low river made the fish easily spooked and reluctant to take a fly.

Back home he sent an email to his grandad, telling him enthusiastically of tomorrow's opportunity and saying he assumed light tackle would again be the way to go. No reply had come in before he decided to sleep, or at least try to, as even with windows open it was unpleasantly close.

He had a brief reply from Granda the next morning saying, 'The warmer it gets, the smaller the fly.'

It felt quite strange heading to the bus stop without his heavy fishing bags, but today he just had a small sports rucksack with some clothes, a towel and the essential phone charger. Seeing him in his shorts and trainers, it would have been difficult to guess where he was going.

He looked over the river where it meandered close to the road. It was a lot smaller and many more features were visible when it was running low like this. As the bus trundled into Banchory he could see Buster's pickup parked ahead of the stop, and Honor standing on the pavement and leaning forward through the open passenger window to chat to her father. She too was in summer clothes, which accentuated her long, athletic legs. Her pale green polo shirt hung down from the window, and a small gap to her denim shorts revealed a little more of her brown skin.

At the sound of the approaching bus she rose and turned towards him, smiling. He caught a sun-filled flash of white teeth and sparkling eyes as he bounced towards the front and out of the door as it opened. She gave him a subtle but public kiss and led him to the waiting truck, urging him to take the front seat, where he could say hello to her father.

"Nice to see you again, Callum," said Buster in his deep, friendly voice. "You're looking well. Must be all the time outside catching those fish."

"Thank you for picking me up and the really kind offer of a lift home, it's been hot and sticky in the city. So glad to be getting back to the river, it's really good of you. How's the fishing been at Cairnton?"

"We had one early this morning – the guy was on the water way before I was even awake. The hot weather is making it tricky, but the fish are there. I don't think you need rush this afternoon, your best chance is after five, I would say. I know our guests are planning to fish into the evening today. After a nice long lunch and a snooze on the riverbank, no doubt." He chuckled. "Honor is planning a stealth approach for you with the water so low, she wants to try using the single-handed rods and light tackle. There are still some sea trout around too, you've a good chance of finding them with that set-up."

Callum nodded, and the three of them chatted during the ten-minute drive to the beat's hut.

"I'm going to drop you at the Lower Woodend hut. I'll be with my guests and we are having a BBQ of our own by the river in the evening," said Buster, "Why don't you two just walk down to us when you're ready, and I can drop Callum back?"

This was music to Callum's ears. He would get to spend the rest of the day with Honor, fishing a beautiful, secluded stretch of the river.

They parked beside the main hut, just a few metres from the river, and transferred their bags onto the outdoor table. They waved to the truck as it disappeared, then simultaneously turned to each other and Honor leapt into Callum's arms. He felt the soft flesh of her bare legs pressing against his as his hands delicately touched the naked base of her back. Then she withdrew and lifted her polo shirt over her head in a single, flirtatious movement. Callum's eyes felt as if they would pop from his head, but as he stepped towards her, she turned her back and held a container of suncream in an outstretched hand.

"Would you screen my shoulders please, handsome?" she asked, and he duly obliged, gently massaging her skin whilst being careful not to rub the cream into her green and white bikini top.

"C'mon, let's explore," she said, and led him towards the river's edge. They walked slowly downstream in the sunshine and though his eyes were mesmerised by her beauty, Callum gradually became aware of the surroundings. Honor had a print of the beat map, and she had already decided which pools they were going to try.

There was a clearly defined long pool in front of the hut, which they walked past. "We'll fish this later," she said as the river started to curve to the right and out of sight. A few metres further on she stopped and said, "But first, welcome to our swimming pool."

Without another word, she pulled off her trainers and stripped off her denim shorts. Now in just a bikini, she took a few steps onto a large boulder and lowered herself into the crystal-clear water, catching Callum completely by surprise. But she had left him with no choice, and he too was soon lowering himself into the cool water sporting just his underwear.

Even on one of the hottest days of the year, the water still felt fresh, but he would have joined her even if it had been full of grue. She splashed him as he got near before submerging her whole head, flicking her dark tresses and allowing him to embrace her.

He could feel her firm nipples as their bodies squeezed together and played in the current as if it was a spa. She turned away and lay back onto him, his arms wrapped round her and he bent his knees so that their eyes were only just above the water. It was like a scene from a movie or some TV ad. The surrounding trees were almost fluorescent green, the branches draping the edge of the river. "Maybe Granda's right," said Callum. "Mother Nature really was a salmon fisherman."

They stared downstream and he held her, one arm across her chest and one around her stomach. He held her like something was trying to prise them apart. She murmured her approval then she turned back towards him and they kissed passionately. "Come on, I'm getting cold," she said softly after a few minutes, drawing away from his clinch.

"Me too," he replied.

"Your blood circulation seems fine to me," she said with a wink.

Once out of the water, they put on their trainers and dried off as they walked back to the hut. With the temperature just starting to drop back, Honor slipped on her polo shirt and removed the bikini top, hanging it on the rail to dry. Then she opened one of the bags she had brought and took out their food.

"Here, can you start the barbecue?" she said. She threw some matches to Callum, who set about his task whilst she put the plates on the table. "The freshest, most organic venison steaks. Medium rare please chef!" she said and removed from the canvas bag a rod tube just 60cm long. Unscrewing the cap, she carefully extracted the rod pieces and proceeded to connect them.

"A ten-foot six weight, my sea-trout weapon of choice," she said as she attached the reel and continued with the set-up. Callum watched as he waited for the charcoal flames to subside. "Full floating line and a twelve-foot tapered leader is what I'm going to try given how low and clear the water is," she continued. Callum stared at her. She was fascinating him even more. "A size fourteen fly tied by my dad. He says you can use any fly for sea trout, so long as its silver and blue. How's the barbecue coming on?"

"It needs a few more minutes before it's ready for the steaks," he replied, "Why don't you have a go in the meantime? Do you have your waders?"

"There are not many things I enjoy more than fishing with bare legs," Honor replied as she stepped down to the pool, "It isn't often possible, especially in Scotland. But when you can it's just another level, reminds me of Nigeria when I was little."

She walked out in her trainers until the water was up to her bikini bottoms and began to cast out the fly much in the way Callum had tried at the trout lakes. Only it wasn't. The smooth coordination of swaying body, curving rod and curling line transfixed him. He forgot about the grill and watched her. The pace and distance of the fly bore no relation to her gentle, rhythmic movement. Her right wrist commanded the rod and at the same time her left wrist worked the line. As she moved the rod backwards with her right, her left hand tugged the line down to accelerate it. The fly was reaching all parts of the river, landing gently and softly swinging across the current. Forget about the fish, this was artistry in itself, and at that moment he saw her as like a beautiful dancer.

A crackle from the charcoal reminded him of the task in hand and he laid the two steaks onto the grill with a hiss. A few minutes later Honor made her way back to the hut, placed the rod in the holder and towelled her legs dry. The sun was heading west, taking the heat with it, and she slipped on her shorts and hoodie. Watercress salad and sliced tomato were heaped onto the plates as Callum transferred the venison into the open soft rolls. "Try my chipotle sauce if you dare," she teased.

For many reasons, what followed was the finest meal of

Callum's life. Honor had opened a container of strawberries which she smothered with cream and they ate with their fingers.

As they did so, two fish simultaneously splashed in the pool in front of them.

"Teach me how to cast like you can," said Callum.

"Come on then, help me pack this away first."

They cleaned off the plates into the garbage bin and packed them with the remaining food into the picnic rucksack. Then Callum put his Polaroids on and followed Honor back to the starting point of the pool. They stepped about ten metres into the pool to where the bottom slowly dropped away from them, and with Callum by her side, Honor began to cast. "Don't pull the rod too far back, stop it when you get a little past upright and pause whilst the line extends behind you, don't rush it," she said. "When you push the rod forward again, try and pull down on the line with your left hand at the same time to add that extra bit of power and you'll see how well it flies."

She swapped places with him and he began to imitate her. It took a few minutes to get the timing right, but before long he was casting a nice line.

"Here, now do it left-handed," he said, handing the rod back, and with a smile she cast equally well without changing position, reaching ten metres further than he had. He grinned at her. She was confident, but humble and unassuming. She turned towards him, but suddenly her expression changed and she began to lift the rod, which had started juddering. "Whoa, fish on!" she cried. "Here, see what it feels like on light tackle."

She offered the rod to Callum, but he was not prepared to take it. "No way, this is your rodeo," he replied and stepped back towards the bank, giving Honor more space as the thin rod buckled. It wasn't a big fish, but it was feisty, and as it leapt from the water Honor lowered the rod tip as if she was controlling a puppet on a string.

Before long she had expertly coaxed it into the edge, where Callum stood, having collected Honor's small net. He unhooked the fish whilst it was in the net as she laid the rod down. "This feels like a role reversal," he simpered as she joined him to release the shiny sea trout.

"There's nothing not to like about summer fly fishing, for me it has it all," said Honor. "It's just a bit crap that we can't take one for the barbecue, but we all have to do our bit to help given how they are disappearing. Maybe one day we could head up to one of the lochs and see if we can catch some wild trout. Completely isolated."

They spent some intimate time together on the grassy bank as the evening set in before deciding it was time to head downstream. There was one pool below that fished well in low water and tended to hold a good stock of sea trout, and they planned to try it before reaching Cairnton. They gathered all their belongings into the two bags and made their way along the path mowed through the grass until they reached the spot, a classic pool. A smallish fish leapt clean out of the water as if to welcome them. Although the sun was no longer on the water it was still very light, and Honor had planned for them to fish for about an hour before reaching the group at Cairnton.

"Your turn, c'mon, I've shown you how easy it is," she said, raising her eyebrows.

"Och, yeah right," replied Callum. Having placed the bags on the grass, he headed to the steps that marked the start of the pool. It was still pleasant enough to wade bare-legged, and he slowly edged until he was up to his knees, when he felt he could comfortably cast over the main channel of flowing water in front.

"Hey Callum, look," she suddenly whispered. He followed her pointing finger back upstream to the far bank, where a pair of otters were playing at the water's edge, completely untroubled by their presence. They watched them play as they scampered away from sight like a courting couple before Callum started casting the single-handed rod under Honor's watchful eye. He wanted to impress her and soon got his timing right; left hand was coordinated with right, and the line looped over the surface and gently landed. As he was some way into the river, there was comfortably enough room behind for the line to extend without snagging the bank.

"Look at you double-hauling!" she said with a laugh. He was now using his left hand to accelerate the line while his right sent the rod forward.

Callum proceeded to fish his way along the pool, covering the section where there had been activity when they arrived. Honor opened her phone and messaged their planned arrival time to her father. Then she heard another loud splash and looked up to see what the cause was.

"I'm in!" said Callum determinedly. He had wanted to make sure the hook was set before alerting her, but the fish had other ideas and was dancing around the surface of the pool. He saw the suspended silver arc as it jumped; clearly it was a bigger fish. It had taken the small blue and silver fly aggressively just as it swept through the tail of the turbulence where the current began to slow down, and now it wanted desperately to escape.

Callum was enjoying the sense of immediate connection the light single-handed rod gave to the fish. Compared to the big double-hander it was like using a car aerial, but when it steamed off downstream, he knew that with the light leader and small fly he could not afford to bully it. Line peeled rapidly off the reel, even though Callum's left hand was applying resistance to slow it down. He reeled in as the nylon began to head upstream, chasing the fish that had changed direction. He could see the fish now and it seemed to have seen him too. It steamed past with a fresh burst of strength, turning cartwheels above the water as it strove for freedom.

Honor had stepped in with the net to join him. "It's a nice one, let's step back a little to see if it helps," she said. "You walk to the bank and I'll stay in the shallows with the net."

As they carefully stepped back, Callum began to feel he was winning. The fish splashed in resistance, but it headed towards Honor and the shine of its flank could be seen. After a few more plunges he was able to steer it over the waiting net, and he couldn't help letting out a cheer of relief under his breath. He pulled some line off the reel so he could lay the rod down on the bank and joined Honor, who carefully removed the hook with her forceps.

"That's a nice fish," he said with admiration. There was no hint of immodesty from the captor; it was a pure factual observation. "Maybe four pounds, would you say?"

"I totally agree, a really pretty fish. But look at its flank, it has no spots below the lateral line." She carefully turned it on its side as it recovered its strength. "And can you see the tail fin has a slightly concave shape rather than straight across?" Callum nodded. "The bad news is that this isn't your best sea trout, but the good news is it's a grilse, so you've caught another salmon. From a new estate!" Honor took a few photos of Callum as he released the fish.

Although it was still plenty light enough to fish, they decided not to continue, as there seemed to be nothing more the river could offer them today. They took down the rod and packed the tackle into the canvas bag, both feeling slightly giddy with happiness. Then they slowly made their way along the bank and past the waterworks to the downstream boundary with Cairnton, where they could see three people sitting round the table in front of the hut. Callum was slightly embarrassed to be seen holding hands, but Honor tightened her grip, and they approached the grouping together. He could see her father a hundred metres further down the river in the same spot where he had caught his fish in February.

"Hello Honor, who have you hooked then?" asked one of the fishermen. All three grinned broadly. They appeared to be enjoying an open magnum of wine.

"Hi Mr Murray, this is my friend Callum. He's just landed a strong grilse in Lower Woodend on my six weight. We reckon he's now leading Win the Fin. How have you got on today?"

"Och, well done you Callum, well done indeed. I bet that gave you a runaround. We've had a lovely day, as always when we fish with your father. He's taken great care of us and managed to get two of us onto fish this evening as well as the one Charlie caught this morning. Our first time fishing this estate and hopefully won't be our last, it's truly stunning." The other two murmured in agreement. "He's just down there with Jean, she's desperate to catch one herself before she drives us to the hotel."

"So pleased you've had a nice day," replied Honor. "It's quite different from the Tweed, but we're loving being here so far. We'll go see Jean and my dad now. Best of luck tomorrow, I'll try to drop by and see how you're getting on."

"Nice to have met you," said Callum as they made off.

"Cheerio, Callum. Break a rod!" was the reply.

They joined Buster and Jean on the bank, and excitedly shared details of their catches with them.

"The owner will be delighted you had success, well done both of you," said Buster. "Specially you Callum, that's great for the competition. I'll run you home now if that's OK, then I can be back here before close of play. I'll grab the pickup and we can head off."

With a common interest like fishing, there was never going to be a shortage of conversational material. Callum and Honor recounted their success with the single-handed rod as well as telling the story of the courting otters. They understandably kept their own swimming escapades to themselves.

"When are you fishing next, Callum?" asked Buster.

"I'm on Culter early next week, then Honor and I have both been able to get rods at Dess the following Saturday through the Twilight programme. So I have a chance to add to my tally, though I'm sure James will have caught more by then, based on his recent form."

"Ah, you just keep enjoying it Callum, there's no such thing as a bad day fishing."

Before long they had reached the outskirts of the city and arrived at Callum's home. With sincere thank-yous for such a fabulous day, he waved them off and opened the front door. Joining his mother in the sitting room, he shared some details of the day's adventure. Then he went upstairs and posted the picture of his Lower Woodend salmon to the ADAA website.

As Callum drifted to sleep later that night, his mind was full of images and memories from the river of that day; of Honor's bare-legged casting, of the tremendous fight from the salmon on the small rod, but mostly of their dip in the river together. After almost six months together, he was feeling secure in their relationship. The day had only added to that. She was hot and cool at the same time, and he longed for her.

CHAPTER 22

On the Friday afternoon Callum went to the tackle shop in Aberdeen to collect a few items he was running low on. He arrived home, pulled his bike into the hallway and burst into the kitchen, where he hugged his mum and called Fergie in from the back garden.

"In a hurry are we, Cal?" his mum said with a grin. He smiled back, switched his shoes for trainers and strode into the street, almost dragging a bewildered Fergie behind him as they headed to the park. As soon as the gate opened, he slipped the lead off Fergie's neck and broke into a jog around the park perimeter, bouncing along so fast that the dog barely had a chance for a sniff or a pee to keep up. They were back home within twenty minutes, both a little out of breath and in need of rehydrating, but equally excited.

"I'll go change, then I'll be off to the bus, if that's OK Ma?" he said as he gulped down the water. Callum felt close to his mum, and their interaction had been more relaxed as the year had progressed. He knew she was pleased that he had taken such an interest in fishing and he felt sure there had been some therapeutic benefit in them talking more of his father and brother. He carried a sense of responsibility he had not had a year ago. He needed to be there for his mum and to make sure the link to those they had lost was strong. He liked this position; he had a responsibility, and he wasn't going to let his dad down.

"I've been OK without your help for long enough now, Callum Anderson, just go and have a nice time," she said. "Enjoy the fishing tomorrow, you lucky lad, and I'll see you back here for tea. Give your Granda a call from the bus if you can, he hasn't been good the last couple of days. I've hardly heard from him but I'm sure he'll have some fishing advice that he'd be glad to share."

Showered and changed, Callum gathered the big rucksack, shouted goodbye and rode off to the Cult's bus stop in plenty of time for the 18.10. With the bike secured and his rucksack in the luggage area, he took his usual seat by the left-hand window and checked his phone. There were a couple of messages wishing him luck with his fishing, a group message confirming the details for the rugby training and one from Honor with intimate emojis that made him smile.

Once he had finished replying he went to his favourite contacts and pressed the number for Granda. They had not spoken for more than a week, though they had exchanged a few texts.

"Callum, lad," said Granda. He spoke softly and slowly, and there was a noticeable rasp in his voice. "Feeling confident about tomorrow?"

"Granda, sorry I haven't called but I seem to be so busy now I've got some work at the hotel. Everything's going great, I've so much to tell you. Are you any better?"

"Aye, nae bad. What's your plan for tomorrow? It's a lovely stretch of water, but the weather's nae with ye. They caught many this week?"

"Aye, they've had a couple, I spoke with the ghillie last night and it sounds promising. Floating lines, light leader and small flies by the sound of it. I'm going to make an early start as it's so warm, and also I have to get to the field for training in the afternoon."

Callum could just make out his reply above the sound of the bus. "Make sure you get one, and send me a picture won't you, the season will be away from us before ye know it."

"I'll do my best Granda and come to see you on Sunday, if that's all right?"

"Aye laddie. My love to Honor." With that he hung up, leaving Callum wondering quite how his grandad knew he would be seeing Honor, before realising with a smile that it could only have come from one person.

To have travelled to the fishing on Saturday morning by bus would have meant getting to the river at 9.00 at the earliest, three hours later than he wanted to start. He had learnt that on a hot and bright day his best chance of a fish was before the sun rose too high, or possibly, as had been the case on Tuesday, later in the afternoon as it began to set.

He had looked into getting a taxi, but it was going to cost more than £50, so that was out of the question. It was Honor's father who offered a solution. Their home on the Cairnton estate was only twenty minutes' bike ride away from the Dess. When Honor chatted with him about their plan, Buster suggested Callum should stay in the tent in their garden, allowing him to depart at first light if he wished without disturbing anyone. Callum had naturally leapt at this opportunity to sleep close to where he would be fishing, but it also meant he and Honor would be together that night.

One complication was that he was expected to attend rugby training Saturday afternoon, as the start of the season was fast approaching. In many ways he would have preferred to fish all day with Honor, but he owed it to the team to train, so he planned to leave the river at lunchtime and had arranged to get a lift with one of the second-row players who conveniently lived just upstream in Aboyne. This meant his only chance to catch was early Saturday morning. The love he had developed for fishing wasn't compromising his rugby in the slightest. In fact, it strangely seemed to complement it, and he would often think about moments of triumph when he was waist-deep in the Dee wondering how to tempt a fish.

Sitting on the bus, looking out to his left, Callum was mature enough to recognise the balancing calm that fishing brought to his life, too. He loved adrenalin-pumping activities as much as he always had but relished the zone that fishing took him to. It was sometimes punctuated with the tensest of moments, nothing compared to that unique feeling of a hooked fish, but it was the unpredictable element of a largely predictable activity. By far the majority of time was spent casting, absorbing the natural and special surroundings and imagining that a fish was about to seize the fly.

Callum estimated that his average day's fishing was eight hours with the rod in his hand, or four hundred and eighty minutes. If he managed to catch a fish every day and it took ten minutes to land, that would still be less than two per cent of the time and from experience, one a day was very, very optimistic. Therefore, salmon fishing was more than ninety-eight per cent of the time a chance to appreciate other things, to reflect on the rest of life and be thankful for it.

He reached Cairnton around 7.30 pm and sat with Buster in the fading sunlight on the lawn facing out over the river, a cold beer in his hand. Honor had shown him to the tent. They had embraced once out of sight, excited and giggling as their lips met. He dropped his rucksack through the unzipped entrance and with huge smiles they walked hand in hand back to the patio just as Honor's mum arrived home from work. Honor went to meet her, leaving just the two of them.

"How's the fishing been this week?" he asked.

"It's been another good week," said Buster. "That rain last Sunday seemed to move the grilse further upstream – there are

quite a few about and some larger summer fish. We've caught nine
so far, all of them around four to five pounds, so can't complain,
especially given that on Monday the river was a bit dirty from the
rain."

It seemed that the grilse, those salmon that spend just one year
at sea, arrived over a window of about two months, generally in
June and July. Fishing could be prolific. If you hit the river just
right when the grilse were running it was not impossible, though
very special, for someone to catch ten in a day.

"They all came on small flies with floating lines, apart from
today when one of our rods was using the riffle hitch," said Buster.
"Now that's a lot of fun, have you tried that? We used to catch a lot
of salmon on the surface in Canada."

Callum had not tried the hitch, but he had seen it on YouTube.
He had learned how it was especially successful on smaller rivers
and particularly in Iceland. Rather than have the current swing a
fly below the surface, hitching was about making a 'wake' with a fly
across the top. To achieve this the 'hitch' was made less streamlined
by attaching the line through the middle of the fly rather than onto
a hook at the nose. If you imagine a stick with string tied around
one end and dangled it into a stream off a bridge the stick would
point downstream and wave in the current. If, however, you tied
the string around the middle of the stick it would lie perpendicular
to the current and create quite a wake. It was this V-shaped wake
on the surface that the small fly created that provoked the salmon
to take it, and all in full view of the angler. Some of the takes he
had watched on the video were explosive.

"You're having a good season, be nice to catch one at Dess
tomorrow," said Buster warmly. "Has your grandad given you some
advice?"

"Yeah, we always have a little chat, he knows so much about
this river. He's a big believer in small flies and light tackle when

the grilse are around. It's very good of you to let me stay, Buster, it gives me all morning on the water."

"It's a pleasure to see you," said a woman's voice. Grace, Honor's mother, had joined them, having changed out of her work suit. Despite the obvious difference there was a very strong resemblance between her and her daughter, who was a step behind. They shared the same elegant figure and curly shoulder-length hair. Same image through a different lens.

"How about getting the lad another beer, Ibrahim?"

"Ignore my mum," said Honor. "Ibrahim is dad's real name, but everyone calls him Buster. Isn't that right, Dad?"

Buster smiled and nodded as he replaced Callum's empty bottle and attended to the food. He handed out juicy burgers straight from the grill and they ate, drank and laughed together until a natural pause led Honor to suggest that she and Callum should take a walk up the riverbank.

"Would you mind checking the top hut door is locked if you're OK to walk that far?" asked Buster. "The guys did say they would pull it to."

"Of course dad, we won't be too long."

"Nice to see you Callum, best of luck tomorrow. The early bird!" said Grace.

"Thank you very much Grace and thank you Buster for the lovely supper as well as kindly letting me stay in the tent, saves me three hours!" he replied in his most polite voice. His Nanna would have approved, for sure.

"Bye now, I'll let Nelly out when I'm back and lock up if you've gone up," said Honor with a smile. She placed her arm around his waist and they strode along the riverbank in the dusk. With such a clear sky there was enough light to walk without a torch for now, and he felt her head soft upon his shoulder. The sound of the river and the occasional splash filled the gaps in their chat.

As they approached the first fishing hut, she gently pulled him towards her, and they began to kiss before laying out the blanket she carried onto the warm dry grass, then sinking onto it.

As they kissed, passion overwhelmed them.

"You OK?" asked Callum.

"Yes, yes I'm ready," whispered Honor and pulled him closer.

He was nervous. Of course, he had thought about this a lot, and he wanted it to be special. As if sensing this, Honor helped, and soon they were together. No fumbling or misguided over-enthusiasm; this felt natural and perfect. She drew her head back from his neck to face him. Their eyes were open, searching each other's and shining with desire. He felt a wave of happiness that left him gasping and as he held onto her, he became aware once again of the sound of the river rushing by. She buried her head in his neck again and murmured her love.

The next morning the alarm on Callum's phone woke him at 5.30 and he sleepily dressed, gathered his belongings, and departed in a sober dawn daze. He passed no other traffic as he cycled peacefully through the countryside, which was fortunate as he was still thinking deliriously about the previous night. He arrived at the Kincardine village stores just as they opened, to pick up some water and some snack food. A few minutes later he reached Dess and kept left down the driveway, where the track took him to the head of Jock Rae. Using the bottled water, he gave himself a good wash and brushed his teeth, all the while captivated by the river.

The river at the estate he was fishing today flowed in an inverted L-shape. From the upstream boundary it ran almost directly west to east before it sharply dog-legged and flowed north before reaching the boundary. It was a beautiful stretch of water known to fish well all through the summer, even when the river was quite low, and he was delighted to get the chance. Callum had read that as their eyes are always moist most types of fish have no eyelids, so they have difficulty looking upwards when the sun is intense. This is particularly true when the sun is upstream, reducing the chances of them rising to a fly. He had spoken to Eoin, the ghillie, who was happy for Callum to fish the lower beat in the morning as that was closest to the hut where he was being collected. Callum knew the sun would be in his face not the fishes. He had described the two main pools for him to focus on, the Mill pool and Jock Rae pool, and outlined the set-up he would recommend. They would swap over with the upper beat in the afternoon, though Callum would not be able to stay. Callum asked if he could make an early start and like most ghillies, Eoin was fine with that so long as he was careful.

With his bike rested against a tree, Callum set up his rod, on which he tied a longer than usual length of leader and attached, without hesitation, a size fourteen black Frances. He slipped off his trainers, placed them on a large rock and carefully pulled on his waders before slipping his feet into his boots. He looped the braces of his waders over his shoulders so they sat tight against the fabric of his brown polo shirt. He then applied some suncream to the backs of his hands and neck before donning his cap, sunglasses and flotation device.

Callum studied the glassy water. The current was easy enough to decipher, and he was confident he could fish this pool well. There were a few large boulders that seemed likely lying spots for any fish, and as the water parted over them, flashes of white shone briefly. He moved confidently but gently down the remaining part of the bank, hoping the river wouldn't notice him.

He had two hours alone, and then she would be here. The last few weeks had been so good. He began to relive the previous night again, but then the splash of a fish some distance below brought him back into the now. He began to roll out his fly and let it swing on quite a short line. Although there was a good clear channel midway across the river it was new water to him, and he knew that coming out of darkness at the start of the day the fish can sometimes be closer in. His casting was improving, and he could probably add another ten metres and still retain control, but he was in no rush to do so just yet as the current was a little closer to his bank at the top of the pool. There was something very special about being in the river when the world was awaking; there was a purity to it.

Another fish showed, this time closer, and then another alongside as if they were trying to catch a look at him. His attention was acute, and he was taut with expectation. He took a step downstream and very delicately rolled out another shortish cast, a little mend to slow it down...

And then, *whack*, he felt the line tighten sharply. Before he could even lift the rod the startled fish was pulling line off his reel as it steamed out into the main current. It was angry, and it crashed around like a wildcat in a box, somersaulting across the water. Callum felt sure it would shake the hook unless he could calm it down. He tried to maintain a constant pressure by reeling in to avoid any slack and allowed the rod to tip forward as pressure increased. It wasn't a big fish, but it tore around the pool.

Callum decided to step back onto the dry stones, hoping to avoid the new burst of energy that often accompanies a fish spotting the angler, but as he did so the fish launched itself into the air in a silver arc, and by the time it had splashed back into the river the hook had come out.

He smiled. That one had deserved to get away, he thought. Although it was only a grilse, it had been a high-speed rollercoaster ride for the minute or so he had hung onto it. Landing the fish was a relatively small part of the excitement of fishing; it was nice to get a close look and ideally a photo, but it was the initial take and the fight that were so special. At the back of his mind, however, was the knowledge that it would not, of course, count in the competition.

He checked the leader and hook and found them in perfect condition, so he took a few paces upstream and started again, positive that he would get another chance.

He worked the pool until he eventually came to the tail, but despite seeing more fish moving there had, surprisingly, been no more offers, although it had looked fishy all the way down and he had moved slowly. Not that you can ever define what makes a pool 'fishy' – unless you can see fish in it – but it had seemed that there had been a real chance of a take at every cast. He had stuck with the same fly, confident it was as likely to tempt a fish as any.

By the height of the sun he realised that he had been fishing for some time now. He had agreed to meet Honor at the hut at 8.30, so he put his rucksack on his back and pushed his bike towards the meeting place, carrying his rod. Just as he was resting the bike, he heard the gentle sound of a bell and caught the glorious sight of Honor cycling down the track towards him. He embraced her before she could dismount. They kissed, then laughed, and he took her tackle-bag. He held her free hand and led her to the outdoor picnic table, where they kissed again. He could smell the bacon even before she retrieved the paper bags, and they tucked into breakfast without needing to say more.

As Honor finished her roll they heard a big splash and looked up simultaneously as if expecting to see the culprit, which had of course already disappeared below the surface. The sound of a fish moving was something no angler could resist.

Then they heard a car's tyres on the stones of the path and turned back together. Once it had parked they rose and slowly walked to meet the driver, who extended his hand with a warm smile. Callum knew this must be Eoin, the ghillie. He was smartly dressed and reminded Callum of his Granda.

"Callum, nice to finally meet you, and you must be Honor, Buster's lass?" said Eoin. They each shook his hand and returned friendly greetings.

"Pleasure to meet you Eoin," said Honor. "My father says you're one of the most experienced ghillies on the river. He sends his best regards."

"That's very kind of him, but I think he may be overstating it a wee bit. He's having a cracking first season down at Cairnton, good on him. So how have you got on this morning Callum, you got yourself a Dess salmon?"

"Not yet, but I came bloody close. Had one on for more than a minute, but he slipped the hook just as I thought he was beginning to tire. There's lots showing but I only connected with that one."

Eoin opened up the hut and went in, and Callum and Honor sat back at the table to finish their coffee and sandwiches. The ghillie reappeared wearing waders and carrying a coffee of his own. He had released a black spaniel from the boot of his car, which ran at his feet as he made his way back to them.

"I've fished all the way down the Jock Rae pool with a small Black Frances," said Callum. "What do you suggest I try next? I've to be away at one." There was an anxious note in his voice. He had felt confident that he would catch one that morning, but with Eoin's arrival he had become aware how much time had already slipped by.

"Why doesn't Honor fish down the same pool?" suggested Eoin. "It'll be well rested at the top by now, but I would suggest she tries a brighter fly now the sun has risen, maybe a small Silver Sheep if you have one? I'll get you going down here in the Mill pool, it's a lovely height for that and I feel sure you'll get something."

As Honor began to assemble her rod, Callum collected his and followed Eoin in front of the hut and down to the water's edge, where the ghillie now described the key features and lies. This was the most productive pool on the beat, Callum learned, with a wide streamy section that opened into a deeper hole where fish often held. But it was quite tricky to fish, with lots of boulders and slippery bedrock, so a wading staff was essential. You could fish it in sections using different tactics, but Eoin advised that a light line and small fly would be as good as any today, so Callum was taking that approach. It was a long pool and would take some time to fish thoroughly.

Eoin wished him luck and turned back towards the hut, nodding to draw his attention to a Land Rover that was now heading towards them. *Friggin' James,* thought Callum, his jaw tightening a little as he started into the water. There was no real animosity between them, but there was definitely a little friction, driven partly by the contest but also by an unspoken rivalry over Honor.

Something nagged at Callum regarding James's success in fishing, too. He was able to get on the best beats whenever he was home from school, which was bound to be the case given who his father was, but it wasn't really that. He seemed to have an inexplicable knowledge of where to cast his fly. Maybe it was specific and expert advice from the ghillies, but whatever it was it seemed to work for him, as his catch rate was phenomenal. More importantly however, James might have caught more fish than him this year, but he had not caught Honor.

Callum gradually worked his way down the Mill pool, sending the fly out nicely with little disturbance and watching the line swing back in towards him. Occasionally, where he had seen fish moving, he would cast twice before taking the next step downstream and on the second cast he would retrieve his line to speed up the fly. At other times he would try to 'twitch' the fly so it moved more in the water.

He continued along the pool, the bright sun reflecting off the shimmering water directly onto his face. He dreaded reaching the end of the pool without a take, but it was only a few steps away, and he knew there was no chance of a salmon in the next stretch, so he reeled in. He looked further upstream towards where he knew James was but could not see him; he must be round the corner of the Pitslug pool. Despondently he trudged back to the hut, feeling sure that James had already caught. He decided to call Granda on his way. Just speaking to someone would help, he felt sure.

"Hi Granda, it's Callum." There was a pause as his grandad cleared his throat. "Hello laddie, how's it?" he croaked. He sounded out of breath; perhaps he had rushed back indoors to answer the phone.

"Ach, Granda. I cannae get one to bloody stick," said Callum. It was quite unlike him to use coarse language. "There's plenty of fish aboot but I lost the only one that I've tempted. It's been frustrating and now it's bright and sunny, not sure what I can do in my last hour or so. Any ideas?" Callum heard the TV in the background before the gentle reply came.

"Just imagine we are there with you, always," he said. Callum was about to answer, but as he rounded the front of the hut he was distracted by the sight of Honor at the picnic table with a bottle of water and wearing a broad grin.

"Aye, I'll try that, Granda," said Callum. "Got to hop now, see you tomorrow. Bye." He placed his rod in the stand and plonked himself down next to her. "Well?" he asked.

She took out her phone and showed him a picture of a small but very fresh grilse lying in the shallows at the river's edge with her rod next to it, Callum could see from the photo that it had been taken at 11.30, twenty minutes ago.

"Well done you, that's grand. Was it on the Silver Sheep?" He gave her a slightly patronising kiss on the cheek.

"Yeah, just towards the tail of the pool, not a big fish but really strong. How have you got on?"

"Ah, nothing. Not sure what I'm doing wrong, but I just can't get one interested and I don't have too much time left. I'll give it one more go."

"Did you want to try the lower pool again?" offered Honor.

Callum paused, considering the options. "Nope, I'll try the Mill again, but I'm going to use something a bit heavier and see if that helps now it's so warm and bright. The sun's right on the water. I really hope he hasn't caught one," he added. "Is it OK with you if I do that?"

"Yes, sure. I'm going to put some more suncream on and watch you from the bank, promise I won't put you off. First, I'm going to send that photo to Dad. Catch you up, hon."

Callum removed the floating tip that was attached to the fly-line and replaced it with one that would sink relatively quickly. He also replaced his small fly with one aptly named the Eternal Optimist, which was much heavier and largely silver and yellow in appearance. Knowing he was short of time, he skipped over the shallower start of the pool and began to cast towards the deeper water. As the fish had stopped jumping he figured they may be lower down in the water. It was a bit trickier to cast the heavier line and fly, and it took him a few attempts to get the timing right so that the line went out straight. He had to slow the action down a little as the heavy fly moved more slowly, but when he got it right the line flew.

It was past twelve now, the sun was overhead and there were no longer fish splashing on the surface. His early confidence was gone, replaced by emptiness. The pressure of needing to catch something was uncomfortable and didn't sit well with him. He should have been delighted that Honor had caught a fish, but that joy was tempered, and he knew why. He was casting aggressively and stripping the line in faster than normal. The calm gracefulness of his fishing had been briefly replaced by a tempestuous thrash and he swore under his breath.

Thankfully, he was distracted by the sound of a whistle and as he looked towards it, he saw her sitting on the grass bank and waving. Her legs were straight in front, and without a cap to restrain it the locks of her hair fell round her neck. She stuck up her thumb to him, and he smiled back. Retrieving the line more gradually, he took a step downstream and cast out more calmly. This time the line flew out effortlessly and landed gently. His anger was now directed inwards, at himself for letting the pressure get to him, but it soon passed as he realised his foolishness.

He listened to the water tumbling by, felt the warmth of the sun on his arms and was just thinking it might be a good idea to join Honor on the bank when without warning the line thumped twice, instantly awaking all his senses. He resisted the temptation to strike and within a second there was another thump, but this time it turned into a firm resistance. He waited; he didn't want to pull too hard unless the hook came straight out of the fish's mouth. It felt as if the fish was stationary, and it seemed to be shaking its head, as if in disbelief at being snagged. But then the thumping turned into a strong pull as it headed away, drawing line against the drag of the reel.

He heard Honor shriek behind him as he stepped downstream to follow the fish. Another few metres of line ran out before the fish stopped, and it was like that moment in a tug-o-war when both sides are pulling but nothing moves. They held there for some time, Callum with the rod nearly vertical and the orange line stretched taut to where it was attached to the grey sinking tip which entered the water below it.

Slowly Callum increased the pressure and very gradually began to reel line back in, almost in slow motion, drawing the salmon slowly back upstream. It felt much less excitable than the grilse and there was certainly no bullying this one. He coaxed it further, and then, with a shake of the head like a stubborn puppy out for its first walk on a lead, it turned back downstream.

"I'll get the net," called Honor, running back to the hut as more line sang out from the reel and Callum stepped after it, avoiding the boulders as best he could, but almost toppling in. This was a strong run.

The fish pulled twenty metres or more of line out, and then suddenly stopped. Callum applied more pressure, but it would not budge. He had read that sometimes a big fish will position itself immovably in the fast current for long periods of time, almost ignoring the fact that it is hooked.

He walked further downstream, reeling in the slack he had created, but still the fish did not move. As he drew level with it he saw that the bottom shelved away in front of him; this was the deepest part of the pool. He applied even more pressure but was anxious the line would part. He could feel faint vibrations that suggested that the fish was still there, but otherwise it was solid, as if snagged.

Honor joined him, net in hand. "Is he still on?" she asked.

"I'm not sure. It's a good fish, but I think it's wrapped itself around a rock. I'm going to get downstream of it a little and see if I can prise it out." Whereupon Callum let the line go loose and stepped fifteen metres downstream before making another attempt to turn the fish his way, but to no avail. *Shit*, he thought, *What now?*

He did not know what he could do other than to try and heave the fish off whatever it was wrapped around, assuming it was still attached. If the line broke, at least the fish would be free, and he was pretty sure it would be able to shake the hook at that point.

He decided to let out some slack line and wait for a minute, just in case that prompted the fish to move. He did so before quickly tightening the line again, hoping to feel the fish, but it was still solid. With no alternative he started to walk backwards, stretching the line and involuntarily gritting his teeth as he anticipated the break.

Two more steps and it came. He reeled in, expecting to find the leader had snapped close to the hook, but was confused to see that as he wound the thin backing line up through the rod eyes and back onto the reel, the orange fly-line failed to follow it. It took Callum a moment to realise that the tackle had snapped where the two lines met; he had lost his fly-line, and worse, it might still be attached to the fish.

He stared into the water incredulously before marching back along the bank, accompanied by a silent Honor. As they rounded the hut, they met Eoin, who had returned for his lunch. They chatted a little, but Callum was not very talkative. After congratulating Honor for her catch, Eoin consoled Callum. He explained how over time the fishing lines can fray and weaken as they rub across rocks. They need checking and replacing periodically. This was of no consolation to Callum. Eoin felt sure that if the fish was still attached it would soon work the hook loose.

Callum packed away his tackle, casually enquiring whether James had caught anything; his sorrow that he had not was almost convincing.

Callum gathered his tracksuit and started to change on the grass behind the hut. As he was slipping on his trainers, Honor appeared, talking on her phone. As she got closer, he heard her say "Blah blah blah", then she placed the phone in her pocket and threw her arms around him. She had not been on the phone at all; she had just wanted to get away from Eoin and kiss Callum before he left. He hugged her, trying not to think of the fish that had got away.

Now in a better mood, Callum headed over to the table, collected his big bag and wheeled his bike to the rear of the car, where he shook hands with Ritchie, the tall teenager who was giving him a lift who had just arrived. He had known Ritchie since they had started at Cult's together, and they had played rugby together over the past five years.

It took about thirty minutes to reach the Academy sports pitches. Ritchie asked probing questions about his relationship with Honor before turning to the morning's fishing. He knew Callum was in with a chance of the prize – lots of people did – and he was sorry to hear what had happened. They reached the ground, parked up and paced over to meet with the rest of the squad before the training began as usual with some warm-ups.

Honor called him later as she was heading home. "How did the rugby go?" she asked.

"Not so good, I've really hurt my finger. I think it's just a dislocation, but my teacher's taking me to the hospital to get it looked at. Don't think my mind was completely on the game today and I fluffed it. Not my day today."

"Oh no, poor you! Does it hurt? Which finger is it?"

"It did initially but it's OK now, problem is it's the index finger on my left hand."

"But you're right-handed, so it isn't so bad, is it?"

"I can write OK, that's not the problem. Issue is I don't know how I'm going to cast and retrieve the line properly and I still need to catch to have any chance of winning."

"Oh Callum, ouch. You'll be OK, you can cast left-handed if you need to! Look, I'm not sure how to tell you what's just happened.

After lunch, James fished the Mill pool and halfway down he seemed to have hooked a fish. It turned out he was actually hooked up to your line, and the fish was still attached. It was a fourteen pounder and I'm afraid it counts as his catch."

There was an initial silence before Callum replied, "What the fuck? I don't believe it! Look, I gotta go." He hung up angrily.

CHAPTER 23

Callum's finger turned out to be dislocated, but once it was back in place and bandaged, most of the pain had receded. There would be no rugby for a couple of weeks, but thankfully he should still be able to fish.

As he left A&E, Callum called Granda to see if he could collect him from the sports ground, as he would not be able to get all his fishing gear back with the bike, but there was no reply; perhaps he was in the garden. Thankfully, his mother had agreed to walk to the Academy after her shift and they headed home on foot together with the bike and the bags. It was still warm, but it was now August, so the days were quite quickly shortening and the sun was no longer overhead.

Thirty minutes later Callum was at the dinner table, refreshed and relaxed, and telling his mother about his night's camping, though again omitting certain details. He received an email with the daily catch report and could see the fourteen-pound fish recorded against Dess, along with a good number of others all along the river. He knew that the weekly report on Sunday night would show James one ahead, but he was hopeful that the following week he could add to his tally, as he had two more days planned. He headed to his room and caught up with some messages. He was tired after the night before and the early start. As soon as he turned the screen off, he fell into a deep sleep.

Callum came to gradually; he had slept well into the morning, despite the throb from his left hand, and he headed to the bathroom to check how it looked. The bruising had come through; it was almost black around the knuckle, but it hadn't swollen too much. He could just about clench his fist.

As he opened his bedroom door, he realised what was missing. On Sunday mornings they always had a cooked breakfast, and the smoked bacon could usually be smelled as he descended the stairs. His mum wasn't in the kitchen. It was still before ten; perhaps they would be having it a bit later. He filled a bowl with cereal, emptying a carton of milk onto it.

Fergie wandered over and sat on his bare feet, comforting and warm. But what was Fergie doing here? He had assumed his mum had taken him for a walk.

He reached for his phone to see if she had sent a message, but there was nothing. She had probably gone to fetch the papers or some milk. He read a message from Honor, intimate, caring and personal. There were a few messages asking about the fishing, friends wanting to know who was in the lead, which irritated him. He worked through these, alternating between typing and lifting the spoon to his mouth. Photos of fish caught had appeared on social media, including one at Dess of James smiling in triumph. Some of the salmon were now showing their autumn colours, the shine replaced by dull but beautiful browns in much the same way as a leaf changes. They were coming towards the end of their journey.

Callum cleared his bowl and wandered into the living room. Unsure whether to walk Fergie, he had started to message his mum when he was distracted by a car pulling up outside. Its roof bore the blue light fitting of a police car. As he watched, a woman police officer walked around to the front and opened the passenger door. His mother stepped out. She seemed to be thanking the officer.

Callum was confused. Had she witnessed something when she had popped out? Could there have been an incident at the newsagents?

"Everything OK, Mum?" he asked as she opened the sitting room door.

She approached him slowly, pain on her face, and extended her hands to him like an image from a children's bible. He instinctively took them, wondering what on earth was wrong.

"Callum, my darling, Granda's gone." She broke down, sobbing in a way he had never heard before, and he drew her into his chest. He wrapped his arms around her protectively, staring at the featureless off-white wall.

After a long embrace, she composed herself enough to sit at the kitchen table while Callum made her a cup of tea. He brought her a tissue and asked her to tell him what had happened.

"I got a call at seven thirty from John Reid, who as you know lives close," she said. "He had been out with his dog and noticed the lunch-bag I had placed for Granda was still on the doorstep and the front room curtains were open. He knocked on the door but there was no reply, which he thought was unusual. Your Granda had been taking a nap during the middle of day over the past few weeks, so I've just been leaving his lunch for him to collect when he awakes rather than disturb him. I tried to call him, but it went straight to voicemail, so I thought I would pop down and just check he was OK. When I opened the lunch-bag I could see it hadn't been touched, I let myself in and there was no sound or reply to my calls."

She stopped to wipe her eyes and blow her nose. Callum rested his hand on her shoulder and she resumed. "I knew something was wrong. I went into the dining room and found Granda lying on a camp bed he had made up. He looked at peace Callum, but he was very pale, and I immediately knew he had gone." She stopped again to catch her breath. "I made some calls and an ambulance came with a police car. They didn't try to resuscitate him, so he must have been gone for some time. I was told to call his doctor, who I know is Dr Morgan, and thankfully he took my call even on a Sunday morning." She paused and it seemed like they both needed to absorb what she had said, but her delay had more purpose than that. "Did you know your Granda was unwell, Callum? Had he mentioned anything to you?"

"No Ma, not at all. I hadn't seen him over the past week as he said he had a summer bug which had laid him low, but I had spoken to him. I even spoke to him yesterday morning. He sounded very tired, but I thought nothing of it. Come to think of it he did say something which sounded a bit sentimental, for him, but I dismissed it as I was with Honor and all I could think about was trying to catch a damn fish. Do you think I could have saved him if I had realised he wasn't well?"

"No love, you definitely couldn't have saved him, nobody could. Your Granda had discovered in the spring that he had pancreatic cancer, and although it was terminal, he must have decided not to share it with us. Dr Morgan was not aware he had kept it to himself, but he assured me he would not have been in any pain. The medication would have removed that and the end would have happened quickly. He has been taken to the funeral home in Peterculter."

They both sat immersed in their thoughts for a few moments. Callum looked out of the window, anger inexplicably building inside him.

"I'd like to go to his house, is that allowed?" asked Callum, calmly and precisely.

"Yes Cal, the doctor is going to provide the medical cause of death and I'll register it tomorrow. We're fine to visit the house and we can visit your Granda in the funeral home too, if we want at some stage."

Callum nodded and rose unsteadily. He placed his hand on his mother's shoulder as he passed and headed upstairs to change into dark jeans and a smarter shirt. He put his black school shoes on. With a flat "Bye Mum" he picked up the door key with the salmon fob and left the house.

He walked slowly along the pavement, with no dog lead and no phone. His right hand was thrust into his front pocket and his left swung slowly at his side, like a pendulum marking time. As he approached his grandad's house, he saw nervous movement from the neighbour's windows as they discreetly looked to see who it was. It must have provided them with some excitement, he thought bitterly.

He opened the door and entered swiftly, closed it behind him, and stopped in the hall to remove his shoes. The house already felt different; it was silent and hollow. There would be no warm welcome today, or ever again.

Callum peered into the front room, which was immaculate; the same two photos still looking back from the dresser. The kitchen was similarly sterile; there wasn't even anything draining next to the sink. The only other room downstairs was a small dining room which a few years ago, when the stairs became mountains, had been converted into a downstairs bedroom for Morag. Over the past few years, the sofa bed had been unused, but that had recently changed. The bedding was ruffled, from where his grandad had been removed. Ironically, it was the only sign of life.

Callum gently sat at the base of the sofa-bed and he looked towards the far wall. There was a watercolour he had not noticed before of a long sweeping bend in the river with a castle he recognised as Balmoral. As he rounded the end of the bed to get a closer look, he stepped on something. Looking down he saw three photos scattered on the carpet and spotted Granda's old mobile phone beside them. He checked the phone, but it too was dead.

He gathered up the photos and placed them on the bed. They were so very familiar. His Nanna had been very pretty, her smile even brighter than the silver salmon held by Granda. Callum could see that he shared the same smile with his brother and his father, happiness bursting from their lips. But he hadn't noticed before any resemblance between him and his Granda. Yet stood together outside Polvier, a glint in both sets of eyes, there was no mistaking it.

Now they were all together, and he was alone. He tried to stand but his knees gave way and he rolled back so his head was on the pillow. He cried until his head hurt and his palms were wet.

When he arrived home he opened the front door as quietly as he could, but Fergie was waiting for him. Callum dropped to his knees and hugged his pal, which gave him a moment to gather himself before heading into the kitchen. His mum started to talk, but when she turned and looked into his face, she stopped.

Callum spent the next few days at home, joining his mum for meals but otherwise cocooning himself away from the outside world. He left his phone on its charger in the kitchen. Each day she would tell him who had been trying to reach him; she had asked them all to give him some space.

He tried to read the Chaytor book he had been given and look through the photos Granda had passed to him. There were two weeks left until school restarted, but his confused mind could not settle on anything.

On the Tuesday he was meant to be with Honor, but that didn't happen. He didn't want any sympathy and was annoyed whenever his mum asked if he was OK. He lacked any clear idea about what he was to do. What would Granda have wanted him to do? What about the competition, did any of it matter? He wanted to hurt himself, to smash that damn weak dislocated finger of his. He lay in the bath, submerging himself until he could hold his breath no more.

Over the next days these feelings subsided, and a sense of responsibility elbowed its way into his mindset. He was the survivor, he had to hold it together and make it better. At dinner on the Wednesday, his mother told him she wanted them to take a walk the following day. She wanted him to show her where he had fished with Granda. It was important, she said, that they should decide together where on the river they were going to sprinkle his ashes. That was Granda's wish.

"OK," Callum replied. "Let's do that, it would be good for Fergie to get a proper walk."

On the Thursday morning, they left the house after breakfast. It had turned cooler, which allowed them the increased anonymity of high-collared coats and hats. Neither of them wanted to get drawn into conversation with their neighbours. They walked along the Garthdee Road and dropped down through the university grounds to the bank of the river, where they stopped at the same bench Granda had sat on whilst Callum had practised casting almost exactly a year ago. He recounted this to his mum.

"I sat on this very bench many times myself," she said with a forlorn smile. "Usually with a book to read as your dad fished below. I remember one day watching two seals playing right in the middle. One of them had caught a salmon and actually gave half of it to the other. Incredible sight for me, but it did upset poor Ian."

Her last word made Callum twitch, as he could not remember ever hearing her say his dad's name before.

Despite being made of granite the bench appeared well worn; it must have hosted so many memories thought Callum as he looked over the rushing water. "Maybe one day your wife will look down on you fishing here with you own child," his mother added hopefully.

"You know Mum, I'm really not sure there will be any salmon left in our rivers by then," said Callum. "And if the salmon disappear, so do our ancestors." That statement hung over them for a moment as they sat in silence, staring into the flow of the river.

"I don't think this is where we should lay Granda," said Callum after a while. "Let's head further upstream." They walked along Deeside Way, chatting openly about things that mattered. They spoke about Granda, about school and eventually about fishing. Callum wasn't sure if he could enjoy being on the water knowing their discussions and reviews would not happen. Winning the competition was within his grasp, but did that matter any more? Would trying to win be a betrayal, or was it his destiny? Their conversation was punctuated with long, pensive pauses.

After a little more than an hour, Callum stopped and pointed to a development of buildings in front of them.

"That's where the Culter Mill was for over two hundred years," he said. "Granda told me how many thousands had worked there during the life of the mill, including him and many generations of Andersons. When the works hooter blasted for the end of the day it often meant it was time for fishing." He pointed to the river ahead on the left as it stretched away. "That's the Culter beat, let's head there."

They left the trail and took a path heading down towards the river; even when it was hidden, they could hear it flowing by. As they passed through a gate, Callum took his mother's hand and they followed the path he and Granda had taken to the bench beside the Greenbank pool. They sat down and Callum took his phone from his pocket and located the picture he wanted from his favourites folder.

"My first salmon, Ma," he said. Although she had seen the picture many times before, she studied it closely.

"Just down there on that shingle beach," he said flatly with a nod of his head in the direction of the river. "I have read other people say that you always remember the first salmon you catch. I am so, so glad it was here with Granda. I'll never forget that day and I think this is where he should rest." He took a deep breath and let out a sigh.

"Your hair looked nicer when it was longer," said his mum. It was a comment that only a mother would make. She smiled and hugged him.

CHAPTER 24

Honor awoke from a deep sleep and lay on her side hugging a pillow. Turning onto her back, she stretched out like a starfish, reaching towards all four corners and arching her back. Lowering her feet onto the soft carpet, she stood and walked towards the curtains, stopping at her dressing table. As she looked in the mirror she pouted and raised her eyebrows in a way she never would do in company. A silken nightie hung from her slender shoulders down to her thighs. Messy hair tumbled onto her prominent collar bones and down onto her breasts.

With a smile she moved to the curtains. Opening them, she saw the river beyond the neat lawn. She looked over the cottage pool, then, turning to the right, she gazed upstream to where they had lain. Transported back thirty-six hours, she looked without seeing, her eyes not focusing, her mind drifting. She headed for the door and took her dressing gown.

At the breakfast table, a tall stack of pancakes sat in front of them. She engaged enthusiastically with her parents, building up courage and awaiting the right moment.

"Can I help tomorrow, Dad?" she asked. "Do we know the rods?"

"No, I don't know them, but we spoke on the phone yesterday and they sound like a nice group. Two families. All four adults fish and their children too apparently. Your help would be much appreciated. It's always a bit of an effort getting everyone going on the first day, especially as they haven't been to Cairnton before."

"Ah sure, I can help all day. On Tuesday Callum's asked me to fish with him on the Association water at Garthdee."

"That sounds great, maybe he can make up for the fish he lost at Dess on Saturday."

"He's already caught at Garthdee so it won't affect the competition, but just a chance for us to do something." Then she casually added, "He said I could maybe stay over at his afterwards. I think it was his mum's idea, they have a spare room."

It was her mum's turn to speak now. "Ah that's kind. I'll have a chat with your dad about our plans and let you know this morning, love."

The topic changed seamlessly and they finished their breakfast together.

Later that morning, there was a knock at Honor's door and her mother entered.

"Getting your schoolwork done? That's good," she said. "Hon, about staying over at Callum's on Tuesday."

"Yes Mum?"

"He's a nice lad, it's good you are getting on so well. You will be careful, won't you?" She spoke in a soft, caring tone.

"Yes of course Mum, he always wears protection," was the unexpected, matter-of-fact reply. Grace frowned in surprise. "I always put it on too as soon as it's my turn to fish."

"Ah! I wasn't talking about a buoyancy aid," said Grace.

They stared at each other for a moment, both suppressing grins.

"Seriously, don't worry, Mum, I've got it covered," said Honor, and she rose to hug her.

She messaged Callum again, excited that she would be allowed to stay over. Earlier she had asked how his dislocated finger was, but he had not replied. She could see that he hadn't even seen the first message yet. Presumably he was getting a good recovery sleep after his eventful day.

When she had still not heard from him by the time her work was done, she sent him another message, but this time through Instagram, thinking that maybe he had a problem with his Snap account or something. Through the afternoon she checked in vain for a response. She could see that neither account had been active. It made no sense. Unless maybe his phone had broken? It had to be that. That was the only logical reason.

In the early evening she tried sending an email, knowing that would reach his computer even if his phone was not working. She felt sure he would respond. It said 'Hey, you ignoring me? No longer want me? ;-)'

Just before ten she got a response. It said, 'Will you please leave me alone.'

Initially she thought Callum must be joking, but when he didn't respond to her reply, she knew something was wrong. It couldn't have been because of Saturday. She knew he was annoyed that he had lost the fish and James had caught it, but he couldn't be cross with *her*, surely? The words sat in her stomach like stones. She had a torrid night, waking up drenched and disturbed, waves of fear washing over her.

She was quiet and distant at breakfast. "I'll meet you at the hut Dad, I'd like to walk up," she announced before heading to the side porch. As she sat on the bench to pull on her waist waders, Nelly approached and pushed her nose into Honor's face as she leant forward. Honor pulled her closer, needing some comfort, building the mental strength to leave the house. She hugged her again then made off on her own. Honor paced along the bank, past the Grey Mare where they had stood together in the February flood. She stopped at the Middle Ferroch, vividly recalling him landing that special fish. How delighted his grandad had been the day they started going out together. What had changed? What had she done to put him off? Did he think there was something between her and James?

"Are you OK, Honor?" asked her father as he drove her to the cottage for lunch.

"Sorry Dad, I know I haven't been much help this morning. I'm not OK, I don't know what I have done but Callum isn't speaking to me. He won't answer any of my messages. He has gone off me and I just don't know why!" She clenched fists of hair and shook her head.

The truck stopped at the side door and Buster turned to face his beautiful daughter, the most important thing in his life. "Call him. Don't rely on emails or text or whatever. Phone him and speak to him, I'm sure it's just a misunderstanding."

Honor sat in the passenger seat staring through the windscreen. Then she turned towards her father and nodded. "I'll be in shortly," she said.

Moments later, she removed her boots outside the door and slipped off the waders, composing herself before opening the door. Her father anxiously looked up from the table.

"His Granda's died. Callum's mum answered his phone and told me." She didn't join her father on the riverbank that afternoon.

Later that day, Honor started to receive messages from her friends and from those who knew Callum, all trying to find out how he was. Nobody had received any contact from him, despite them all trying to reach out to him. It remained that way for the rest of the week and whilst she respected his need for some space, Honor grew increasingly concerned; she needed to know how he was. Besides, she was missing the contact with him; they had grown so close over the past months.

On Friday evening as her mother returned from work, Honor intercepted her as she stepped from the car. "Mum, I need your help.

I've still not heard back from him and I'm getting really worried. They were so close, so this will be devastating. I know I can help him, Mum, but he won't speak to me."

"Of course, darling. Come with me, I have an idea."

Honor followed her upstairs and they chatted whilst Grace changed out of her work clothes. As they made their way back to the kitchen, Honor's mood had changed a little. For the first time all week, she felt some positivity.

Mid-morning on Sunday, Honor waited nervously in her father's truck. She peered across at the sitting room window of Callum's house, through which she could see the back of his head. His hair looked curlier than usual. Her father stood opposite him, and she could see his lips moving but could not make out the words. Callum occasionally shook his head and sometimes nodded; she could only wonder about what he was saying and what he was responding to.

A few minutes later, she saw Callum's mother join him at his side. Her arm reached as far as she could manage around his back and she pulled him to her. Honor watched her father shake Callum's hand and then disappear from sight.

When Honor's father stepped out of the front door, she saw Callum turn to look out onto the street. She stared at him and their eyes met. The driver's door opened and then shut again as her father got back into the car, but her eyes stayed on Callum's. As the car rolled away, Callum's expression changed. He managed a thin smile and raised his right hand in a wave. Honor involuntarily raised her left as they turned out of sight.

"He's coming," said her father.

CHAPTER 25

Family traditions meant a lot to Grace Garba, as they had to her own parents. Christmas Day had always meant a big gathering at her grandmother's house, an annual convention of cousins, aunts and uncles. Each summer, from as early as she could remember, her parents had rented a house on the south coast with the same two other families. But these occasions both came to an end around the same time. Death and divorce were the enemies of tradition. Because of Buster's work on the river they had not taken any summer holidays in the past six years, just the occasional weekend, but this was partly compensated by a trip to South Africa for three weeks each New Year.

Since moving to Scotland, Grace and her sister had started a new tradition. Every November they returned to their family home in Hampshire for their father's birthday, and they would all go out together in the morning and pick blackthorn berries from the hedgerows to make sloe gin. Before lunch they would sample the previous year's infusion, her mother would roast a joint of beef and in the afternoon they would play cards. Such small things wove the generations together, and perhaps something similar would replace them after he was gone.

Grace found she could watch her husband for hours as he stood in the water; she had tried fishing herself whilst in Nigeria, but once they moved to Canada her attention was always on her daughter. Honor seldom fished with her father as she was usually at school, or during the season, he was working. Most of her fishing time was spent supervising others, or occasionally she could grab an hour before dark. But for the past few years, in mid-August, he had arranged a day off and they had spent it together in this way. There was extra excitement this year as they had been very kindly invited by the owners to join them at Lower Crathes and West Durris, the most sought-after beat on the river.

It had been Grace's idea to ask Callum. His relationship with their daughter this last year had made the transition to Deeside much easier for all of them. He was a nice young man, polite but funny, and the passion he had developed for salmon fishing with his grandad was very special. But now his cast had become tangled again and she hoped they could help him through it by getting him re-engaged in his fishing. She knew there was still a good chance that he could win the prize, something she felt sure his grandad would have wanted. Robert, the head ghillie at Lower Crathes, knowing the situation, had been keen to do what he could to help. His knowledge of Callum had been a fortunate coincidence.

As was usually the case, Grace had spent Saturday morning working. She enjoyed the challenge that had come with her promotion, but it came with a big commitment that included part of her weekend. It didn't quite beat the position of her desk in the window at home, but this fishing hut overlooking the river was still a very special home office.

She raised her eyes from the screen, contentedly closed the laptop and pushed the wooden chair back from the table. The panelled wall behind her was adorned with notices and photographs. All the pictures had two common features: a salmon and a smiling face. There were a few empty aged wine bottles, each no doubt witness to a highly enjoyable lunch. Although this wasn't really her scene, she could appreciate the history and character of such a room. A lot of the photos were of male anglers, but she knew from Honor that more and more women were taking up the sport. She reflected with a grin that there ought to be a UNESCO list of the world's best salmon fishing huts.

She left the hut and strolled upstream towards the Mill pool before stopping so that she could see Buster and Honor without being seen herself. She watched her daughter casting; they were clearly chatting and occasionally her husband would point to the water. The two of them had been together for three hours, standing in a river talking. It was not lost on Grace that getting a sixteen-year-old to do that with a parent was not common these days.

As if to order, just as she was about to join them, she saw that Honor had hooked a fish. She stayed back watching them, intently focused on the fight. Gradually they overcame the salmon and she smiled as her husband lifted the bulging net and high-fived his daughter, who flung an arm round him. Yes, this end of summer day fishing was a new tradition that she hoped would continue forever.

CHAPTER 26

Callum caught the 201 bus, as he had numerous times in the past year, but his feeling today was quite different. He rubbed the zip of his jacket between his fingers and adjusted his cap. There was no reason for him to be apprehensive about the fishing, as he was more than competent, nor about spending time with Honor's family. Yet his routine was different, and this was unsettling him. He needed the reassuring voice or text message, wishing him luck and offering some advice; just the knowledge that he was there, that someone was in his corner. Today it felt like he was heading out on his bike knowing he had a slow puncture.

There was a bus stop just outside Crathes Castle, and there he had arranged to meet the Garbas. He could see the truck waiting as he arrived. Callum straightened his cap again as they all got out to meet him. He didn't dare return their well-meaning hugs. He couldn't afford to think about anything other than the fishing.

It was just a two-minute drive to the hut, but he was relieved when they stopped and he could get out. The two ghillies stood outside the hut to greet them, along with two other anglers. It was overcast but not too cold, and the rain early in the week had passed.

They introduced themselves to the other two rods, who, they discovered, were from the owner's family. Callum and Honor busied themselves setting up their tackle with the help of the younger ghillie whilst Buster and Grace chatted with Robert, the head ghillie, who occasionally looked over.

With the rods set up, they all gathered in front of Robert.

"Morning all," said Robert. "The Pearsons will start on the far bank with Daniel. I'll look after the near bank. Buster, if you can take Honor to the Mill pool. Callum, come with me down to the Bridge pool and we can swap over a bit later. Can you each please put on a flotation device, too. Grace, please make yourself at home in the hut." Friendly but businesslike.

Callum hadn't considered how the fishing would go; in some ways he was sorry he wasn't with Honor, but in others he welcomed some space, at least this morning. They had been in touch again since Buster's visit, speaking later that night when Callum could not keep his composure. He apologised for excluding her, for pushing her away. It was all he could offer for now. She accepted his apology through tears of relief.

He attached his rod to the holders on Robert's truck roof and with a tip of his cap to Honor, jumped into the front. It was just a minute's drive to the parking bay that signified the start of the famous pool.

"Right Callum, there's no shortage of fish in this pool, but they aren't guaranteed to cooperate," Robert began. "That Cascade you've tied on will be just fine. Let's take a walk to the neck, as they're showing all along with this height, it's ideal." He led Callum about fifty metres upstream and out across the shallow shingle to the clearly defined main flow of the river toward the far bank.

"This will be grand. Try and get your fly across the current into the slack water beyond, then hold the rod tip straight out in front of you so it swings across slowly. See if you can hold the fly in the main current as long as possible. There are good taking spots all the way down to the bridge, but particularly where the big rocks stick out."

Callum surveyed the length of the pool all the way down to the bridge as a large logging lorry drove over it. He had seen some videos online the previous day of big fish being fought and landed in the past right where he was now looking. He took a deep breath. It felt once again as if he was taking to the stage, but this wasn't the first night; it felt more like the last. Amongst the emotions stirred by the river was an underlying sense of apprehension. What if he messed it up, what if he didn't catch? Who would he be letting down?

"Take your time, there's no rush lad, he'll wait," said Robert comfortingly, though the words swirled round Callum's head as he began to roll out the fly. Once the line was reaching across the current he started to step downstream after each cast and began to build up a nice rhythm. Regular splashes along the pool drew their attention. Robert made gentle conversation, and they spoke about how the competition stood.

Callum cast again and was just talking about how close it was between him and James when his line tugged three times. Something had snatched at his fly. Callum's heart quickened, but there was no follow-up tension in the line and the fly continued to swing through the water. He looked forlornly at Robert, who grimaced. That was his chance gone, thought Callum. It was going to be another of those days, like at Dess. He sucked his lips between his teeth, something he always did when he concentrated.

He cast out again, but the line landed in a splash. He felt frustrated, and anger was creeping in. He paused, composed himself and tried again, keen to impress the ghillie. Thankfully the line flew out as he had hoped, almost onto the large boulder on the other bank, and gently fell to the surface. "Finally done something right," he muttered cynically to himself.

Just then there came a swirling spray of water a metre away from where the fly had landed. He felt the line tighten, and this time it stuck. The fish leapt clean out of the water, slapping back down as it landed, and he felt the ecstatic, unique thrill of a hooked salmon. Adrenalin fuelling the surge of his pulse.

"Gotcha!" said Robert with a broad smile.

Callum couldn't speak. His lips remained pressed firmly together as he fought to tame the fish. It shook its head aggressively, and each time Callum felt sure the hook would be thrown, but he kept up the pressure as much as he dared. The fish turned with the current and headed for the bridge, but Callum was making it work really hard to take line and as it tired, he drew it back towards him.

"That's it, step slowly towards this big rock and see if we can land him here," said Robert. He lifted the strap of the net over his head and held the shaft firmly in his right hand.

Callum was gripped with fear, still convinced he would lose the fish. The thrill of the take had been replaced by a sense of dread as it struggled to escape. He was imagining telling Honor he had dropped another and was trying to stay positive but secretly he felt distraught. At every run the fish made he expected the line to go loose, but the hook remained fast. His finger throbbed as it slowed the reel until finally he began to guide the fish towards the waiting net.

"Step back onto the bank and draw him smoothly with you," said Robert, and as Callum followed the instructions the fish followed him.

"Yes, oh yes, thank fuck for that," said Callum before he could stop himself. "Sorry Robert, sorry for my language, it just felt like I would never land another one." He put his free hand onto his hip, closed his eyes and looked up to the sky.

"Nae bother Callum, we often get colourful language from our anglers, especially when they've lost a fish," said Robert with a smile as he removed the hook. "Come, let's just take the net a few yards downstream and get a photo before we release him."

Positioned as directed by Robert, Callum briefly held the fish before releasing it. It was a cock, and surprisingly silver for an autumn fish. "This one's come late to the party," said Robert as he took the picture.

With the fish safely back, a smiling Callum stepped up to look at the screen on Robert's phone. As he stared at the picture, the smile slowly drained from his face, replaced by confusion. "That's not me," he murmured, puzzled. It was the same scene of a salmon being landed from the same pool, but the angler in the picture was much older and there were no leaves on the trees.

"That's... my dad, isn't it?" and he turned from the screen to the ghillie's face.

"That's right Callum, it's your father. It was taken just a few weeks before the accident. I went to school with your dad, we were good mates and we fished together many times. He always managed to catch more than me, no idea how he did it, but he just seemed to have a knack. This was the last time I saw him, and I'm pretty sure the last time he fished. You've just caught that one right in his footsteps."

Robert gave Callum a sympathetic smile, swiped to the picture he had just taken and handed it over. Now Callum saw himself in an identical pose at the same spot on the river, almost a copy of the previous one. The blood returned to his face, which broke into a smile. "Mine's bigger," he said with a nod before passing the phone back to Robert. He stood tall, taller than he had ever stood, and turned to add, "I'm going to change the fly for the rest of the pool."

Robert patted him on the shoulder. "Good lad, I'm going to check on Buster and Honor now, I'll be back for you when it is time for lunch."

At eight o'clock that evening Callum was sitting opposite his mum at the table in their kitchen. Still in the clothes he had worn to the river, but with his hands thoroughly cleaned as instructed, he watched as she scooped a large portion of lasagne onto the garlic bread on his plate.

"Carry on," she said, and he talked her through the day, answering her questions in detail. He showed her the two pictures Robert had sent him and heard more from his mother about what good friends he and his father had been.

"I knew it was going to happen, I've no idea how but I did," he said. "We had an awesome lunch, both ghillies joined us and we were in no rush. I felt so relaxed, there was no pressure as I had already caught one. Then I went with Honor up to the Mill pool. She was sitting watching from the bank and when it took, I just turned to her and we looked into each other's eyes. I could feel the fish tugging the line but I just lifted the rod without taking my eyes off her. She netted it and we got a photo with the Anderson's Last Resort sticking from the side of its mouth. It was so cool, Mum."

"What a special day, Cal. They are so kind to have invited you and I'm sure they spoke to Robert in advance. He's always been such a lovely man and such a cannie ghillie. I'm sure he was nearly as pleased as you were today. So, what does that mean for the competition?"

"James is on nine and I don't think he'll be fishing any more this season as he is apparently abroad until he goes back to school in Edinburgh. I'm on nine too, but he would win if it stayed like that as he got to nine first. The thing is, I have now caught in pretty much every beat I can access, and school starts next week so I don't think I can add another. The only chance I have is the September break on Saturday 25th if I can get on somewhere new, but many places are already booked, and the Twilight programme is only running until the end of this month."

"Well, I hope you can find somewhere. I know I'm biased, but I think you deserve to win. You've tried all year, even in the ice and snow. I'm sure your Granda will have some hand in it even from afar."

Callum smiled; he wanted her to be right, though he felt a pang of anxiety at the same time. He changed the subject and once dinner was finished he made his way up to his room, opened the spreadsheet 'winthefin.xls' and looked once more at the columns. Invery, Cairnton, Commonty, Lower Woodend, Banchory, Garthdee, Banchory Devenick, Culter, Lower Crathes/West Durris were the nine beneath his own name. If only one of those he had hooked at Dess had stuck, or even the crazy one that had been taken from him at Balmoral.

He went onto the Fishpal website again to see which estate had a single rod available for the day he was free at the end of September. He had no idea which would be best other than to base it on the price; he needed someone to ask, but that person was no longer here. He would have to work it out himself, but he had no idea how he'd find time what with his final school year beginning next week.

Gina Rees

CHAPTER 27

Returning to school had been uneventful for Callum. Normality was creeping back into life. Gone were many of the painful protocols and rules that had been needed over the past eighteen months. The rugby team had won both their opening games, but otherwise he kept a low profile. His favourite part of the day was when he got to spend lunchtimes with Honor. They were back on track, closer than ever.

There had been a lot of planning for the funeral, which his mum had largely arranged, but he had been involved in some respects, particularly the communications with guests. As they went through the schedule the night before, she decided to show him some photos from that earlier funeral he had attended. He could not remember what must have been a traumatic day for everyone, but he instantly recognised the small boy dressed in black holding his mum's gloved hand as they walked in front of two raised coffins. He stared at the figure of his Granda, stoic and upright in his own black suit, like a granite statue.

There would be little sense of tragedy this time. There would be a form of poignant celebration as outlined by Granda's wishes. He was to be cremated in his full fishing outfit, including his waders, and all attendees were to be handed a special ADAA cap bearing the date; Callum hoped many of them would wear it when fishing. The wake was to take place on the banks of the river.

There had been a proper turnout. As well as the Garbas, many of the other ghillies from the river were there, along with a large proportion of the ADAA membership. Each took time to speak with Callum, and the message was a consistent one. His grandad had been a highly respected man, and the river had been central to his life. It had been essential to his work at the papermill and integral to his family and social life. They all understood how circumstances had driven him away from the river but knew how important it was for him to have returned. Everybody seemed to have their own favourite amusing story; Callum listened intently to them all.

Robert from Lower Crathes shared an entertaining story that involved an inflatable dinghy and a bottle of whisky, Callum then took the opportunity to mention that he was looking to book fishing for the end of the month to try and win the Golden Fin along with the prize cheque. Robert suggested a couple of beats and when Callum was home he booked another day at Crathes Castle for the last Saturday of the month.

As the end of the month approached, Callum found he was increasingly checking the weather forecast and each night he could not wait to see the daily catch reports. There had been regular rain through the month but without a big spate, so there was plenty of water in the river just now. The nights had become much cooler with frosts creeping in, especially further upstream. Catches all along the system were encouraging.

Historically, the two most prolific beats on the Dee in September had been Park and Lower Crathes, both of which were usually full, taken by rods who had been fishing those weeks for many years. Callum was lucky to have caught at Lower Crathes but had not managed to catch at neighbouring Crathes Castle when he had visited at Easter. These estates were all catching fish each day, and this would be his chance to get the missing salmon. He sent a text to John, the ghillie, and received an encouraging reply with details of the most productive flies.

Everyone at school seemed to know how close he was to winning, and as Saturday approached he was constantly receiving messages of good luck. Even his sports teacher took him aside after their Wednesday training to pass on his support. It was a relief to be home on the Friday, because he felt that if anyone else said 'tight lines' to him he might well throttle them.

Callum woke early and was unable to get back to sleep, so he left the house earlier than needed. He packed the lunch his mum had made but avoided seeing her before leaving. With the days now shorter than the nights, he had needed the lights on his bike as he headed to the Cult's bus stop. He arrived at the Crathes Castle stop just before eight, and a short walk later he was at the estate fishing hut, to see smoke already rising from the chimney.

As he tapped on the open door, John turned and raised his coffee mug in recognition. He came outside and they chatted whilst Callum hastily assembled his rod and line.

"The other rods won't be here for a while yet, one of them had his fiftieth birthday yesterday and I know they were planning a big dinner," said John. "They caught three between them and lost two others. The conditions haven't changed, so I would say you would be as well to use a similar fly."

Before long they were attaching the rod to his truck roof and heading to the first pool. Callum felt like he was stepping up to take a deciding penalty in front of a full house, and the whole season came down to him slotting this one.

The door slammed behind Callum as he leaned his bike against the hallway wall. He dropped the bag and the rod case on the floor and ran upstairs before even Fergie appeared. He had flailed away on the river all day and would have carried on all night had it been possible, but no matter how hard he tried, he had not been able to tempt a salmon.

There had been an awkward farewell at the end of the day; one of the other rods was seemingly embarrassed to report he had caught two that afternoon from the pool Callum had unsuccessfully fished in the morning. Callum had shrugged it off, stiff upper lip and all that, but now, in the sanctuary of his room, anger built up within him. He was briefly even tempted to contact Jake and see what he was doing, but memories of those nights last summer now made him feel sick.

He jumped when his phone rang. Hardly anyone actually called these days as it was all text and voice messages, so he looked to see who it was and was surprised to see it was the ghillie at Balmoral.

"Hi Dave, how are you?" he said, trying to sound casual.

"Hi Callum, all good here thanks, all good. I am sorry I couldnae make it to the funeral, I heard there was a grand turnout for your Granda. Very respected man."

"No problem at all, we got your kind card. You must have the Royal Family in residence at the moment?"

"Aye, we're kept pretty busy in August and September, on the hill and the river. I'm sorry to disturb you this evening, I heard from a friend about your day today, bad luck my man. It is about that I called. I have been given permission for you to have another go up here on Monday if you're free? I'm pretty sure you get a long weekend and there's no school? No charge, and I would collect and return you."

Callum couldn't reply. It was completely unexpected, and he was off guard.

"Ask Honor along too if you like," David added. "She hasn't seen the estate yet and it would be nice for her to join in."

"Yes, thanks Dave, that would be awesome. See you then." He lay back on his bed and mouthed *thank you* to the ceiling. It was fate, it had to be. But he already had plans for Monday.

CHAPTER 28

Grace dropped Honor at Callum's house on her way to work. It was a misty morning, but you could tell it would soon burn off. It was the perfect day to say goodbye.

The rucksack sat in the hallway and whilst Honor waited, Callum pulled on his trainers. He took the lead from the hook and Fergie appeared, closely followed by his mum. They filed silently out of the door, and Callum put his arm around her. They followed the road until they met Deeside Way, where he slipped the lead off Fergie and took Honor's hand in his. They walked like this as the mist lifted with just a few remaining ghostly wisps lingering over the river. The swifts had gone already, but a few swallows skimmed the surface scooping up insects. Occasionally, for no particular reason, he would squeeze her hand, prompting a smile, and they chatted until arriving at the chosen place.

Mary and Honor linked arms as they stood by the bench watching Callum carefully step down the riverbank. He reached the gravel bar and took the rucksack from his back, then placed it gently beside him and squatted down next to it, breathing slowly and heavily. He turned and looked up at the two most important people left in his life. They smiled as he nodded to them and removed the urn. It took just a few seconds to release his grandad into the river, the final step in his long journey. At the top of the bank the three of them hugged. The river gushed on, hiding their sobs.

David collected them at one o'clock in a shining black Range Rover, opening the rear door as if they were royalty. Callum and Honor had been home for an hour and eaten lunch together, anticipation and excitement building all the way back from Culter. It somehow felt appropriate to fish on the same day they had said goodbye to Granda. They sat side by side in the back smiling as they drove off westwards. Within five minutes they were crossing the Dee on to the south side near Peterculter, and with very little traffic they made good progress. They both peered down at the river once it was in sight.

"Looks good, it's nae a bad day," said Callum. "How's it looking at Balmoral?"

"Aye it's pretty braw," replied David. "Water's a good height and it's cooled down these past few days nicely, there's certainly a good chance. We're going straight to the castle. I've been given clearance for you to fish the Balmoral beat, which has been very lightly fished since July and the pools are holding a lot of fish."

They crossed the Falls of Feugh, where in the past weeks hundreds of precious salmon must have flung themselves at the gushing water, relentless in their urge to continue to their journey's end. The car crossed back to the north side again and Callum looked down over the bridge at the Banchory beat. This was the scene of his memorable birthday fish with Honor a few months earlier, but it was those who had gone that he was thinking about now.

They continued through Banchory and onto the A93 and were soon approaching Kincardine. Callum had fallen silent, his head full of flashbacks from the last time he had travelled to

Balmoral with Granda. There was one image he couldn't get out of his mind; that moment when Granda had placed his hand on his shoulder on the riverbank and Callum had imagined it was his father.

He looked out of the window at the scenery; it was very different from April. Now the leaves were turning brown and the bright colours of spring had gone.

If he could catch just one more fish, he would win the competition. His success would be for all of them. He had to get it done, close it out.

They continued along the main road and he started to imagine being on the water, rolling out his cast and anticipating a take. But each time his thoughts were interrupted by images of his Granda almost in tears telling him how much their day together had meant to him. Why had he been left alone? Why had they all been taken from him?

He tried to concentrate, peering out of the left window at the river, but his eyes were misting over, and he felt a lump in his throat. Where had this come from? Honor's soft hand placed on top of his right soothed him, and he closed his eyes.

He must have drifted off and was woken by a squeeze from her hand. They were crossing the old bridge, and soon the main gates were opened for them. They stopped by the stables next to other cars which had their windows blacked out. It was quieter today; there were no tourists this time. The restaurant was closed, no ice creams or audio guidebooks.

They paused a moment, admiring the majesty of the castle, and Callum smiled at Honor before opening the door. It had grown warm during the morning, but there were more clouds up towards the Highlands. Callum slipped on his waders as David collected the rucksack and rod case before leading the way to the river.

"Here you are then, by royal appointment no less," said David. "Let's get the rod set up and make a start as the days aren't so long now. This is your chance Callum. You can do it, I have no doubt."

Making an effort to smile, Callum reached for the fly he had decided well in advance he was going to use and began to tie it onto the line, but something nagged at him. Initially he thought it was just the memory of the previous time he had been there, but that wasn't it. The pressure to catch a fish and win the competition had altered the dynamics. The sentimentality had gone; he just didn't feel the enthusiasm to fish any more. The best times had been when he could immerse himself in the surroundings, the unfolding of nature around him and the person he was with, the pure enjoyment of common happiness he had felt. They had not caught a fish, but that time was irreplaceable and indelible.

He stood upright, rod beside him, as Honor and David walked over. Callum had made a decision, and it felt as if a weight had been lifted from his shoulders.

"Right, start by that large rock and work your way down," said David. "Keep a good pace so if you don't connect, we can rush up to the Queen's pool further upstream and give that a go before I drive you to the Brig O'Dee pool, which is the last resort. Think of that prize money and the gold just waiting for you."

But Callum handed the rod to Honor. "You fish," he whispered.

She looked into his eyes. "Callum, you just need one more fish to win, you can do this. Everyone's on your side."

Calmly, with a brief smile, he replied, "No, it's OK, I'd much rather you fish. I needed to come here but I don't want to try today. I'm happy here, and I know he would understand, I know they all would. I just want to be here, part of this scene with them. Go on, go get some silver!"

They froze for a moment, then Honor and David nodded silently to each other and made their way to the river.

Callum stood alone. His thoughts were of the generations that had been before and what connected them, what was lost and what could be saved.

Callum watched Honor as she started to cast from the bank below, the familiar smooth motion dissolved into the serenity of the stream. There was a plateau of grass between them and at that moment, an image appeared. He saw the same tartan rug laid out and sat on it was his mum, Buster and Grace smiling as they watched her. To the side was an old collapsible chair and Granda was nestled into it. Never before had Callum felt so sure that they would be OK.

As he started towards them, he turned and stared up at the magnificence of the castle behind, his eyes drawn to a presence he had not noticed. He felt certain the lady in tweed and wearing a headscarf was looking back at him.

EPILOGUE

Yes, of course she did.

In fact, she caught two within the first hour, but Callum still didn't want to try. He was as happy as he had been for months. And she caught two more on the last Saturday of the season, 9th October, when Callum joined Honor, Grace and Buster at Cairnton. It was a very different scene from the snowy, flooded day in February, and different again from the scorching day they had spent at Lower Woodend. It was cold first thing, but by mid-morning there was a pleasant late summer warmth to the air that lasted through the afternoon. The cooling water temperature had triggered a reaction in the salmon, and the cock fish had become more aggressive as they headed for their spawning grounds. The colours of the fish resembled those of the leaves that now littered the river, the pattern of the males like their own special tartan.

Callum had accepted the invitation on the condition that he provided the lunch. It wasn't that he hadn't enjoyed the feast at Lower Crathes; he knew that if this was his responsibility, his mum would be sure to join them. If there was one thing she did not trust Callum with, it was preparing a suitable picnic. She arrived laden with Scotch pies and flapjacks prepared that morning, which they enjoyed on the outside table. There was laughter and warm praise for the surroundings, with recognition that it would be another year and a new generation of salmon when they next fished. With much nudging from her son, Mary even had a cast herself in front of the hut. Callum's mouth hung open as he watched the fly land delicately on the water.

As the season was about to close, so too would the Win the Fin competition. Although Callum had caught fish on as many beats as James, James had reached his total of nine first, so the rules stated he would be the winner. The prize money had no doubt been doubled by his proud and confident father.

Opening the WTF email on Sunday evening, Callum fully expected to see the leader board for the under-eighteens unchanged, so he was shocked to see his name at the top. As he puzzled over this his phone started pinging with messages asking him why James had withdrawn from the competition. He had no answers.

Although there were rumours, the actual chain of events was never made public. It was only the Chairman of the Trust and the most senior board members who were permitted to view, confidentially, the video footage. Following an anonymous tip-off, they retrieved the recording from a camera that was used to observe the water height and conditions of a beat just below one of the bridges. The footage was dated mid-July and showed two teenagers fishing the beat, although only one of them had a rod. They could clearly be seen lowering an object into the river, and one of them appeared to be navigating it with a radio controller whilst the other stared at the screen he was holding. Use of underwater drones to locate fish was not just considered unsporting; it contravened the rules of the river and of the competition.

With the season over, Callum and Honor decided that they would use the winter months to launch an initiative they had been talking about for some time. They wanted more people of their own age to be aware of the threatened disappearance of the incredible king of fish, the silver ghosts. Using the prize money from the competition they were able to launch their own awareness campaign.

You can find it at www.silver-ghosts.com.

"The salmon is the king of fish. Their journeys up rivers are some of the most thrilling spectacles in the natural world. And yet, now, their very survival is at risk."

- Sir David Attenborough

Numbers of wild salmon are estimated to have fallen by 70% in the last 40 years.

Will Shropshire worked in finance for over twenty years, a career that included more than ten years in Asia. Whilst enjoying his time abroad, he missed nothing more than the British seasons and the countryside of home. Since returning to the UK in 2014 and living just a short roll-cast from the river Test, he has developed a love of fly-fishing. He caught his first Scottish salmon in 2016 and made his first visit to Deeside in April 2019. Struck by the beauty of the river Dee, the stunning countryside and the friendliness of the people, he has frequently returned, often with his wife Josie, his son Frankie and daughter Kitty.